Stephen Bywater left school at sixteen to join the Merchant Navy. He now lives with his family in Bedford, where he teaches English. *The Devil's Ark* is his first novel.

D1008180

STEPHEN BYWATER

THE DEVIL'S ARK

headline

First published in 2014 by
HEADLINE PUBLISHING GROUP

1

Cataloguing in Publication Data is available from the British Library

ISBN 978 1 4722 1039 5

Typeset in Sabon LT Std by Palimpsest Book Production Limited,
Falkirk, Stirlingshire

Printed and bound by CPI Group (UK) Ltd, Croydon CR0 4YY

Headline's policy is to use papers that are natural, renewable and recyclable
products and made from wood grown in sustainable forests. The logging and
manufacturing processes are expected to conform to the environmental
regulations of the country of origin.

HEADLINE PUBLISHING GROUP
An Hachette UK Company
338 Euston Road
London NW1 3BH

www.headline.co.uk
www.hachette.co.uk

For Lucy, Matilda and Eva

Wildcats shall meet with hyenas,
goat-demons shall call to each other;
there too Lilith shall repose,
and find a place to rest.
There shall the owl nest
and lay and hatch and brood in its shadow.

Isaiah 34:14f

The devil's finest trick was to convince the world
that he doesn't exist.

Charles Baudelaire

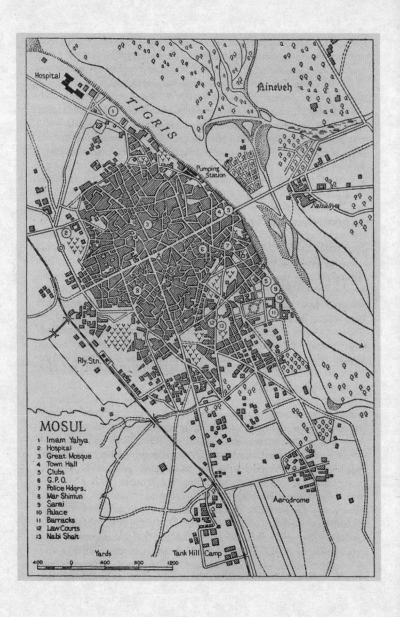

Hospital

TIGRIS

Nineveh

Pumping
Station

Faisaliya

Rly. Stn.

MOSUL

1 Imam Yahya
2 Hospital
3 Great Mosque
4 Town Hall
5 Clubs
6 G.P.O.
7 Police Hdqrs.
8 Mar Shimun
9 Sarai
10 Palace
11 Barracks
12 Law Courts
13 Nabi Shait

Aerodrome

Yards

400   0   400   800   1200

Tank Hill Camp

Prologue

December 6th 1930
Rue d'Andenne, Brussels

She came to me last night, little more than a shadow settling at the foot of the bed. Sometimes she stands a yard away and I hear her breathing: a soft, slow rhythm rolling in and out across the darkness above me. I sense her brooding presence, her vast hunger. Perhaps it's her scent that announces her arrival; a scent that's raw and vulgar, sensual and strong. Not that it's always the same. There are times, even in the coldest of houses, when a fog of heat and sand silently gathers.

My eyes are closed, but I can picture her bending towards me, her supple limbs descending in one balletic movement, her bestial, primeval smell pouring through the cold air. I feel her weight on the mattress as she kneels down. Her lips are swollen and bleeding, yet I allow her mouth to brush against mine. I feel her finger tracing the scar that runs across my lips, I feel her lashes on my cheek, her warm hands holding my sides. She pulls on the cord round my waist and I succumb to her caresses. Nothing can foil her seduction, the art she's been perfecting for countless centuries. Whether it's just a recurring dream or not is almost immaterial. Last night she discovered my room and I allowed her to take me. She is lust and loss of reason and my faith in her is unshakeable for I know she will always find me. There isn't a house or byre that can give me sanctuary.

This has been the longest I've managed to elude her, a month hidden in a squalid boarding house. A month spent sleeping in the day, trying to stay awake during the night; nights sitting alone and staring into the blackness that lurks beyond the candle's flame. And now it's over. As the curtain edge grows light I record her appearance. Notebooks lie around me. Exercise books filled with murky sketches and indecipherable lines written in an unsteady hand. I will return to London and find new lodgings with what little money I have left, but before I leave I want to give an account, to put the record straight. It sounds hideously melodramatic, the tired, cliché-ridden thoughts of a deranged man, but she's still haunting me. What we discovered disturbs every waking hour, shatters what little sleep I can snatch. A year on and I sit here trembling, even with the sunlight streaming through the

2

window. That I'm still alive is a marvel I find it hard to fathom. Ink runs across the paper, marking the page, scratching out a warning before the darkness descends, before the harvest begins again.

1

Baghdad, early November, 1929. A city of dust and flies, of covered bazaars filled with the sound of guttural tongues and the heavy smell of sunlit canvas and bitter coffee. This was my opportunity to make a fresh start, to glimpse again the half-forgotten empire we'd left behind. It was a chance taken with little thought, other than the ill-conceived idea that, after twelve years, a return to the country where I'd spectacularly failed might restore my faith. And it had been easy for them to organise – a Methodist subscription, a publisher willing to invest. *The Study of the Bible* was almost finished, but they needed a photographer prepared to travel across Palestine and Iraq.

This was my modern pilgrimage, one spent retracing my steps, viewing the relics that had survived the war, outfacing memories that had haunted me since we'd smashed the Ottoman Empire with bayonet, rifle and shell. That's how we'd made history, in a mechanical war across mud and sand, crushing together bone and flesh beside silent antediluvian towns that had never witnessed such carnage before.

Returning to Iraq I was able to photograph some of the more recent discoveries: clay tablets, golden amulets, carvings of mythical creatures unseen for over three thousand years. I still have some of the photographs: braying donkey in the foreground, the ruins of a tower behind, a boy shepherd beside a mud wall. Recently, I've even been bold enough to keep a print beside the bed, Babylon's Tower of Babel. At Babylon all was well. I had kept to my schedule and kept my thoughts from dwelling too much on the past. What had once been a battlefield was now no more than an undulating strip of scrubland. Where blood had been spilled, goats peacefully grazed. The flies were the same, but a wafted cigarette still kept them at bay. There was nothing there to trouble me other than the heat. Up until Baghdad my only concern was that I'd miss some biblical ruin.

My arrival in the Iraqi capital signalled the end of my odyssey. I understood the obligation I was under to return to England as the decent God-fearing man who'd first left its shores in 1915. It wasn't meant to be my road to Damascus, nothing as grand as that. I didn't expect an epiphany, just the beginnings of a campaign against doubt. In Iraq, floundering in the blood-black mud of war, all certainty had been knocked out of me. Yet now I felt I was making progress. My melancholia had begun to lift. The trepidation with which I had disembarked in Haifa had been replaced with the cheery suspicion that I was on the path to salvation. I'd found a room at the Clarendon Hotel and had one further excursion to make before taking the train to Mosul. From Mosul I'd travel to Constantinople and from the Turkish capital I'd make my way to London. On a small desk in my hotel room I composed a succinct telegram to the editor at Browns, telling him I'd come to the end and asking for the price of a ticket home.

The Clarendon was one of the cheapest hotels in Baghdad and what served as a bar was a dark, damp-smelling cellar. There were dust-covered bottles, four or five round tables and the obligatory picture of King Faisal. On the second night I felt I had the measure of the place and, with the last excursion in mind, was content to wait for my railway fare to be wired to the Anglo-Persian Petroleum office. Along with the British and American oil companies, there was still an army presence in Iraq and it wasn't uncommon to see soldiers in certain bars. In the Clarendon you'd find the occasional pilot, or several junior officers. It wasn't the place for a major, or for the swilling sapper and his painted doxy.

The bar was almost empty, except for two young officers and a middle-aged man in a fawn-coloured jacket. The man, sitting in a corner, had his tie loose round his unbuttoned collar. He was reading a well-thumbed newspaper which he'd spread out on the table in front of him. I decided to sit at the bar. I ordered a pale ale and placed my hat on the wooden counter.

The scraping of chairs behind me signalled the departure of the officers. I turned to see again if I'd come across either of them before. On several occasions the army had obligingly taken me to remote ruins. I was a veteran and my lips served as my service medal. The sight of the scar and what I had to say, when pushed to recall my own share of the slaughter, were validation enough; enough, at least, to be treated with a mix of respect and sympathy, occasionally enough to gain a bed for a night, or a tour of the local sights. With the officers leaving I felt that I'd missed an opportunity, which at the start of my odyssey could easily have soured my mood.

I was about to turn back to my drink when the man in the corner looked up from his paper. He caught my eye and, as the two young men disappeared up the stone steps, he smiled congenially. 'Care to join me?' he asked, or words to that effect.

In the Middle East I was every fair-skinned fellow's cousin. The fact that he was Irish, given the lilt in his voice, certainly didn't make any difference.

'Same again?' he asked, pointing at the glass in my hand as I crossed the bar.

'That's very kind,' I said, though it had hardly been touched.

He gestured to the barman and pushed out a seat with his foot.

His name was O'Neil and he was a doctor. He was talkative and, having been starved of conversation, I was happy to sit and listen. During the war he had served at one of the hospitals but was now growing fat at the consulate in Mosul. It was his final stint of service and in the summer he planned to return to his practice in Exmouth. He'd seen me earlier in the lobby with my camera and the conversation turned to photography and my commission. I told him that I'd already spent several days working at Babylon and Ur, sites that had punctuated our march in the spring of 1916.

'You know there's a dig outside Mosul you should visit. The chap in charge has been there since the start of the month.'

'And he's hoping to m-match Woolley's success at Ur?'

'He is,' O'Neil said. 'You've heard of Kipling's poem, the one that starts with "dominion over palm and pine . . . yet all our pomp of yesterday is one with Nineveh and Tyre"?'

'No. I've heard of Nineveh, but not the poem.'

'Then you'll know it from the Bible. Of course Babylon eclipses it, and the newspapers have put Ur firmly on the map. Though Tilden's keen to find something that'll do the same. Argues the Assyrian city will soon be as famous.'

'Hard to imagine he'll uncover anything to rival Woolley's discovery. And as for Babylon . . .'

'I know. I keep telling him that Nineveh's been forgotten. You should see the walls though, they go on for several miles. In fact, you should meet Tilden. He's taken his dig outside one of the gates. Thinks he's onto something.'

'Did he say what?'

'No. But this might interest you: his photographer, a queer fellow, has just left them high and dry.'

'In the middle of a dig?'

'Just when they needed him the most.'

'Why did he leave?'

'No one knows. They say he walked out into a filthy storm; drunk, no doubt. Captain Fowler conducted some sort of investigation, but there's no reason to suspect foul play.'

'And the Arabs aren't to blame?'

'If they were there would have been some kind of song and dance. No, they've been quiet for the past year or so; bombed into submission. Since Sheik Mahomet's departure things have settled down.' O'Neil paused. I could tell he was wondering if I was some sort of Arab sympathiser. 'There's always tension, of course, Muslim, Christian, Jew, all cheek-by-jowl.'

He wiped his glistening forehead with his handkerchief. 'It doesn't bother you, does it, what you've heard about the tribes in the north?'

'Why should it?' I replied, as though unaware of what had been happening. 'These things have a tendency to boil over.'

'Such unrest can easily spread. I've seen it in Ireland. A firm hand's required.' O'Neil leaned forward. 'A couple of years ago, when the insurrection was at its height, there was talk of gassing the Arabs; dropping canisters from aeroplanes. Even Lawrence supported it, couldn't understand why some were being so prissy about its use.'

'Lawrence,' I repeated.

'Have you heard what they've been saying about the colonel, why he's been transferred again?'

I shook my head. I had my suspicions, which he was clearly willing to confirm, but I preferred to discuss the dig.

O'Neil drained his glass and signalled to the barman for the next round. 'It's going well,' he replied after a moment's reflection. 'Tilden says he's close to uncovering something significant and I'm inclined to believe him. It's an opportunity for a fellow like yourself, if you're in no rush.'

'And this other chap isn't planning to return?'

'It's been two weeks, and they've still no idea where he is. My guess is he's either rotting in some bar in Aleppo, or working his passage home. Not the most popular man. I can't imagine why they'd welcome him back, even if he had the nerve to show his face again. He was highly strung, unbearable towards the end. Seems to have put everyone on edge.'

'What do you mean?'

'Well,' said O'Neil, weighing his words carefully, 'last season it was all very happy; all laughter and high spirits. This year it's different. Right from the start, with Bateman's arrival, it soured very quickly.'

'Bateman?'

'The photographer who's disappeared. He wasn't here last year.'

'And last year?'

'It was a young chap named Munro. Pity he didn't return.'

'Why didn't he?'

'Not sure why. Tilden seemed happy with his work. I should think Bateman had a lot to live up to. Still, strange for him to wander off like that.'

'Artistic temperament,' I suggested.

'In a photographer?' said O'Neil dismissively.

'Perhaps being cooped up together?'

'It's too early in the season, though there are few other newcomers this year, which can always unsettle things. Dr Tilden's been there from the start, and Mrs Jackson's an old hand. Secretary and general bottle-washer. Her husband was an archaeologist. Died in the war. She's a charity case, really. Tilden worked with her husband in Syria. Feels the least he can do is keep her occupied. Tom Suarez, the architect, has been out here nearly as long as Mrs Jackson.' He lifted his tumbler of whisky and swirled it around, the ice cubes clinking against the glass. 'They didn't have ice last year. Now that's what I call progress.' He took a sip, and nodded in approval. 'The Russian's new.'

'The Russian?'

'It's an Anglo-American dig, but they've a chap called Stanislav who deciphers their clay tablets. Not sure about his background. Fought during the civil war, but can't be a Bolshevik – otherwise he'd still be there now.'

'New faces can unsettle things.'

'Quite so. It's a pretty close community. All the same there seems to be something not quite right. Tilden leads by example and, although he has little tact, he's always managed to keep his expedition happy before, everyone on good terms and yet . . . well, it's just a little tense at the moment.'

'Are you trying to put me off?

O'Neil smiled. 'I just think it's worth you knowing. I tell you what, I'm heading back to Mosul tomorrow, I'll mention your name to Tilden. If you turn up in the next couple of days you'll have at least a fortnight's work, which means board and lodgings, and a few rupees in your pocket.'

The doctor paused. He seemed to be studying my face. You're not in any hurry to get back to Blighty are you?'

'I won't be sorry to leave the blasted heat behind. Easy to forget how much of a furnace this place is, even in November.'

'Believe me, you'll soon be shivering and wishing you were back here. Are you married?'

'No,' I answered. 'I was engaged, b-but . . .' Throughout the conversation I had hardly stuttered at all, but I couldn't trust myself to talk about her without making a mess of it.

O'Neil nodded, and glanced again at my lips.

13

2

I had no serious intention of joining the dig at Nineveh. My conversation with O'Neil, at least until the thought of her, had been almost flawless and I was keen to get back to England. I didn't want anything to spoil my triumphant return. The problems I had suffered appeared to have more or less disappeared. I was admittedly curious to visit the site, and if they were onto something significant then I felt almost obliged to stop by, but the talk of trouble was enough to put me off.

I sat down at the breakfast table and brushed a few crumbs that had been left behind onto the tiled floor. It was late and the room was emptying. When the waiter came over I asked him if he'd seen the doctor. The man shook his head. I ordered and he returned to the kitchen through the revolving door. I sat and watched the net curtains billow gently an inch or two towards my table.

In the grey, filtered light I wondered if I'd ever see O'Neil again.

After breakfast I wandered out towards the bazaar. By mid-afternoon I'd managed to hitch a ride to a barren plain just beyond the outskirts of the city. What some say is Adam's grave is little more than a depression in the sand, though it's almost a hundred yards in length. Noah, at the age of six hundred, is said to have found the site. It was a deserted spot, made all the more forsaken by the lack of any vegetation.

The light was fading and I remember feeling quite alone. There was the emptiness of a Sunday afternoon, and the stillness in the air began to breed melancholy thoughts. Buildings must once have stood around it as piles of rubble lay scattered across the plain. It was easy to imagine the site as a place of pilgrimage, as having had a shrine of some sort. Had it all been smashed by the war, another unrecorded spasm of destruction in a worthless corner of the world? It had become convenient for me to blame others, to see peace as the thing we should desire above all else. Yet even after witnessing the bloodshed and brutality I can still recall the ache of excitement I'd felt, when the idea of fighting in some distant land appealed far more than a suburban life with its washing lines and carpet slippers. My loathing for monotony was therefore to blame for the thrill I felt when I heard the bugle's call. There's nothing noble about running away from boredom, but doing your bit for king and country makes it laudable, even heroic. In England

I'd been prone to dwell on my unbearably dull life, my self-destructive nature, my propensity for evil. Standing beside a grave, no matter how unlikely a spot, was like picking at the scab.

Yet I'd been lucky. I'd returned almost physically unharmed. It had been an ignominious end, but I'd survived; sound in body if not in mind. I don't remember much about the last day, though I can still see myself running, squelching through marshland towards the Turkish line, the mud sucking at my boots, sweat pouring into my eyes. My mouth is dry, but others are shouting, yelling obscenities as they run towards the canal. The Turks respond with cries of '*Allah hu Akbar*'. It's a shouting match. Bullets fizz by. Shells whistle overhead. Shells explode. Shells begin to fill everything in front of me with flying metal. A deafening roar suddenly engulfs every other sound and a giant's fist smashes the air out of my lungs. I'm catapulted into the sky. Thrown into the marsh. Debris rains down, pressing me into the slime. I can't hear or see anything. There's a throbbing silence, a stillness that is briefly welcomed. At first I don't know where I am. Mud and blood start to fill my mouth. I can hardly move, with no sense of up or down. Stuck in the cloying ground, I begin to swallow. I'm trying to breathe, but I'm trapped.

A sergeant had seen my aeronautical cartwheel, saw one of my boots sticking out of the mud. It was kicking and he was curious. I know I was crying when they pulled me out. The sergeant thought it remarkable that I hadn't

17

lost a limb. My lips had split, my tunic was singed and several ribs had cracked, but I was still in one piece. A miracle, he was saying as he pressed a dressing to my mouth. I was crying, wiping mud from my eyes, squirming in his arms, twisting in pain. I'd been reborn, ejected from the earth's slimy womb. What had once been Eden, what we were ploughing with shells and watering with men's blood, had given birth to me. A foolish notion to have had in the middle of a battlefield, but it filled my mind. I became troubled, confused. The tears wouldn't stop.

I don't remember much else, other than being taken downriver. They gave me morphine and managed to stem the flow of blood from my lips. The injured slept on the open deck as we slowly steamed back towards Basra. Only fragments of the journey remain: the oppressive heat, the constant burr of bloated flies, the groans of other men. I can't say whether it was the fear of being buried alive, or the heat, or simply the strain of serving on the front line that sent me over the edge, but my mind began to unravel. I started to see things. Sleek, beautiful creatures: half-girl, half-hyena. They sat quietly for hours, staring down into my eyes. There were other visitors too: strange amphibious lizards, strutting around with a bulldog's gait. They paraded across the deck at night and then, later, through the ward in Amarah. Some sort of story was unfolding in front of me; I had a vague understanding that it meant something, that there was more to it. Even now I'm convinced it had some significance. I know it's irrelevant, reason dictates that the dreams of a madman

18

have no logic, yet I can't escape the feeling that there's an answer.

On the slow river journey I was oblivious to those around me. I ignored all the things that others deemed important. Beyond my own thoughts, my own world, nothing mattered; unless something found its way through, some innocuous scene or phrase: a wireless broadcast, a nurse's greeting. On certain days they would burrow into my mind, until there was little room for anything else. But gradually it all started to make sense and the hallucinations subsided. In England I started to understand again, to recover my senses, to find my place, my function. To understand where I was, what I'd been and what I'd become.

My rehabilitation at Napsbury was relatively swift. Some cerebral sensitivity to the suffering I'd witnessed, and a scar which passes for a harelip, but otherwise unharmed. Up until Nineveh the most unpalatable effect was probably the conceited belief that I had gained a unique understanding of how miserably mankind had failed, with our slavish response to the factory whistle and our subsequent readiness to shed blood.

The sun had begun to set. I turned away from the grave and started to walk back to the dirt road. A black dog sauntered towards me. I eyed it warily. It was panting, though I hadn't seen it running. It stopped about ten yards ahead and seemed to be staring beyond me, its head tilted to one side; looking either through me or just to my left. I gazed at its wide jaws, its thick, scarred muzzle and dark, protruding eyes. It was an ugly scavenger, about the size of a boxer, though it was patently a mongrel or pariah dog. Its mangy carcass was painfully thin, which made its bulbous head monstrously outsized. I was about to turn my gaze away, convinced that it was looking past me, when it started to growl. The sound, a hoarse, uneven rumbling, annoyed me more than anything else, though when it bared its yellow teeth I began to feel a little uneasy. With its black lips pulled back, it started to paw the ground. I glanced behind me, but there was nobody there. Rather than face it again, I looked out of the corner of my eye. It had stopped growling, but what appeared to be an involuntary ripple was contorting its upper lip. I wasn't afraid of the dog; I knew I could land a hefty kick to its muzzle if it came any closer, but I didn't relish the idea of having to defend myself against it.

I took a step away, and was glad to see it remained stationary. I was prepared to make a short detour back to the road to avoid any sort of confrontation when several other pariah dogs suddenly appeared from behind a mound of earth. Their eyes shone like blood rubies, a trick of the setting sun, but enough to unsettle me. The black dog, emboldened by the appearance of the pack, started its advance. It strutted towards me. I headed purposefully for the road, one hand holding the Leica against my side. The other dogs descended from the summit of the mound and joined their black companion. They were three or four yards behind, snarling and barking. The fear of being bitten, of feeling their teeth

20

snapping into my flesh, reared up inside me. The dogs, as though sensing my nerve was about to collapse, inched closer. There was no stick to beat them with, no stone near enough to throw. The only thing I could do was to keep walking. To look back or to run would surely have given them a reason to attack.

I was thirty yards from the road when in the distance I saw a cart kicking up the dust as it made its way to Baghdad. The dogs continued to track me, their barking a cacophony of fury and hunger. One grizzled muzzle was sniffing at my calf. With an ungainly step I lifted my heel sharply and caught its jaw from below. It fell back with an angry yelp, while the others continued in their chase. The cart was making its slow journey towards me. I crossed the road, for no other reason than to keep moving. The heat was taking its toll. My hands were sweating. The black pariah followed me for a yard or two then turned round. I glanced back and saw to my relief that the dogs had stopped on the other side. I started in the direction of the cart. The pack moved in unison with me, but for some inexplicable reason the road kept us apart.

The cart and mule were coming closer. I could see a father and son sitting together. The barking continued, their anger unabated by my crossing to the other side. I wondered whether or not it would alarm the driver and his mule, but their progress remained steady. As the dark features of their faces became visible I waved at them. With a pull of the reins the mule lifted its head, and its soft shambling stopped. I walked up to the cart. The driver, wrapped in a grey robe, paid no heed to the barking dogs, but kept his eyes on me. I greeted them with what little Arabic I know and gestured towards Baghdad. The son, a boy of no more than ten, nimbly climbed into the back of the cart, which was full of pomegranates. The man leaned towards me, offering me his hand. He pulled me up onto the rickety frame and then shuffled over in order to give me some room. With one flick of his thin rod, the mule staggered forward. I looked over his shoulder to see if the dogs were still following, but they were nowhere to be seen. The man beside me turned his head briefly. He said a few words and laughed, not in an unfriendly manner, but amused by something beyond my comprehension.

I took off my hat and wiped the sweat from my brow with the back of my hand. The boy tapped me on my shoulder. He held up a goatskin sack. I smiled and took it from him. He watched me as I drank and when I handed the sack back to him he shyly pointed at my lips. With my hands I mimed an explosion. 'Boom,' I said, and then slowly drew my finger across my mouth. The boy's face took on a hurt expression and he softly muttered something which I could only interpret as words of sympathy.

When we arrived in Baghdad I offered the father a couple of rupees. He refused at first, but when I made a play at giving the coins to the boy he accepted the fare, albeit with a reluctance which did him credit. I took a picture of the boy standing beside the mule. It's one of the few that I've kept.

Back at the Clarendon I was given a scribbled message

left by O'Neil. The desk clerk told me it was the doctor's habit to sleep in and that he'd left the message around midday. It was an invitation to visit him in Mosul, to see the dig and meet Tilden. I was curious to see what was going on there, but that afternoon's incident with the pariah dogs had understandably strengthened my conviction that it was time to quit.

3

The railway journey up until Mosul was uneventful. Most of Iraq is marsh or scrubland and looking out of the carriage's open window it was hard to believe that it had once been a fertile plain. Between the Tigris and the Euphrates the Sumerians, the Assyrians and the Babylonians had all farmed the land. It was the Sumerians who had founded the first city-state and it was the Assyrians and the Babylonians who, after conquering them, had added to those cities now being excavated up and down Iraq. The cradle of civilisation, and all that was left was sand, scrub and rubble. Though we mustn't forget the people who still inhabit the land: Chaldeans, Kurds, Arabs, Armenians. Since the Turks had been defeated they were all enjoying a degree of autonomy – at least that was what the politicians in Parliament were saying. On the street the Iraqi men were often wary at first, though once you'd shown them you meant no harm they could be disarmingly hospitable. In the Iraqi soul there's a warmth, even humour, a way of comprehending the world that is unashamedly poetic. Ours is a prosaic world of mechanical efficiency, and therein lies the division which exists. In many ways the Bible is our last link with what we once had. Its pages reveal a use of language far from leaden, a way of seeing unlike our own.

The train stopped at Mosul. Doors clattered and people disembarked. I expected, within a few minutes, to hear a whistle and for the locomotive to shudder forward. I had no intention of getting off. In my mind I had turned down O'Neil's invitation. I had visited Ur and had no desire to visit another dig.

In the stationary carriage the heat quickly became intolerable. I leaned my head out of the window and was met by the sulphurous smell of the engine. In what little shade the station platform afforded I saw a Jew with corkscrew curls shepherding several men in tattered, ill-fitting dressing gowns. Dismay swept over me as I realised that nobody was climbing aboard. I looked around. The carriage was empty. I had no choice but to gather up my pack and haversack and step down. Looking towards the front of the train I saw that the Jewish foreman and his men had gathered beside a flat-bed wagon. On the wagon were long lengths of pipe and a great black object, like some sort of boiler. Ropes were being untied and a man had arrived with a two-wheeled cart of galvanised tin.

I wandered into the ticket office. The stationmaster, a

stout Arab with a handlebar moustache, spoke enough English to explain that the offloading would take at least an hour. The loading, however, would take considerably longer. The train wouldn't be leaving until four o'clock at the earliest. I could wait at the station, or there were cafés in town. He offered to look after my luggage but, with the wariness that dogs every Englishman, I pretended that my pack was lighter than it was and walked away.

At the entrance to the station I glanced at my wristwatch before stepping into the glare of the midday sun. The *mu'addin*'s call to prayers had sounded and the streets of Mosul were practically deserted. Dogs lay in the empty streets with their backs against kerbstones. They briefly lifted their mangy heads at the sound of my footsteps, but otherwise didn't stir. In the main thoroughfare shops and cafés were veiled beneath fragile balconies, while the occasional merchant was to be spied lying half asleep in front of his stall. It was a place of lethargy and decay. I was glancing from one inebriated building to another when I saw her: a white woman in a straw boater and powder-blue dress. She skipped, with one hand holding onto her hat, across the street to a waiting lorry. Her sudden and skittish appearance had all the enchantment of a mirage. It wasn't so much her face, half hidden in shadow, that captivated me, but the graceful briskness with which she moved. After opening the cab door, she glanced back at me and smiled. She climbed inside, the engine started and the lorry drove away.

O'Neil had said something about an elderly widow, but

I couldn't recall him mentioning another woman. Of course she could have been the wife of some consulate official or petroleum engineer, yet I was convinced that she belonged to the dig. Her appearance had been fleeting, but I was enthralled; she seemed, in the stifling heat and torpid air, to be the apotheosis of the modern woman. As the lorry turned out of sight I felt an unaccountably strong sense of loss. With little more than the semblance of an idea, I unbuttoned a pocket and began to search for the scrap of paper O'Neil had left me.

4

The consulate was a large two-storey house of grey stone. Apart from the narrow balconies and their ornate metalwork, it was an ugly, functional building. At the wooden doors I was asked for my papers by an Indian sergeant. They were given a cursory glance and I was ushered towards a desk that had been placed in the middle of the entrance hall. In the cool stillness of the tiled hall I was greeted by a dark-haired fellow seated behind the desk. He had a thin moustache and a sallow face. Once he'd realised I was English his features softened a little and, with some difficulty, he rose up from his chair. 'It's my leg,' he said quietly, 'gone beneath the knee.'

'Don't get up on my account,' I responded, spreading my fingers in an unsuccessful attempt to deter him.

'It's quite all right.' He reached for a silver-tipped cane

that was leaning against a bookcase. 'All for king and country.'

'Here or Europe?' I asked.

'Not far from here. Landing a Bristol.'

'You were in the Flying Corps?'

He nodded. 'And Air Force, or was until two years ago.' He glanced at my lips.

'Shrapnel,' I said, 'at least that's what the surgeon thought, or possibly a bayonet.'

'Couldn't you tell him?'

'I was blown over. An exploding shell. I prefer to think of it as a piece of shrapnel; if it was a bayonet it could only have been my own.'

He nodded sympathetically and put out his hand. 'Crabtree,' he said, 'James Crabtree.'

'Harry Ward.'

'And what brings you to this land of milk and honey?'

'I'm here to see Dr O'Neil.'

'There's nothing the matter with you, is there?'

'No. It's just that he told me about an archaeological dig nearby, and I would like to take a look before my train leaves.'

'You're not a reporter, are you?'

'Far from it. I'm here to take pictures for a Methodist publication. Photographs of holy sites, that sort of thing.'

'And Nineveh is all you're interested in?'

'Yes. Is there a problem?'

'No, it's nothing really.' He inched forward, his cane dismally clicking on the tiled floor. 'It's just that we had this bloody awful reporter here last month, kicking up a fuss about the Arabs. Place was a powder keg until recently.'

'Well, I'm not here to cause any trouble.'

'Things will get better,' he said, as though he'd decided to take me into his confidence. 'The Anglo-Persian Oil Company will help to see to it. Once we send their sons to our schools to learn table manners and to play tennis the place will improve enormously. You see, this country lacks a proper ruling class.'

'Is Dr O'Neil around?'

He frowned. He was only just getting started. 'Are you in a hurry?'

'I'm afraid so.'

'Then I won't detain you any longer. Clinic's down the corridor,' he said, tilting his head to the right.

Soft yellow sunlight filled the clinic. After the dust and dirt it was almost disorientating to be in such an orderly room. In a glass cabinet chrome instruments glimmered in the half-light and in the air there hung the smell of disinfectant. A young nurse with dark-brown hair put down her book and smiled at me from behind her desk. I licked my lips and stuttered an introduction.

She listened politely and then, after gesturing for me to sit down on the bench beneath the window, went through the door behind her. Through the panel of frosted glass I could see her talking to someone. I sat on the wooden bench holding my hat in my hand, revolving the felt brim through my fingers. The room was silent except for the soft indecipherable words being spoken on the other side of the door. I'd spent too much time in clinics after the war to feel at ease and I began to think my being there was a mistake. I was on the brink of leaving when the nurse reappeared. She smiled reassuringly and ushered me through.

'My dear fellow, I didn't expect to see you quite so soon. Come in, come in.' He shook my hand, and steered me towards a chair. 'It's good to see you, though I'm afraid I haven't had a chance to speak to Tilden. But I did see Mrs Tilden this morning, and mentioned I'd met a photographer. You are here about the post, aren't you?'

'I'm sorry, I'm not staying,' I replied, conscious of his disappointment. 'My train's delayed until four. I just thought I'd take a few photographs of the site.'

'You can't be persuaded?'

'No, I don't think so.'

'I tell you what,' he said, glancing at his watch, 'I'll be finished here shortly and then I'll take you over. We'll see if Tilden can change your mind?'

'So the other chap's still missing?'

'I think I can confidently say Bateman won't be showing his face again.'

Back in the waiting room I sat down beneath the slow rotation of the reception's fan. An awkward silence descended. The nurse lifted herself an inch from her seat and smoothed the hem of her dress under her thighs. She returned to her novel and I gazed around the clinic as though such a setting was an unfamiliar one.

It was just before two when O'Neil reappeared. He led me out to the back of the consulate and to a black Mercedes, which was parked beneath a shelter of corrugated iron and wood. 'It's an extravagance, I know, but having my own motor is an enormous help. Apparently it used to belong to a friend of King Faisal's.'

'It's kind of you to take me over there, I'm sure . . .'

'Don't mention it. Besides, it gives me a chance to see how things are progressing. Wind down the windows before you get in, it'll be as hot as hell in there.'

Driving along the narrow streets towards the Tigris the doctor ran through the names of those working at the site as though he had the intention of introducing me to as many as possible. 'There's the Russian, Stanislav, Mr and Mrs Suarez, they're Americans from Chicago, and Mrs Jackson. I think I mentioned she's a bit long in the tooth, but good value. She's thoroughly loyal and completely trustworthy. Very bright, studied theology at Oxford. It's Tilden I'll introduce you to, and no doubt his wife will be around somewhere.'

Prayers had ended and the streets had started to fill. I turned away from the dark limbs and striped gowns that surrounded the car and looked at the doctor.

'Is she an archaeologist too?'

'No, and to be honest I believe she has little interest in the dig. Tilden's her second husband. Can't tell you where they met, but this is her second season out here.'

33

'And Tilden's been out here for . . .?'

'For six years now, though this is only his fourth at Nineveh. Didn't you say you served out here during the war?'

'Yes.'

'Whereabouts?'

'The siege of Kut.'

'Not under siege?'

'No, with the Norfolks.'

'Bad business.'

'Dreadful,' I replied automatically, not wanting to start a weary reckoning of the suffering that had piled up along the Tigris.

I saw the bridge ahead. It was a narrow stone strip that, for the last twenty yards, was covered with planks that had become warped in the sun. The car started to shake. 'It's ancient,' explained O'Neil, slowing the car down. 'Two-thirds intact, and finished with a wooden pontoon. It's the only thing that connects the dig. Three years ago part of the bridge was washed away. Tilden was left stranded for a week.'

Less than a mile after we'd crossed the Tigris we turned off the old road which led to the ancient city and travelled over a rutted track towards a large, flat building. The vegetation was thin and feverish and the few twisted trees were frantically leaning back to the river. In the distance I could see the walls of Nineveh. Beyond what I assumed to be the expedition house were several large mounds of dirt and rubble on which Arab workmen staggered up and down. A tall man, fanning himself with his homburg, was walking in our direction. Though the afternoon sun was shining across his face he glanced up at the sound of the doctor's Mercedes and watched as we turned into the house.

5

We drove through iron gates set in a narrow arch and into a courtyard. O'Neil parked beneath a palm tree which stood in the centre. The only other vehicle was a Ford lorry. Its bonnet was an oxblood red, though it was covered in dust. The expedition house was rectangular in shape with the four walls surrounding the courtyard and broken only by the narrow entrance through which we had driven. It was similar to Woolley's in that each room opened out into the yard. The roof was flat and in one corner stone steps led up to where sheets on a washing line were gently flapping. 'Reminds me of a stable block,' said O'Neil. 'Those working on the expedition have a stall and a window each.' As we crossed the courtyard he started pointing. 'Accommodation for the workers runs along the south wall. Those rooms over there are where the real work takes place. Across here is the common room, mess and kitchen.'

I followed the doctor into the expedition's common room. There were three easy chairs and one pea-green divan along the far wall. Sitting on the divan, with her bare legs tucked beneath her, sat a slender woman in a floral dress. One elbow rested on the back of the divan, the hand partly hidden behind her red hair. At the sound of footsteps she looked up from the periodical which lay across her lap. With some reluctance, her bare feet slid across the divan and into her dusty shoes. O'Neil stood on the Persian rug in the centre of the room while I advanced towards her. 'Mrs Tilden,' I heard him say behind me.

The woman rose to meet me. Her freckled face remained impassive as she shook my hand.

I introduced myself and explained my arrival. My explanation was met with a stony silence. For want of anything better to say I asked her if the photographer had returned.

'Oh no,' Mrs Tilden reassured me, her voice as soft as a lullaby. 'He's gone, and wouldn't have the nerve to return.'

'Then there's something to be done,' announced O'Neil.

'If it's employment you're looking for, Mr . . .'

'Ward,' I said for the second time. 'But I'm not staying.'

'Well,' she continued, her thin red lips giving me the briefest of smiles, 'we can certainly use another man.'

'And where's your husband, Susan?' asked O'Neil, his tone a little brusque.

'Where else but up at the dig.'

Her pale green eyes drifted briefly down to my lips as

38

she answered the doctor. Manicured fingers absently rubbed the delicate jade necklace that lay across the neckline of her frock. I found her gaze disconcerting, almost brazen. She smiled again, either unaware of the signal she was sending, or deriving some sort of kick from confusing the man in front of her. 'I thought you were an American, another geologist come to talk about oil wells. Have you seen them?'

'No,' I replied.

'They're all over,' she said, frowning as though I'd been travelling with my eyes shut. 'Always the smell of gas. A nightmare of hammers, drills, gas flares.' She wanted to jog my memory. 'Their paved roads shimmer in the heat.'

'I'm sorry,' I said, 'I haven't seen any.'

'Then you don't know Walt?'

'No.'

'Well, it doesn't matter. Don't let me keep you from your business.'

I nodded a goodbye and followed O'Neil back outside.

In the courtyard the doctor paused in the shade of the overhanging roof and lit his pipe. We crossed the yard in silence, but once we'd walked beyond the gates he turned his face to me. 'I'm afraid Mrs Tilden's recently found there's little here to entertain her.'

'She doesn't take an interest in her husband's work?'

'Not since . . . not for a while. She finds the heat and the flies quite difficult to cope with.'

'I've yet to meet a woman who likes being here.'

'Well, you've yet to meet Mrs Jackson.' O'Neil looked

ahead as we walked towards the dig. 'While you were serving out here did you ever suffer from heatstroke?'

'Something of the sort.'

'Then you'll know just how irrational some people can become. I don't normally share a concern with anyone outside the clinic, but Susan, Mrs Tilden, has trouble sleeping. Her mind's overwrought. It's some sort of neurosis, nothing too serious you understand. I honestly don't know why Bateman took off like he did, though it's easy to surmise what might have happened.'

'I see.'

'Her husband's a little older than she is. We all thought he was a confirmed bachelor when he first arrived. As for Bateman . . .' He paused as if to allow me time to reflect on men like Bateman. 'You're not a ladies' man are you, Mr Ward?'

'I don't think of myself as a Valentino, if that's what you mean.'

'Oh it doesn't matter about looks,' said O'Neil. 'It's how you cast yourself that counts.'

'Well, I can't see myself playing the lead, can you?'

'Not since the war?'

'Not even before the war, if you must know.'

'It's just that Susan means a great deal to Tilden. But there's no foundation for her fears, her neurosis.'

'Sometimes being abroad, surrounded by Arabs . . .'

'Oh no, she likes Arabs, appreciates their simplicity.' He paused and placed a hand on my arm in order to stop me from walking ahead. 'Listen, if I can persuade you to stay I'd like you to keep an eye on her for me. I believe you're a decent man, Mr Ward. What little time we've spent together makes me think you wouldn't betray someone's trust.'

'Of course not, though I still intend to catch the train to Constantinople.'

'Then we don't have much time. But if you were just to stay for a few weeks I know it would be an enormous help to everyone.'

'I understand.'

'I knew you would. Anyone that's served out here should be able to sympathise.'

We continued on our way towards the largest mound at the corner of the excavation site. The dusty, windswept area had been churned up over the course of several seasons and what Tilden now seemed to be focused on was quite a distance from the city's wall. Arabs were swarming over the large mound. I saw the man with the homburg I'd seen earlier reappear as if from beneath the earth.

O'Neil called out to him and Tilden turned round. He was a gaunt-looking man with stooping shoulders, a narrow face and spectacles. Mrs Tilden was in her thirties, but her husband looked much older. 'Why if it isn't O'Neil,' he cried, his voice deep and authoritative. 'Come to see what all the fuss is about?'

'Oh, there's always something to be excited about it seems.'

'And it often ends in disappointment, I know. But this

41

is—' Tilden's sentence ended abruptly as if registering my presence for the first time. 'Hello,' he said a little warily, 'a new face?'

'This is Mr Ward,' replied O'Neil. 'He's a photographer by trade and I thought . . .'

Behind Tilden's shoulder I saw the woman walking towards us. The hat was gone, but she was wearing the same powder-blue dress.

'A photographer,' said Tilden. 'You know ours has gone missing?'

'Yes,' I replied, though I was hardly listening.

'Ah Clara,' said O'Neil, 'let me introduce you to Mr Ward.'

With an accomplished movement she flicked her cigarette away and put out her slender hand. She was a comparatively slight woman with dark eyes and jet-black hair cut fashionably short. I took her to be in her early thirties, yet there was a girlish frankness to her face which, like her bare arms, was tanned by the sun. 'I saw you in town,' she said with an American drawl, the mellowness of it almost out of sorts with the vernal woman before me. 'What's your business, Mr Ward? You don't look like another oil man?'

'No, I'm a photographer.'

'A photographer,' she repeated as though amused by my answer.

'I've been travelling across Palestine and Iraq.'

'Snapping belly dancers and temple virgins?'

'Not quite. Scenes for a book, *The Study of the Bible*.'

'And before you began your pilgrimage?' asked Tilden, doing his best to disguise his annoyance at having been interrupted.

'Weddings, landscapes.'

'And you now want to throw in your lot with us?'

'Well, not exactly. I thought I could take some photographs and then . . .'

'Stay the night,' said O'Neil. 'That'd be all right, wouldn't it, Henry?'

'But my railway ticket . . .'

'The consulate can sort that out. And you can't do this place justice in under an hour.' O'Neil turned to Tilden, who stood impassively staring at me. 'You need the help, and Mr Ward served out here during the war. Who knows, we might even be able to persuade him to stay for the season.'

O'Neil was doing his best, but Tilden wasn't having any of it. I had the feeling he could see right through me and understood perfectly why I was hardly protesting.

'I'm sorry,' he said, wiping his brow with a grimy handkerchief, 'there's no need for Mr Ward to stay. I spent most of this morning speaking to the official photographer for the Department of Antiquities in Mosul.'

'Did you tell them where we're digging?' asked Clara. 'They aren't going to like you digging outside of the city.'

'There won't be any fuss.'

'You want to take that chance? Tom says we need that permit.'

Her questions annoyed him, but he wasn't so easily

defeated. 'And how will it look if I have to go back to the Antiquities and tell them we don't need their photographer?' he asked.

'It's going to look a damn sight better than having to stop the dig. Tom's just itching to write to Chicago, you know he is.'

'But this photographer,' he said, gesturing towards me, 'stays for a night or two and then what?'

'How long can you stay for, Mr Ward?' Clara asked. 'Tell me you're not in any hurry to get back to those damp islands of yours. Who knows,' she quickly added, 'if you hang around we may even light upon more golden rams than Woolley.'

I was caught between the two of them but it wasn't a difficult decision to make and, by the look on her face, she knew what I was thinking. 'A week,' I said, 'if it's warranted, though the train will need to be sorted out and I'll have to send a telegram.'

O'Neil nodded and Clara smiled.

'It needs to be a month,' said Tilden. 'If I'm going to have to deal with Antiquities it must be longer.'

I paused in an attempt to weigh up the reasons for and against, but having risen to the challenge once I wasn't about to let him beat me. 'All right,' I heard myself saying, 'a month.' Again there was a nod and a smile and I felt like a man who, having been encouraged by his wife to bid at an auction, had finally triumphed.

Tilden grunted. 'I take it you do know how to develop and enlarge?'

'Of course. You have an enlarger here?'

'We have one somewhere. Bateman left all his stuff. You've your own equipment?'

'A Leica,' I replied, lifting the case, 'and several rolls of film.'

'Well I dare say that'd give me time to find somebody else.' Tilden spat into the dust. 'We can't pay you much, you understand, but there's board and lodging.'

'And if you find something he'll get his share?' asked O'Neil.

'That's for Tom to decide.' Tilden turned to me. 'I expect you'd like to see your quarters if you're set on staying. Clara, you can take Mr Ward back to the house. Tell your husband I'll be there soon. I need to talk to O'Neil.'

6

'You won't regret staying,' said Clara, as we walked towards the house. 'Tilden's all right, he's just bloody-minded when he feels like it. Bateman's disappearance didn't help, though in some ways he wasn't sorry to see the back of him. You've never worked on a dig before?'

'No, but I've visited a few.'

'Well some folk find it hard to get along, especially when things aren't going to plan. Did O'Neil tell you about the dig?'

'Not really.'

'Would you like to know? Some people say I talk too much, but I reckon you're a good listener.'

'I'd like to know,' I replied. Listening to her was easy, though a slight awkwardness had seized me. I wasn't saying much, but it didn't seem to matter. Her shoulder lightly fell against my arm as we crossed the uneven ground. It was hard to say whether or not she'd noticed. There was something girlish about her, like a divine carelessness. She looked to be in her thirties, but her vitality made her seem much younger.

'It's what he thinks is a temple that Tilden's most excited about, though it's beyond the city's wall. He's hoping it's the great temple of Ishtar, but so far there's nothing to confirm his hunch.'

'Isn't it unusual to have a temple outside the city?'

'Sure is,' she agreed, 'though we've yet to find out why it's there.'

'Any theory?'

'Nope, no reason why it should be placed out on its own, but it is.' She glanced behind us. 'You can't see it now, and anyway most of it is still buried beneath sand and rubble. Imagine a rectangular tower built in stages, a stepped pyramid like the one at Ur, but totally covered. Or at least it was until a month ago.'

'What made him dig beyond the wall?'

'A local rumour that there was something beyond the Shamash gate. He had trouble persuading Tom to let him dig outside the city.'

'Tom's your husband?'

'He is.' Her short answer was neither the declaration of a lover, nor the anguished confession of a broken woman.

'You say it's a temple?'

'Yes, though there's nothing to indicate worship.

48

There's a pit thirty feet deep and all they've found is an inscription.'

'You think it's been pillaged?'

'Perhaps,' she said reluctantly, as though the thought of an empty ruin could make me change my mind, 'but there's something strange about the place. If it was a temple then you'd think they would have uncovered a series of carvings by now or some sort of decoration. We've gone from the uppermost chamber down to the next level but both chambers are bare.'

'Could it have been a watchtower?' I asked.

'I doubt it. Each level appears to be almost twice the size of the one above. It seems too grand for such a simple purpose. The one inscription they've found is also unusual.'

'In what way?'

'I'm not sure, other than Tilden says he's seen nothing like it before.'

'It's been translated?'

'Not quite. Stanislav is struggling with its meaning.'

'How many levels does this thing have?'

'They're guessing at least four. Maybe more. We haven't found a single artefact yet. We did in the eastern corner of the city.' She pointed towards the vast expanse of ruins which sat beside the Tigris. 'Nineveh's down there, or what's left of it after being ransacked by the Babylonians. Beneath the earth we found jewellery and offerings, strange stone carvings of creatures. I'll show you back at the house, though I doubt they'll ever be on public display. Say, you're not easily spooked are you, Mr Ward? You know Nineveh was a very wicked place. They say if you wander through it at night you can hear the crack of whips and the rattling of wheels.'

'But the city's deserted isn't it? I mean it's just a ruin?'

'A ruin, but cursed by so many. No one's lived there for over two thousand years. You see the wall that surrounds the city; sun-baked brick and stone. Once it was covered with human skins, from one gate to the next. At night, when the wind blows, it echoes with the screams of men, crowds baying for blood. Soldiers flayed alive. Imagine that.'

'I'd rather not.'

'Oh you're just yellow,' she innocently teased. 'Before being flayed they were forced to parade naked through the city, swinging their general's head by its beard.' There was a pause as she studied my face, and then she apologised, fingers hovering, nails bitten. 'It's just the thought of all that history excites me. I didn't mean to cause offence.'

I waited at the entrance to the house and began to wonder if I'd made the right decision. There was Clara, and there was the war, and I wondered if my staying had anything to do with the latter. Was the idea that salvation comes from serving others so ingrained as to make me want to serve, to atone for what had happened? I watched Tilden and O'Neil approach the house. The sun was beginning to set and for a second the mounds and hummocks in the pitted earth seemed to hold grotesque shapes; no more than shadows playing tricks on my mind, but enough to swell the landscape's malevolence. I held my breath. With the boundless desert it's not what can be seen, but what lies beyond our grasp. I exhaled. An infinite sea of sand at dusk is a melancholy landscape and I was not immune to its morbidity. I began to breathe again.

Not so fast.

Take a deep breath.

Before charging our breathing was irregular, shallow, rapid; an attack of nerves being as contagious as it is. Then it would start to fall into a rhythm. Just briefly, breathing together, as though forged by our desperate longing to go on living. It begins to slow, the harmony of breath and spirit unwinding. One licks his lips, another swallows with difficulty. Some murmur a prayer, some sob a little. The harmony is broken and each one of us is alone again.

I tried to focus on the two men coming towards me, but my mind was caught by the moving blotches of shadow. There was the sound of a whistle or a bird, and in the yellow light a soldier pirouetted like a skater, knocked sideways by a shell. I saw him twist and fall. On his face there was the expectation of pain. He'd tried to keep his balance but had failed. He staggered on one foot, as though he was convinced that if he was able to stay standing he wouldn't die. What was his last thought? That we were laughing at him and his odd arabesque?

I looked across at his body lying in the reeds as I staggered through the sliding mud. I didn't want to, but there was the faintest possibility that he might be alive. Only

51

one leg was still attached, broken at the knee. His head was hanging loose across his shoulder. It was the last thing I saw before I was blown off my feet.

Their voices were clear. 'Did you hear Woolley's been asked to speak on the wireless when he gets back to London? He says he's sick to death of finding gold headdresses.'

O'Neil laughed.

I think Tilden was glad to see me on my own. We walked through to the courtyard and stopped next to the car. 'O'Neil tells me he's introduced you to my wife, but you've yet to meet Mrs Jackson. She keeps precise records of the finds and will tell you what needs photographing. I'll introduce you to her.'

I tried to rouse myself from my stupor. Tilden continued to talk. 'Suarez organises the workforce and draws up plans of the excavation. I write up the field reports for *The Philadelphian*, which also requires photographs. Just wait here for a moment.' He went off to the washroom.

'Keep an eye on Mrs Tilden,' said O'Neil quietly as he handed me my pack. 'Henry's not the most sympathetic of husbands, but she imagines things . . . gets herself all worked up over nothing.' He shut the boot of the car and walked round to the driver's door. 'I've given her something to help, but just watch her for me.'

I nodded as he climbed in and started the motor.

'I'll be back next week,' he shouted above the engine. I watched him reverse through the gates. A song thrush flew above the palm trees and landed on the roof of the house.

'You travel light,' observed Tilden as he came out of the washroom, a towel wrapped round his neck.

'I was starting to think I was sleeping in the y-yard.'

A smile played across his lips. 'Follow me. I'll give you Bateman's old room.'

7

My room was sparsely furnished: a narrow bed, a bedside cabinet, and chest of drawers, its mirror held at an angle with a squashed matchbox. A bare bulb was hanging from the centre of the ceiling while the small window that looked out into the yard was covered with a net curtain. On the tiled sill were five dead flies, their black bodies desiccated by the sun. The equally small window in the south wall had an iron grille across it. The view was uninspiring: banks of earth and stone, no sight of the Tigris. I pulled across the makeshift curtain and the room turned a dirty yellow.

After unpacking my few belongings I went to the communal washroom and then made my way back to where I'd met Mrs Tilden. She'd left, but sitting in her place was a man reading a novel, the title of which I assumed to be in Russian. On hearing me enter he put the novel aside and stood up to shake my hand. I took him to be in his early forties. His dark hair was shaved close to the skull, and his eyes, behind his horn-rimmed spectacles, appeared to be the tired eyes of someone who'd seen a great deal of life. 'You are Mr Ward,' he said, with hardly an accent. 'I am Victor Stanislav. I hear you have come to join us.'

'For a little while, at least.'

'A little longer, I hope, than Mr Bateman.'

'I certainly won't be leaving without saying goodbye.'

Stanislav smiled. 'I'm in charge of translating the clay tablets and inscriptions.'

'So I've been told.'

'I prefer to think of it as deciphering, rather than translating. It's a subtle difference and one lost on most people. You know you've come at a most inopportune time. All we have left to photograph are a few tablets. Can you read cuneiform?'

'I can hardly speak Arabic.'

'Of course, you're English. It is a pity though that you'll have to take my translation as gospel.'

'I've always thought that there's very little we can take as gospel.'

'Is that right?' asked Stanislav, who appeared to be amused by my answer. 'Dr Tilden tells me you've been tramping around the Middle East taking pictures of biblical scenes. Have you visited Sodom or Gomorrah?'

'I believe they've yet to be found.'

'If they ever existed.' Stanislav poured himself a drink from the decanter. 'It's whisky. Would you like one?'

'Thanks.'

'Are you a religious man?' he asked as he handed me a glass.

'My parents are Methodists.'

'Which means?'

'Salvation comes from helping others. A worker is equal to a king in the eyes of God. And hymns must be sung.'

'And you are . . .?'

'The son of Methodists.'

'Bravo, but this is neither one thing, nor the other.' He was staring into my eyes with such an intense look of curiosity on his sun-browned face that I thought he must have been mocking me. 'Which means the war didn't entirely destroy your ability to believe?'

'No,' I replied, 'not entirely. What man inflicts upon himself has nothing to do with what I believe.'

'Well, belief systems have their uses. Religion has oiled the wheels of society for thousands of years. Though whether we need it now is debatable. Whether or not it is merely glorified superstition is something we should all ask ourselves. Isn't that right?'

'It sounds as if you have doubts?'

'On the contrary, Mr Ward, I am an atheist; of that I am very certain. Does that shock you?'

'No, not at all.'

'You see, I'm here to work, to earn a crust as they say, and to see where the Bible and Assyrian mythology overlap.'

57

'In order to see how the Hebrews turned base metal into gold?'

'Exactly,' he said. 'How, as Suarez would say, the Bible has gilded earlier beliefs, refined their meaning, deciphered the kernel of truth that was always there. But I'm guessing you're not convinced. For me, every similar event, every shared miracle undermines your Bible. When we're finished in Iraq everyone should be able to see it as a book laced with ancient lies.'

'But you remain objective?'

'I always try and keep an open mind,' he replied with a wry smile.

A dark-haired woman wrapped in a plain white smock appeared at the door. 'Victor,' she said, followed by a sentence which could easily have been Russian.

Stanislav answered her in the same language and then beckoned her forward. Somewhat hesitantly she walked into the common room.

'Mr Ward, may I introduce my wife, Sasha.'

She offered me her hand. I took it, thought of pressing it to my lips as she seemed to expect, but settled on shaking it at an unnaturally high angle. It was no doubt the most awkward introduction she'd ever had to suffer, and it didn't help to hear Stanislav laughing to himself. 'You English are so coy. My wife is Slovak and therefore she expects you to flirt.'

The woman shot him a disapproving look and replied again in her own tongue.

Stanislav said something in response and then laughed.

Sasha, her dark eyes fixed upon me like those of a wary child, went over to the gramophone.

'I am sorry, Mr Ward. My wife understands English better than she speaks it, but she is keen to learn your language.'

'I'm glad to hear it.'

'Are you hungry?'

'Very,' I admitted, having had very little since breakfast.

'Well, we dine at seven in what they insist on calling the mess. It's almost a formal affair, with Tilden at one end of the table and his wife at the other. The food is good: mostly lamb and goat. We have an Indian cook. You like curries? Of course you do. I expect you'll be sitting opposite me, in Bateman's place.'

'I suppose so,' I said.

'We have a generator, which runs until ten o'clock. We can work or read under electric light until then.'

The gramophone had begun to play some sort of slow Arabic tune; all windpipes, cymbals and drums. Mrs Stanislav turned and whispered something to her husband. 'She wants to know if you like Arabic music?'

'Yes,' I said. 'Outside there was a song thrush. Reminded me of England.'

'This is called "The Persian Market". It's very derivative, don't you think?'

'I couldn't say.'

Behind Stanislav's shoulder a thin lady in her fifties entered the common room. Her grey hair was pinned in a bun and she had on spectacles similar to those worn by the Russian.

'Ah, Mrs Jackson,' said Stanislav. 'May I introduce you to Mr Ward?'

Mrs Jackson nodded curtly at Stanislav. 'Mr Ward, I hear you've come to join us.' Her manner was brusque, but not unfriendly. She smiled and firmly shook my hand.

'I'm glad to be here. I've been told Dr Tilden is on to something.'

'He's a good man, Mr Ward. No doubt you'll repay his kindness with hard work.'

'Your predecessor certainly lacked—' The peal of a bell interrupted the Russian's sentence. 'Ah, it seems supper is ready.'

8

Clara and her husband were already seated at the table. We smiled at one another and they told me more about the dig and the cataloguing of the artefacts. Bateman's name was briefly mentioned, but Mr Suarez, or Tom as he insisted I call him, steered the conversation away from the missing photographer and spoke about his tenure at the University of Chicago. Clara, whom he'd met in Detroit, didn't have any formal training, but they'd worked as archaeologists in Greece and had been excavating in Mesopotamia for the last five years.

Suarez, like his wife, was talkative and in his thirties, although he was somewhat slovenly in appearance. He had the stocky frame of a prizefighter and his face was unshaven. His fingernails were an unpleasant yellow from smoking and on one of his fingers he wore a gold ring with a peculiar scarab. Clara, in contrast, was neat and decorous. She had painted her lips and from beneath her black fringe her dark eyes shone brightly. Over supper I noticed that they were slightly misaligned in movement, the left eye dragging a fraction behind the right. At first there was merely the suspicion, her quick movement of her head disguising the slightest of squints. Like her husband, she smoked throughout the meal, only putting down her cigarette to pick up her knife. In a blue haze of smoke I watched her cutting up her chicken into neat strips and then, with a fork in one hand and a cigarette in the other, she conducted her way through supper.

Mrs Tilden joined the table after we'd begun eating and sat opposite her husband. She smiled weakly at those who met her gaze, said very little and left before we'd finished our tinned pears.

At the end of the meal Stanislav asked me if I'd like to join him for a whisky. I was about to accept his offer, but I noticed Tilden shaking his head. 'I think Mr Ward should have an early night. Besides, there's work to be done. You've only partly translated the inscription.'

Stanislav shrugged his shoulders and repeated what Tilden had just said to his wife.

'I think we all agreed to speak English at the table,' said Tilden rather sharply.

'Sorry,' answered Stanislav without any rancour. 'I think, Sasha, it is time to go back to our books. Goodnight, Mr Ward. We will celebrate your arrival another evening.'

I also got up to leave, but Tilden waved me back down.

'I want to speak to you, Ward. Mina, I'd like you to stay behind.'

Mrs Jackson nodded. Suarez looked up from rolling a cigarette. I waited, but the doctor failed to say anything else. An awkward silence descended before Suarez cleared his throat. 'I guess we'd better head back to the *antika*.'

'There are still a few items that need cataloguing,' said Clara. 'No doubt we'll be seeing you in there soon, Mr Ward.'

'Of course,' I replied. 'I'd like to see what you've uncovered so far.'

'Well, goodnight,' said her husband, patting his jacket for the outline of his pouch of tobacco.

Tilden lifted a hand, but didn't look up. They rose and left the three of us sitting there. The table was cleared by the houseboy, except for the glass that the doctor was holding and a jug of water. 'That'll be all,' said Tilden. 'Go back to the kitchen.'

'Amuda's just been promoted from basket-boy,' explained Mrs Jackson. 'He speaks a little English.'

'He's Iraqi?'

'Armenian, or at least his parents were. His mother died crossing the Syrian desert.'

'From Turkey?' I asked.

'Yes.'

'Then he's lucky to have survived.'

'Have you heard of the Blacksmith of Arkantz, Mr Ward?' asked Tilden, leaning forward.

'I'm afraid I haven't.'

'He was the governor of Amuda's province. When the Russians were fighting nearby the Armenians were accused of helping them. This gave the governor the chance to set about mercilessly torturing men and women. For inspiration he delved into the records of the Spanish Inquisition. He was soon nailing horseshoes to men's feet, hence the Blacksmith of Arkantz.' Tilden paused to take a sip of water while I sat and waited. 'Men were roped together and massacred. Women and girls were raped by cutthroats from half-savage tribes. Inflamed by such stories Amuda attacked a Turk in the market, though how serious the attack was I've never been able to uncover. Captain Fowler brought him here last year. I'm telling you this because you're bound to see him sharpening his knife in the evening. It's something he insists on keeping beneath his pillow, but it's nothing to worry about.'

'He thinks of himself as a Christian, yet he obviously can't abide Turks,' added Mrs Jackson. 'When he arrived he had the unfortunate habit of spitting behind the back of any Kurd. The cook's Hindu, which leaves him rather puzzled. He has no reason to hate Hindus, and thankfully they work well together.'

'Gurvinder's teaching him to cook,' said Tilden, 'and the boy speaks enough English to understand what he's being told. And despite his deep-seated desire for revenge he's always smiling. According to Stanislav he wants to own his own café in Mosul and to marry a Circassian slave girl. Apparently they were bred on farms for the sultan's harem.'

'Of course Tom refuses to call him anything other than boy,' said Mrs Jackson.

'What does Amuda think of Methodists?'

Mrs Jackson smiled. 'Is that what you are?'

'Up until the war.'

'And then?'

'Well, the war . . .'

'The war changed a lot of things,' said Tilden. He'd sat back in his seat and was looking at the table. 'Is your room all right?'

'It's fine,' I replied. 'It lacks a sea view, but . . .'

Mrs Jackson had taken off her spectacles and was gently massaging her forehead.

I felt that they were waiting for me to continue. 'It's as good as any since I disembarked in Haifa.'

'Haifa,' Tilden repeated distractedly.

'Where I disembarked.' I smiled, but couldn't abide the silence. 'You wanted to talk to me?'

'I want to explain what I've done, why I've chosen to dig outside the city walls.' He refilled his glass and then looked at me. 'Do you ever act on a hunch?'

'Rarely,' I replied. 'When I have I've always regretted it.'

'It sometimes works in the field.'

'I imagine a lot of it is guesswork.'

He frowned.

Mrs Jackson coiled one wire at a time behind her ears and returned her spectacles to her narrow face. We waited for him to continue.

He took another sip of water and forced himself to smile, though it was more like a grimace; his brown, weather-beaten skin creasing under the strain. Yet it was a signal that he was ready. 'I want you to know how things work around here. How, as with every other dig, we give a share of what we find to Bell's museum in Baghdad. We excavate here at the expense of our patrons: Chicago, Danvers, private investors. Don't be deluded into thinking that it's all about expanding our knowledge of Assyrian society. For some it's driven by the market, as with every other venture. Assyrian artefacts are in vogue and collectors – public or private – will pay a tidy sum for certain items. Once it became clear there was a monetary value to antiquities, Mr Ward, archaeology became very fashionable.'

'I know Woolley's fired the public's imagination,' I said. 'I visited his expedition house at Ur. The *antika* room was filled to the brim with statues, and helmets of beaten gold.'

Tilden seemed to wince at the mention of Woolley's success. 'Quite,' he replied. 'But it's not all about statues and gold, is it?'

'Of course not,' I answered. 'I imagine working towards an understanding of how people lived is just as important, if not more so.'

'And keeping an open mind? On occasion what we uncover can transform our way of thinking, even our understanding of who we are.'

'Absolutely.'

'Let me tell you about what we're doing here.' He glanced at Mrs Jackson and she faintly nodded. 'You see, there was a mound which had been puzzling me. Tom thought that it was simply an Assyrian tip: broken bricks, clay shards, that sort of thing. Easy pickings, a glimpse into a world through what was thrown away. It didn't take me long to realise there was some sort of structure buried beneath almost three thousand years of accumulated sand and rubble. It's a ziggurat, a primitive kind of block pyramid, but the first two chambers are empty. As we begin to dig further down we should find something tangible, otherwise it could turn into a wasted season, and I'll have to acknowledge that Tom was right.'

'Meaning?'

'That we should have stayed within the city and excavated near the Shamash gate, as we'd agreed.'

'And where we have a permit to dig,' added Mrs Jackson.

'Is it too late to switch back?' I asked.

'It's not, but I'm not quite ready to admit defeat. You see, they wouldn't build a ziggurat outside the city without good reason. What I've seen, from what I understand, it's worth staking my reputation on. Today . . .' Tilden paused and rubbed his face.

'What happened today?' I asked, his false start only serving to increase my curiosity.

He stared at me as though wondering whether or not he should say anything. 'Few on this dig are convinced that what we're uncovering has any real significance. They

67

think it's an abandoned temple, an early folly, that its purpose will never come to light. Looking back, it's easy to see that some things should be left to rot.'

'Left to rot?'

'Mr Ward,' said Mrs Jackson, 'if you were on the brink of finding something that could change what people have believed for the last two thousand years, would you want to share that knowledge? If, say, I was able to challenge our understanding of the Bible, would you want to listen?'

'I don't understand.'

'Let me try and explain,' said Tilden. 'This afternoon Stanislav finished translating the first part of the inscription. Your arrival today worried me. We're not quite ready to share what we've found. There must be more to uncover, to understand. Stanislav knows his cuneiform, but he's damned slow. Meticulous, I suppose.'

'What did you find?'

'Something that I want you to photograph tomorrow.'

'And that is?'

Dr Tilden shook his head. 'How much do you know about Adam and Eve?'

'I know that the Garden of Eden is said to lie between the Tigris and the Euphrates.'

'Do you know the story of Lamashtu?'

'Lamashtu?' I repeated.

'Or Lilith, as she later became?'

'I'm sorry, I don't.'

'It's not surprising. There's little mention of her in the Bible. And what there is doesn't really convey anything.

68

Lilith, according to Hebrew and Assyrian mythology, was created before Eve, created as an equal for Adam. And as she was his equal they argued and, ultimately, Lilith was cast out of the Garden of Eden.'

'And this Lilith appears in the Bible?'

'Briefly; buried somewhere in Isaiah.'

'And she has something to do with what you've uncovered?'

'Perhaps,' answered Mrs Jackson. 'You see Lamashtu, as Lilith was once called, was an Assyrian goddess, daughter of the sky god Anu. Her name means "she who erases". According to the Talmud she would come in the night to steal infants and the unborn, though she also preyed on adults, sucking blood from young men, and bringing disease, sterility and nightmares. Accounts of Lilith vary considerably, but she's always been depicted with wings and sharp, birdlike talons.'

'And this all happened after she was cast out of Eden?'

Tilden waved Mrs Jackson on. 'If the Hebrews are to be believed. In one version of the legend, Lilith left Eden and began birthing her own children. God sent three angels to bring her back, and when she refused, they promised to kill a hundred of her children every day until she returned. Lilith, in turn, vowed to murder all the infants she could find. Accounts of Lilith as a child-killer seem to be taken directly from the Lamashtu legend. Most likely the Jews assimilated the figure of Lamashtu into their tradition.'

'And this has something to do with the ziggurat?'

'Today,' said Tilden, 'we found Lamashtu's name carved into a stone. "Preserve thyself from Lamashtu and her daughters. Bountiful breeder of demons". If this building's dedicated to her it could alter our whole understanding of Genesis.'

9

Clara is perched on the divan under the small window in the common room. She sits with one leg tucked beneath her. Her face appears self-absorbed, brooding, almost predatory. She says quietly, 'I ought not to let you, really.' She is needlessly tapping her cigarette over the ashtray. 'I ought not to let you, really,' she repeats in the same mocking and suggestive way. Taking a puff at her cigarette she throws her head back and blows out the smoke in a thin blue stream. She returns to tapping her cigarette over the ashtray. The animal prints on the wall fade slowly from view.

The tapping grows louder, becomes increasingly insistent. Out of a grey obscurity comes the hammering of a machine gun. I look down. My legs feel as if they are bound together, but a smoky haze from shellfire hides my puttees from sight. I'm stumbling away from the

71

Turkish line, trying to run. I'm the only one still moving. Behind me the Turks are cursing and firing. My shirt is clinging to my back. They're cursing in disbelief. Their patience is at an end. They're climbing out of their trench, fixing bayonets, running after me. They're sprinting towards me, their feet pounding on the flat plain, growing louder, while I'm shuffling forward, dragging my legs, wading through the air with my hands, trying to escape the thrusting bayonet, the stabbing pain that will drill into my back.

I'm arching away from the mattress, anticipating the first cold thrust which will cause me to writhe around in agony. Yet the drumming of feet falls away and an eerie silence descends. I continue to shuffle forward. I'm breathing fast and shallow, and finding it difficult to swallow. There's a horrible buzzing in my head. I turn to see what has happened. The Turks are staring up into the sky, shielding their eyes. A shadow is sweeping over the plain, racing towards them. I can't see what it is, yet I know it's not an aeroplane. It's silent and far more sinister. I try to look up but my vision is blurred, sweat is running into my eyes. The men start to scatter. I hear the machine gun's rattle, and the beating of wings behind me.

The noise surrounds me and I stir beneath the twisted sheet. The oppressive air is alive with the invisible flight of a shapeless thing and my first rational thought is that a bird is trapped in the room. I stretch out a hand, feeling for the box of matches, half expecting a brush of feathers or the scratching of a claw. A book falls to the floor. I strike a match: a flare, the smell of phosphorus. A shadow slides across the floor, cast by the light. But nothing is there. The room stands motionless. I light the candle on the bedside cabinet. I try the switch; an empty noise; clicking through the silence. The brick floor is cold beneath my bare feet. I pull back the curtain and the window pane buckles in the candlelight. Behind the grille a half-formed shape falls to the ground. It falls too rapidly for me to be certain. I rub my eyes. A face stares back, a smeared and bleary reflection. I press my nose against the cold glass, straining to see below the brick sill. Was there a bird, a bat? Beyond the grille there's nothing. Whatever it was has gone. My breath spreads across the pane. The window is bolted. It's quiet and the air makes me shiver. I pull on my woollen jersey and return to bed.

Silence. I blow out the candle. The noise returns. It's not in the room but somewhere above me. A heron or a large rat scratching and running around on the flat roof of the house. I lie awake, listening. Every time I close my eyes it starts up again: frenetic bursts, followed by a long, slow clawing that peters out after a minute or so; always stopping just before I can muster the resolve to do something about it.

10

There was a hammering on my door. A voice was saying something about breakfast. It took me a second or two to work out where I was. The room was cold and dark. I lay in bed, gathering my senses, recalling the dream, the sounds that had kept me awake. I thought of Clara and then tried to focus on the work ahead. I tried to recall what Mrs Jackson had said about Lilith, about uncovering something as significant as Woolley's discovery at Ur.

After a quick flannel wash and a cold shave in the washroom I joined the others in the mess. Everyone was gathered round the table, though Mrs Tilden had yet to appear.

'We have a cup of coffee and a slice of toast before we set out,' said Stanislav. 'We rise at dawn, work for a couple of hours and then return for something more substantial.'

'You mean porridge with goat's milk,' added Suarez.

'You've film in that thing?' asked Tilden, pointing to the brown leather case slung round my shoulder.

'Of course.'

'And you know how to develop?'

'I've been developing pictures since the age of twelve. I don't expect—'

'Spare me the potted biography. All I want to know is whether or not you have what is required to develop the pictures you're going to be taking?'

'Yes,' I replied calmly.

'I'm glad to hear it. Right, shall we set off?'

Those who were still standing round the table murmured their assent and we started to follow Tilden out of the mess. Clara briefly took hold of my arm. There was the smell of tobacco and lavender. With her lips close to my ear she whispered, 'Don't worry, he's always insufferable before breakfast.'

'Are you trying to convince me there are times when he's not?'

She smiled back as we stepped out into the weak sunlight and followed the others across the courtyard towards the narrow arch. Stanislav and his wife returned to their room to continue working on the inscription.

'They should accompany us after we've had a proper breakfast,' explained Tilden, 'though Sasha can't really contribute much.'

'She sketches a little,' said Mrs Jackson.

'A little's about right,' added Tilden.

It was a dusty, dry track. The sun was shining yet it

was cold. Mrs Jackson and Clara had linked arms at the back of the party. With Tilden striding ahead, Tom and I fell into step. After he'd lit his cigarette I asked him if he'd heard anything during the night.

The American looked at me. 'What kind of thing?'

'A rat or a bird scratching on the roof.'

'I didn't hear anything,' he replied. 'Tilden used to have a terrier, but it disappeared just before Bateman. It could have been a fox.' He addressed the two women behind. 'Ward heard something on the roof last night. Either of you hear anything?'

'Nothing at all,' said Mrs Jackson, 'but then once my head hits the pillow I'm out like a light.'

'Why don't you ask Susan?' suggested Clara. 'Her room's just the other side of the studio. She has trouble sleeping. She could have heard something.'

I nodded in appreciation, though their response troubled me. Mrs Tilden must have heard it, unless my mind was sliding back into its old ways.

Ahead of us were thirty or so Arabs moving around what they'd uncovered. From a distance the ziggurat itself was hardly an impressive sight. The topmost chamber, which stood a yard or two above the bank of earth, looked no larger than a brick outhouse.

We stopped at the edge of the dig and gazed down on the covered heads of the workmen. They stood on the outer edge of the second chamber and were digging round what they'd cleared in order to reach the next floor. The second chamber, the exposed lip of which was made of the same grey bricks as the walls, was roughly twice the size of the one above. I wondered how far the structure continued down into the earth, if it continued doubling in size.

'We've made an entrance on the other side,' said Tilden. 'Suarez and his wife will supervise the digging out here. I want you to follow me inside.'

I nodded and, treading carefully along the rim, followed the doctor and Mrs Jackson. We walked across planks that had been laid over as a walkway. It was a yard wide and on either side the earth fell away to just below the roof of the second chamber. We clambered inside through an opening that had been hacked through almost a yard of burnt brick. It was thicker than any wall I'd seen before and cold to the touch. An Arab with a paraffin lamp followed us, though Tilden produced an electric torch from his canvas knapsack. The air was thick and heavy. 'There's nothing to see in here,' he said, switching on his torch and shining it into a corner where a hole had been made in the floor. He gestured towards the ladder which went down to the next chamber. The Arab descended first, followed by Mrs Jackson.

'This is what I want to show you,' said Tilden as he stepped off the last rung. He pointed his torch at the far wall and we crossed to where the beam was shining. 'It's cuneiform, several sentences, I believe. Mrs Jackson copied it down, but I'd like a photograph.'

I stared at what appeared to be a block of indecipherable scratches. 'And this is the biblical Lilith?'

'Her name appears here,' said Mrs Jackson, her finger tracing across two lines.

'And there's this over here,' said Tilden, moving the torch's beam away from the wall and down to the floor.

In one corner the dust had been brushed aside and there was a carving, no larger than a manhole cover, of a winged demon with talons. I walked over and looked down at the figure. It was a detailed picture of a forbidding, full-breasted goddess. The embossed talons and feathers gave the carving an impression of depth, but it was the face that transfixed the viewer: the face of a proud woman. I can't say whether it was my imagination or not, but across her lips there appeared to be a coyness that was intended to seduce, a coyness completely at odds with the monstrous claws and owl-like wings. I crouched down and ran a finger along her straight nose, and then traced her smiling lips.

'We think that's the way down to the next chamber,' said Tilden. 'It seems they plugged each floor with a stone slab. Dragged into place when they sealed the building.'

'You think this is a warning?' I asked, still staring into the stone face.

'Could be,' answered Tilden. 'If this is a temple dedicated to Lilith then it's the only one of its kind. Is there enough light?'

'Bring your torch closer,' I said, kneeling in front of the carving. I beckoned the Arab with the lamp towards me and took out my camera. I brought the figure into focus. Holding the Leica in both hands, and with an elbow propped on one knee, I gently pressed down. The click of the shutter echoed in the stillness. I wound the film forward and walked over to the inscription. I took another photograph with the torch and the Arab's lamp behind me.

'You'll have them developed before supper?' asked Tilden, motioning me towards the ladder.

'Possibly before lunch.'

'Well, I suggest we take a few more outside and then you can return to the house.'

Climbing back into the daylight I shaded my eyes from the sun and followed Mrs Jackson across the planks and the dusty earth towards Suarez. Behind me Tilden was ordering a party of workmen into the ziggurat with pickaxes and shovels.

'So what do you think of our brick pyramid, Mr Ward?' asked Suarez.

'It's a strange building.'

'It's a ransacked temple dedicated to another dead goddess; nothing more.'

'But we don't know that for certain,' said Mrs Jackson.

Suarez shrugged as if her opinion wasn't worth discussing.

'Tilden wants some photographs of the outside,' I said.

'Well, try not to get in the way. These Arabs are easily distracted.'

I nodded, but for some reason he didn't appear to be satisfied.

'Bilal!' he suddenly shouted. 'Snappy, snappy!' With one hand he mimed the taking of a photograph.

The foreman, an old man with skin like leather and a cropped grey beard, warily glanced at me as I approached. He started to harangue the work gang in the trench and their melancholy chant briefly faltered beneath his cursing. The basket-boys, weaving around me, quickened their pace as they carried their piles of earth to a growing mound.

I took several pictures and then walked to the other side of the ziggurat. Clara, in what shade the building afforded, was perched on a shooting stick. She was sketching an artefact which she'd placed on a block of stone. In front of her there was scrubland and then, far in the distance, a mountain range lit by the morning sun.

'OK if I take a picture?' I asked.

'Go ahead.'

'What's that you're drawing?'

She held up a small headless statue. 'It's an Assyrian gentleman of about eight hundred BC. His name's written on his back. It was found in the city, near the Shamash gate. It's bronze, though fire-damaged. You haven't visited Nineveh yet have you?'

'Not yet,' I said.

'Then we ought to arrange something. You can see the city wall better from here.' She tipped her head towards the Tigris. 'Eight miles long, and still fifty foot high, at least in places. Isn't it incredible? I'll take you to the gate. It's not far from the house.'

'And between here and the mountains?' I asked, lifting my gaze from her face and staring in the opposite direction.

'Nothing for thirty miles but scrubland, though there's the occasional wadi, and the odd viper. Along the river there's poplar and willow. The foothills are worth seeing: filled with vines and pretty almond trees.' She looked up from her sketching and pointed a finger due north. 'See the long hog's back of Jabal Sinjar; its slopes are the home of the Yazidis. Kurdish in speech, and probably by descent. The Kurds live above and below them. You've heard of the Yazidis?' she asked.

'Aren't they devil worshippers?'

'Do you know why they're called that?'

'If it isn't obvious, then I've no idea.'

Clara smiled. 'It stems from their worship of Shaytan, the Peacock Angel. The name's awkward, upsets most Christians and Muslims.'

'And their Shaytan is our Satan?'

'Their Shaytan's a prophet, not an evil one, but a prophet who's yet to come to power. They believe that the age of Shaytan will succeed the age of Jesus. They also believe his name must never be mentioned, or any word that sounds similar. Onomatophobia, is what O'Neil calls it; the fear of a particular sound. Their founder's tomb is over there,' she nodded towards the mountains, 'in the valley of Lalish.'

'Lalish,' I repeated.

'I know. It sounds like Lilith.'

'Any connection?'

'Hard to say.'

'Have you visited the valley?'

'We visited the tomb when we first arrived. You can drive most of the way, though once you reach the foothills you have to walk. You follow a mountain stream. The valley's a beautiful place, utterly peaceful.'

'And their women bathe naked in the streams,' added Suarez, who had crept up behind me. 'Their morals are loose and they drink an awful lot.'

'Then I imagine we're not going to be mixing socially.'

'Oh, their women look swell when they're young, but it's the devil worshipping that I can't stomach.'

'And the tomb you visited?'

'Repeatedly destroyed by the Turks,' answered Clara, 'but it's recently been rebuilt: white walls, carefully tended gardens. In the entrance there's a carving of a black serpent, and across the floor trickles a sacred spring, runs all the way to Mecca according to the high priestess. In the autumn the image of the peacock is placed in the tomb.'

'A peacock?'

'Some say it's the word most different from the forbidden name. Last month they had their feast of the assembly, when they wash their idols and celebrate the four elements. You know they don't spit or pour hot water on the ground.'

'Why's that?'

'They believe that spirits are harmed or offended by such actions.'

'Are there any Yazidis working on the site?'

'One or two,' answered Suarez. 'You can't fail to spot

them. Their Mir's a tall, seedy-looking old man, dresses all in black. He's their religious leader, visited us just before you arrived, wanted to know why we were digging away from the city. You should speak to Tilden about him. He seems to think they're worth fraternising with. Personally, I wouldn't employ them. They're nothing but trouble. In Syria the Yazidis refused to drink the water on the site because someone had thrown a lettuce leaf down the well.'

'What have they got against lettuce?'

'What they've got depends on what you want to believe; either Shaytan resides in the lettuce, or their word for lettuce sounds similar to Shaytan. If you ask me it's a dumb faith, and it's not surprising they've been persecuted for centuries.'

'I think we should feel a little sorry for them,' said Clara.

Suarez took a final drag on his cigarette and flicked what was left away. 'You taken enough pictures?'

'I think so.'

'Then you'd better head back. We'll be finishing for lunch soon.'

Clara started to get up, but her husband put a hand on her shoulder. 'I think Mrs Jackson would like you to wait for her, don't you?'

11

In the studio I suddenly felt very tired. I was reminded of how sleep at the front had been easy, even in the midst of the most awful horrors. A hammock or bed had only become a place of torment after my collapse; something which my return to England had failed to resolve. I didn't realise that I was trapped, that the grotesque images I had entertained on my voyage back would never fade. At first I didn't discuss it with the medical officer. He referred to it as a mutism of the mind, an inability to talk about what had happened, or even to dwell upon it. It was only when they started to think my behaviour constituted a successful repression of what I had experienced, and was therefore fit to return to active service, that I began to share my troubled thoughts; bedevilled as I was by dreams and imaginings of the most hideous sort. In front of the Medical Board I listened to them deliberating on my confused and erratic behaviour. There was talk of me as feeble-minded, as a weak and degenerate specimen whose madness would inevitably have manifested itself regardless of whether or not I was in the army. They were in agreement that the fighting hadn't caused my breakdown. It was my own lack of moral fibre or backbone or mental plasticity. To go on killing required a sanity which I evidently lacked. After a short deliberation they decided that they didn't want anyone doolally at the front and gave me home service.

I was sent to a small town and billeted with two privates in a terraced house not far from the station. In the goods yard we took delivery of timber and coal and in August land girls in linen overalls came with farm wagons filled with hay. The land girls stick in my mind; the way they coolly appraised us and whispered between themselves. It was then that the nightmares became muddled up with sex. When, in my fever-addled dreams, I squeezed the revolver's trigger I fired pearly seed. Grinding out curses I watched it fly, but instead of carrying life it carried death. And when the shell hit the ammunition barge, land girls floated by like splintered logs. Often the backdrop remained the same: the smell of damp sandbags and charred flesh, the whoosh of shells and the groans of dying men. I carried with me the guilt of killing, the guilt of surviving, the guilt of absconding. My screaming would wake the other two and at first they made light of it. But by the end of the summer their faces at breakfast began to display more irritation than sympathy.

Why then had I agreed to return to where it had all

86

started to unravel? It wasn't for the flies or for the heat or the lingering scent of war. Was it because I hadn't acquitted myself? Did I feel that I'd let everyone down? They knew, just by looking at me, that I'd lost the convictions of my youth, and I longed to regain my sense of right and wrong, to have the courage again to judge my own behaviour. In some ways it was an exorcism I was searching for, an attempt to slay the demons that had plagued me since I had left the front. Such a delicious irony almost brings a smile to my lips.

'Not bad,' said Suarez, holding the edge of a print by his thumb and forefinger, 'though word around the campfire is you're more a travelling salesman than a professional photographer. Catalogues and weddings, Tilden says. Hardly the graduate archaeologist, Mr Ward.'

'I did Latin at school if that's any help,' I said, continuing to clear the bench. 'And my understanding is that you're in a bit of a fix.'

Suarez didn't appear to be listening. 'Munro swore by his Kodak,' he said, picking up my Leica. 'You know he'd a couple of his published in *The London Illustrated* last year.'

'Really,' I replied, trying not to sound irritated. I extended a hand for the camera. 'Then let's hope we find something worth putting on the cover.'

'I doubt that. Tilden's too caught up with his plundered temple. Between you and me, Ward, this season's already trashed. It was tired before Bateman ran away, but since he flit there's not much of a circus left.'

'How long have you worked with Tilden?'

'Too long is the glib answer, the one you suspected, but it just so happens to be true. But I'll tell you something for nothing, I don't trust any of them. Neither did Bateman, though he ploughed his own field.'

I didn't understand what he meant, but chose not to flatter him by asking. 'Have they broken through to the third chamber yet?'

'They have,' he replied while sorting through Bateman's pile of discarded pictures. 'Not a bad one of Susan, is it? I don't know if you've noticed but she has the most remarkable grey-green eyes.' He flourished the photograph in front of my face. 'See the mountains in the background. Well worth a trip.'

'When did they break through?'

'Just after lunch. I'm surprised nobody told you. But then we're full of surprises. Do you know what they've found?'

'How could I?'

'Rainwater. Foul-smelling rainwater. The room's flooded.'

'It's watertight?'

'More or less.' Suarez looked up from Bateman's pictures. 'Isn't that bizarre? Mother Jackson thinks it was sealed with bitumen, though there must have been a crack somewhere. Drip by drip over the last three thousand years, collecting, rising, stagnating. The Arabs were heaving the gorge.' The memory seemed to amuse him. 'Tilden's annoyed. He wants them to empty it. Bucket by stinking bucket. You should run along and take some pictures; but no more of Susan; we seem to have plenty here already.'

The smell hit me before I'd walked five hundred yards from the gates of the house; a foul, stomach-churning stench. I did my best to cover my nose and mouth with a handkerchief. The Arabs had wrapped cloths round their faces. Tilden was there, making the basket-boys carry slopping buckets downwind. The sun had started to sink and in the distance the Kurdish mountains were lit by its golden light. I asked Tilden how long it would take to empty the chamber. 'Another day,' he replied bitterly.

I stood and watched the Arabs by the entrance passing buckets from one hand to another. 'Do you want me to photograph the line?'

'What do you think?'

I left the camera in its case and watched the boys struggling over dirt and sand, crossing the trackless desert to fashion a stinking oasis.

'It's God-awful work,' said Tilden. 'How it came to be flooded is a mystery.'

'Suarez said something about rainwater.'

'It's a possibility.'

'At least they seem to be sticking to the task.'

'It probably isn't the worst thing they've ever smelled. And they're quite loyal. You know the Germans found them impossible – building their railway: Berlin to Baghdad.' Tilden slowly moved his outstretched fingers in front of him as if across the title of a film. 'Berlin to

Baghdad.' He turned to look at me, his lean face softened by the setting sun. 'It's knowing how to treat them that makes all the difference. I was with Allenby when we liberated Palestine. They cheered as we entered Jerusalem. Just the same in Baghdad too. You weren't there were you?'

'I never made it as far as Baghdad.'

'O'Neil tells me they were busy stealing the benches from the parks before we arrived.' He shook his head. 'And now we're left with a cesspit to empty.'

The foreman, wearing a black camel-hair robe over his thin shoulders, walked towards Tilden and then stood passively waiting for the white man to give his final order of the day.

'This is Bilal,' said Tilden. 'He's in charge of the labourers, and not a bad chief.'

'We've already met,' I said, and nodded in acknowledge-ment. The foreman looked at me blankly.

'All right,' said Tilden, having taken the precaution of glancing down at his watch, 'that'll do.'

Bilal turned away and let out a shrill whistle to signal the end of the working day. The boys immediately put down their buckets. Men slowly emerged from the trench and the ziggurat.

'Come on,' said Tilden. 'Let's see if Stanislav's made any progress on the inscription.'

12

We gathered in the mess to hear what Stanislav had deciphered. There was a brief discussion about whether he should read it out before or after supper. I watched Clara give her opinion. By then I had realised that there was no tenderness or desire in the way Suarez spoke to his wife. He seemed to take no pleasure from her company, and invariably responded to any suggestion she made with cool criticism.

Suarez said it was customary to have any translation read out after they'd eaten, but the feeling that evening was that such a significant find couldn't wait. Stanislav stood up. 'You've all heard the first part, but before I read the rest I want to remind you that this is simply my interpretation of its intent. You know it's impossible to give you a literal translation. Ours, like theirs, is a bright but haunted age. While we struggle with our own inner demons they had others to contend with.' He glanced at Mrs Tilden.

'Save your preaching for later,' warned her husband, 'and just get on with it.'

Stanislav cleared his throat theatrically while Amuda waited patiently at the door. He brought out a folded piece of paper from his jacket pocket. '"Lamashtu lives here. Lamashtu is here".'

We waited for more, but Stanislav remained silent.

'Is that it?' asked Tilden.

A smile crossed the Russian's face. 'That's the gist of it. There are some words I've never seen before, adjectives to describe the creature: blood-lapping crawler of the moonless night. But the message is clear. It's Lamashtu's or Lilith's temple.'

Tilden looked up at the Russian. 'There must be more. Christ, you've spent all day on half an inscription just to tell me what I could have guessed.'

'You don't understand,' said Stanislav defensively. 'It's not simply what is said, but how. This isn't an invitation to pray. It's written as a warning – as an imperative, not a declarative. An order to leave well alone, it's not merely a neutral observation.'

'A warning?' echoed Tilden.

'To keep away.'

'Since when does a goddess warn her worshippers away?' Suarez shook his head. 'There's something wrong here. We're digging outside the city wall – where we don't have a permit to dig, and in a place that makes no sense.

I'll tell you what will happen if we continue. We'll waste at least another day emptying a chamber that's flooded and find there's nothing in the next floor other than dust. It's a waste of time.'

'There's precious little left in Nineveh,' answered Tilden. 'And because there's something wrong, because it's unusual, that makes it worth continuing with. It's why we're here.' He signalled to Amuda to start bringing in supper.

'No, we're here because universities are funding our expedition. We can't just simply dig somewhere because we feel like it. We're not permitted to dig outside of the city, and if there's anything left in your worthless folly do you really think that we're going to be allowed to keep it?'

'Listen, I'm leading this excavation. The universities have put their trust in me. If you feel that this is a waste of time then you're perfectly at liberty to leave.'

'Like Bateman,' muttered Suarez.

'Henry,' said Mrs Tilden softly, 'if the chambers are empty doesn't it mean they've been robbed?'

'Is that all you're interested in: amulets, rings, precious stones?'

'Of course not. I just thought . . .'

'Doesn't anyone care about why this temple is where it is? What we might learn? Or have we simply become graverobbers?'

'The universities do expect results,' said Clara.

'Something that glitters, something they can keep, put

on display in their glass cabinets. Isn't uncovering a lost temple enough?'

'Before Carter, before Woolley, it would have been,' replied Suarez, 'but success or failure depend on what we find.'

'Tilden's right,' said Stanislav, taking his plate from the houseboy. 'We shouldn't be worried about finding gold and jewels. We're here to increase our understanding of the past, not simply to plunder it.'

Suarez shook his head in dismay.

'Besides,' continued Stanislav, 'each chamber was sealed. No thief is going to worry about repairing an entrance.'

I turned towards Tilden. 'How long do you think it will take to empty the third chamber?'

'No more than a day or two.'

'Couldn't you just blow a hole in the wall and let the water flow into the trench?' asked Mrs Tilden. 'We still have the dynamite, don't we?'

'You're not seriously suggesting using dynamite?' said Stanislav.

'We couldn't risk it. Who knows what lies beneath,' said her husband quietly.

'I can guess,' said Suarez.

Tilden ignored him. 'We continue emptying the chamber tomorrow. I expect we'll find another inscription, perhaps even an illustration of some sort.'

Clara put down her fork and lit a cigarette. 'Let's change the subject, shall we?' She motioned towards me with the dying match. 'Didn't you want to ask Henry about the Yazidis?'

'It's not about lettuce, is it?'

'No,' I replied, 'it's just I was told that they live in the foothills.'

'And you were told they worship Satan?'

'Which they do,' said Suarez.

'You know it's more complicated than that.' Tilden looked back at me. 'And you know their religion can be traced back to the Assyrians, a religion arguably no less ridiculous than Christianity or Islam? Did anyone tell you about the lettuce?'

Suarez raised his hand.

'You shouldn't be so quick to ridicule them.'

'Just stating the facts.'

'The facts are that they believe Shaytan is a fallen angel, the leader of the archangels, who'll return to his former state. Not very different from our own Satan, but there's more to it than that. The being who refused to submit to Adam is celebrated as Shaytan by Yazidis, though the Islamic version curses him for refusing to submit.'

'Just as Lilith refused to submit?' I asked.

'They're possibly one and the same,' replied Mrs Jackson. 'You see, the Yazidis argue that the order for Shaytan to bow to Adam was only a test, since if God commands anything then it must happen. In other words, God could have made him, or her, submit to Adam, but gave Shaytan the choice as a test. They believe that their praise for him is a way to acknowledge his majestic nature, his sublime knowledge.'

'Could this sublime knowledge be linked to what we have here?'

95

'Possibly,' answered Mrs Jackson, 'though so many myths are built upon one another. They're said to possess a Black Book, which is generally supposed to be the Koran with the name of Shaytan blacked out wherever it occurs. It's believed that any Yazidi who pronounces the name Shaytan will be struck blind.'

'Did Tom tell you the story of the ploughman?' Tilden asked.

'No.'

'I'm surprised.' Tilden glanced in his direction. 'It's an interesting tale – as old as the hills.'

'Well that's technically a lie,' muttered Suarez to himself.

'A Yazidi was out ploughing his father's fields. And as he ploughed, all sorts of thoughts kept passing through his mind, until he happened to think of the prohibition against the word Shaytan and the penalty for breaking it. His curiosity got the better of him, until finally, focusing his vision on a stone, he said, very low, "Sh – Sh – Sh". Nothing happened, and he ventured as far as "Shay" and by degrees he progressed further and further, until at last, in a firm clear voice, he said "Shaytan" and found his vision unimpaired.

'Elated, he returned home to his father. He proudly told him that he had said the word which is forbidden, and that he was not blind.

'"Aren't you?" said the father, as he felt his way towards the door. "Then if I ever see you again you will be".'

'The father's miraculously blinded by his son's behaviour,' explained Suarez with a weary look on his face.

'Thank you,' I replied. The sarcasm was lost on all but Clara and Stanislav.

'They claim they're descended only from Adam and not from Eve,' added Mrs Jackson, 'and believe that the source of evil is in the heart and spirit of humans themselves.'

'And before we get carried away with these sons of Adam,' said Suarez, 'let's not forget that they're prepared to stone any woman who marries outside the faith. And that the priests throw crops into a bottomless pit; a nonsensical offering for Satan while all around their people starve.'

13

This time I saw a face, a sneer, a flickering picture, an emerging silhouette standing out in the moonlight. I couldn't remember how she'd appeared, couldn't shake the notion that her entrance had some significance. Yet it was a fleeting visitation, the prelude to a floorshow. Fingers tapping lightly, faces at the window, flapping wings while the earth shifts as shells thump the ground. Eyes are staring, marbles in their shattered sockets, the night oozing through the hours, sweating through the glass.

Another shell rocks the bed. A bursting mass of molten metal. I close my eyes and it rocks again, hands covering my ears.

I fill my lungs and shout obscenities, words that fly beyond the parapet. The red mist is there. The cheeks damp, dewy. The anguish rises up and it all just comes flooding out. 'Fuck you, you fucking Turk, you fucking cunt, you fucking whore!'

Such a popular show; running for weeks, night after night, always a front-row seat, always the same faces, the same rapturous applause.

They expected it, the young nurses.

Why the revival?

I couldn't say; a growing anxiety, the daily routine, a word that inadvertently triggered the host of this grisly act to return? Or was it something else, something casting its spell? Was the world in which I thought I lived a mere hallucination, the product of my own recurring nightmare?

The door of the common room is ajar and the electric light is burning inside.

Clara is wearing a pair of linen trousers, wide round the ankles, tight round the hips. She carries with her a smart silver cigarette case. The rain beats on the window and the tireless wind tears around the house. She offers me the open case. Inside there is a half-hidden snapshot of a broad-shouldered man.

I lift a cigarette out from behind its elastic ribbon.

Clara lights my cigarette, takes one for herself and sits down on the divan. She crosses her legs and taps the cigarette on the silver case. Thankfully the tapping stops and I watch as the cigarette is lit. She is an accomplished smoker: neatly flicking away the ash, delicately removing minute specks of tobacco from her lips.

The dark, drowsy voice drags me towards her. 'I was present when Adam was living in Paradise, and also when Nimrod threw Abraham in the fire. I was present when God, the compassionate, said to me: You are the ruler on the Earth.'

The silence that follows is only broken by our breathing.

She smiles flirtatiously. 'I think you're wonderful,' she says, and then the wind blows her words away, and a mist begins to cover her face.

Through the cordite I see her shadowy, heavy-lidded eyes staring up at me. The girl's turning from Lilith to Eve, from the conniving Eve to the whore of Babylon. Her skin blisters, the face starts to fall away. There's terror in her eyes. She's shrieking, a continuous high-pitched wail as the countless dead climb through her window and march past her bed.

My heart is hammering as her painted mouth appears: chock full of teeth, black-rooted and damned. There's the ghost of a song on a baby grand, and a sadness falling like burnt skin. 'F-fuck off, Clara,' I stammer, 'get away from me. Just fuck off.'

Her face is a mirage, her mouth a rabbit hole.

The sheet binds me like a straitjacket.

I'm left shivering, cowering against the wall, unpicking the symptoms of a psychological distemper. Yet this wasn't just a painful amalgam of fear and history. These apprehensions were not groundless fears, but an insight into what was happening, a glimpse of what lay ahead. I was the social botanist, the observer of its mating ritual.

101

It wouldn't take me long to realise Tilden could barely tolerate her. It was class and it was history, her history. Stanislav told me the whole sorry story, about how she'd met Suarez at some speakeasy in Detroit. He was all jutting jaw and oily hair; out of some high-priced Catholic school, Yale and Chicago, engaged to some sorority girl, only a month or so away from the society wedding, the respectable marriage.

But Clara was different. A cool, infuriating body and a smart mind; quick-witted, playful, a tongue that promised the happiest of indiscretions, the assurance of a woman who understood men, had seen through their play-acting. She knew that what men wanted to do to her was the same as what boys had done to her. She went to Detroit to study art but never finished the first year. Instead of going to class she went to the Clam House. Men were happy to buy her drinks and Suarez soon fell under her spell. When confronted on the telephone by his fiancée he made his decision. He was happy with Clara, the happiest he'd ever been. And then he became an associate professor, and they moved to Chicago, and Clara continued to drink. He taught classes and she drank. Soon she became known as the girl with the one-trick mind. The invitations petered out. It was then that Suarez became interested in fieldwork.

14

In the morning we mustered in the mess, all except for Mrs Tilden. Her husband looked morose and nobody was looking forward to spending a day emptying the chamber. Stanislav asked me if I was all right. A little tired, nothing more. Why burden others with things they'd find difficult to comprehend? Tilden told me to stay behind. He didn't want me getting in his way and there were some artefacts, small trinkets that Clara had been cleaning. They'd been found within the city walls at the start of the season and now that they were clean I was to make a photographic record of what had been discovered.

The artefacts were kept in the *antika* room. Clara unlocked the padlock and I followed her in. 'The smell's paraffin,' she said, 'we boil it and it's poured over the objects. The wax protects them.' In the middle of the room was a table with papers scattered across it. Running along each wall, from floor to ceiling, were wooden shelves. They were bare except for several small boxes which had been placed on the top shelf above the door. Clara dragged a chair over to the door. 'It's Tilden's system. He believes the cataloguing should get easier as we work our way down to the floor.' She climbed onto the chair and reached above her head for one of the cardboard boxes. I glanced at her bare calves before stepping forward to help her down.

She placed the small box on the table and set out the pieces in front of me. There were shards of broken pottery and little terracotta figurines. Each piece of pottery had some sort of pattern, bulls' horns, or intertwining serpents. The figurines were rather unusual. The female figures had grotesquely large breasts, hips and buttocks. One was on all fours, another was holding her legs apart. Not all of them were intact, but those that were made their purpose very plain. The male figurines were no better. They either had a rampant phallus snaking across their chest or one sticking out a good inch or two.

'They're washed in a pan and then we pour a weak solution of hydrochloric acid over them,' explained Clara. 'Tilden thinks they're quite special.'

'I've never seen the like before.'

'Really?' she exclaimed, her voice underpinned with incredulity.

'Well, you don't see such things in museums.'

'No, not on display.' Clara paused for a moment. I felt her watching me as I looked through the viewfinder. 'I think they're quite pretty,' she said as though daring me to contradict her. 'Tom doesn't like them. He thinks they're vulgar.'

She stared at me expectantly, but I tried to concentrate on my work.

After I'd finished photographing the figures I asked if I could see where they'd been found. I expected her to point the way, or get Amuda to take me across to the site, but she offered to accompany me.

The sun was warm and Clara soon had her olive cardigan tied round her waist. We chatted about bathtub gin and the devil's candy as we made our way to the Shamash gate, conversation proving easier than it had been for a while. She was smart, and her hands were never still, yet I found my thoughts were gradually drifting away from what was being said. It began with me surreptitiously admiring her lips. They were scarlet and noticeably moist. She had the habit of licking her lips after speaking for any length of time and this gave them an attractive sheen. I tried to focus on what she was saying, which had moved on from Prohibition to Assyrian pottery, but the more I tried to follow her talk the more I found myself gazing at her lips. I wasn't sure if she was aware of this sudden compulsion, but as we wandered away from the house I became convinced that she'd noticed a distinct change in the atmosphere. For no reason the air had become taut. Conversation and civility weren't enough to mask our thoughts. Her lecture started to falter. We were both thinking of something else, unspeakable images surfacing in our minds. Or at least that's how I remember it. We could see it in each other's eyes, in every measured gesture, in every smile.

We arrived at the site, which was some fifty yards inside the gate. 'The city wall can be traced for the whole of its circuit,' she explained, her finger pointing, tracing an imaginary outline. 'The gates turned on hinge sockets made of stone.'

Through her parted lips I could see inside her mouth, her pink tongue. 'There are fifteen gates . . .' Perhaps it was the heat, the lack of conscience, or her brazen stare. She was looking into my eyes, fixing me with her eyes. It suddenly seemed inevitable.

'Would you like me to pose for you?' The provocative question coursed through my mind. I thought of Bateman and Susan, and wondered if this was what had happened, if their sense of decency had simply evaporated. I made some glib response and she lifted her frock to just above her knees. The sun's warmth caressed my neck. Standing in the past it's easy to see how transient life is, how little it all means.

I wiped my brow, focused the camera and took a picture. 'For your husband.'

A grinning Clara shook her head, her dark hair gently swinging, brushing against her flushed cheeks. 'Keep it beneath your pillow,' she said, 'or on your mantelpiece at home.'

'Like an invitation to a party?'

'Exactly.'

Still holding her frock, she came towards me. 'Do you know what Herodotus said about the Assyrians?'

My mouth was dry. I was finding it difficult to speak.

'That every woman must once in her lifetime sit in the temple of Mylitta and there give herself to a stranger. Most, Mr Ward . . .'

'Harry,' I managed to say.

'Most, Harry, sat in the precinct of the temple, a band of plaited strings around their heads, dark ringlets cascading down swan-like necks. And once they've sat down they cannot leave until someone's thrown a silver coin into their lap. As he throws the coin the man has to say, "In the name of the goddess Mylitta". And once he's lain with her, taken her, her duty to Mylitta is discharged.'

I watched as Clara, hitching her frock up across her thighs, sat down on a carved block of limestone.

'Do you have a silver coin, Harry?'

We walked back to the expedition house in silence. Aloof from one another, from what had just happened. We were already cultivating a distance, taking stock of who we were, what had just happened, how our understanding of ourselves and one another had changed within minutes. It wasn't shame we were feeling. It wasn't guilt we were wrestling with. It was more a process we were trying to hide from one another, a readjustment, an event we were preparing to conceal from others. She was a married woman, a woman I hardly knew. As her hand had betrayed her husband her wedding ring hadn't stopped broadcasting its message. Was it worth it: bliss, with its irresistible loss of reason? I was tainted with sin, and the stain was spreading.

Yet this was different. From the moment she'd started walking towards me I knew we were about to set ourselves adrift. Entwined in the dust: honest and dishonest, loyal and disloyal. And now the yearning for her smooth skin, for the caressing and lifting, had almost disappeared, but not quite. Before the buttoning up of flies and the brushing down of a frock, lust had crawled back into its cave. Lust was sleeping while the mind was racing. Was this the first time she'd allowed something like this to happen? I couldn't tell what she was thinking. As we drew closer to the house she appeared almost unperturbed.

I quietly wiped my lips on the back of my hand in an attempt to rid me of the taste of impropriety, to dislodge from my mind the rash, indecent act.

Mrs Tilden, clutching a handkerchief to her bosom, was standing at the gates. She was there to greet us. Her cheeks were flushed, her eyes shining. 'Bloody hell,' she screamed, wringing the handkerchief she held. 'Bloody hell,' she cried again.

Clara glanced nervously at me. She wasn't a good actress. Her first 'Hello' was too light, too breezy to be natural. Only her second conveyed curiosity, a suitable degree of anxiety.

But Mrs Tilden wasn't gauging the pitch of our greeting. With the palm of her hand she clumsily wiped a wisp of hair from her brow. 'They've gone . . . gone and found a dead b-bloody Arab,' she cried, her voice tripping with anger.

'Where?' I asked.

'Where do you think?'

'The desert?'

'No! He bloody drowned,' she spat. 'He was trying to steal from us. Henry had to get him out. The Arabs refused to touch his slimy . . . his slimy . . . stinking like a drain.'

'Is your husband here?'

Mrs Tilden was shaking her head, twisting her handkerchief round her fingers. 'He came back to wash. His skin was covered . . . the stench . . . they're over there.' She gestured wildly behind her.

'What are?' asked Clara softly.

'His shorts – stinking of piss. Worse than a drain.'

'It's all right,' said Clara, gently putting a hand on her shoulder.

'I told Henry we'll have to burn them. It's the stench. They refuse to touch them. I can't wash them . . . I shouldn't have to. Why should I have to wash them?'

'It's all right,' repeated Clara. 'I'll see to them.'

'How dare he,' cried Mrs Tilden, 'how fucking dare he!'

15

The bloated corpse of a boy was drying in the sun. Flies were crawling over his face; others hovered above as if the smell was too strong for them to settle. Tied to his waist was the hook that he'd been using to scour the bottom of the chamber. 'Tilden's not the only one who thinks there's something worth pursuing,' said Stanislav, wiping his spectacles with his shirttail. 'He had to get him out.'

'I heard,' I said and looked again at the abandoned corpse. His eyes had lost their sheen and his mouth was black with flies. The boy had been an obstacle, a tedious delay. He was a graverobber and though we pretended to care the lament was shallow. Those around me were more interested in the long dead, and thought that they alone had a proper grasp of what a thing was worth.

'Shouldn't we bury him?' I asked.

Stanislav turned, the sun flashing across his glasses. 'Bilal is seeing if anyone will claim him.'

'If they don't, we should bury him.'

'Someone will come forward. Tilden's offering to make a donation. He was at pains to stress it is a gift, and not compensation. Bilal says our generosity is the stamp of a noble nature and he will make it known in Mosul. It will enhance our reputation.' Stanislav smiled wryly, aware of an irony which almost eluded me.

Later I saw Suarez performing a dumb show of the boy's death for Sasha.

After we'd failed to relieve Kut, three Indian riflemen were shot for cowardice. They were told to dig three pits: four foot deep, four foot long, two foot wide. One had asked for water, which was duly given. Just before noon their shovels were taken away. They were told to lie down. Obediently they settled themselves at the bottom of their pit: knees raised, arms crossed, eyes closed. The officer then removed his revolver from its holster and checked the barrel. He stood over each one in turn, his legs straddling the grave they'd just finished digging. Above the first one he muttered, 'May God have mercy on your soul,' then lowered his revolver and shot the Indian in the heart. He repeated the same action over the other two. The last rifleman was crying, a pitiful sound which was immediately silenced by the thunderous clap of the revolver.

Once he'd finished, the earth was shovelled back, the

soil softly drumming against their chests. Curiosity got the better of me and I peered into the nearest grave. He had his eyes open, staring up at the sky, the sweat still glistening on his forehead.

It wasn't my place to say anything. To whom could I speak? The world had been a place I'd been happy to go along with. The world had turned into a place of wanton destruction and grotesque cruelty.

16

'We'll have a proper look around the chamber tomorrow when the smell's gone,' said a weary-looking Tilden. 'I'm paying two Kurds to stand guard tonight, but I'd like you to check on them just before midnight. Do you think you can do that?'

'Of course,' I replied.

'Good.' Tilden winced.

'Something wrong?' asked Mrs Jackson.

He briefly shut his eyes and shook his head. 'We'll leave the generator running till you return. Just make sure they're still there and more or less awake. I doubt we'll be troubled with another visitor now we've emptied the chamber.'

'And the fourth level is the last?' asked Mrs Tilden.

'It appears so. I thought there'd be more. We can't always be right.' Tilden shifted in his seat. 'But who knows what we'll find in the chamber underneath.'

'And if it's empty, what then?'

He waved Suarez's question away. 'You'll find my torch in the common room.'

'If there's nothing there, what then?' asked Suarez again. 'Shouldn't we return to where we're supposed to be digging?'

'It should be on top of the bookcase,' said Tilden, continuing to ignore him.

'Listen to me. Do you seriously believe we'll be able to keep anything? This is a goddamn waste of time. You know it is, but you just won't see it, will you?'

Tilden silently regarded the American.

'This is Nineveh, not Ur, not the Valley of the Kings. We fight for scraps in the city, where we're licensed to dig. And when you submit your report I insist that what I've said is recorded. Chicago must know I wanted no part in this folly.'

'What is it you're afraid of finding?' asked Tilden.

'Nothing,' replied Suarez. 'I've told you already.'

'It doesn't sound like it,' said Mrs Jackson.

'What's that supposed to mean?'

'That's enough, Tom. Now why don't you . . .' Tilden winced again.

'Tom, you've said enough,' warned Mrs Jackson.

'Then I won't stay to offend you any further.' Suarez picked up his hat and, with a final shake of his head, walked out of the mess.

I thought Clara would follow him but she remained in her chair. Amuda entered and placed the coffee pot in the centre of the table.

'Are you all right, Henry?' asked Mrs Jackson.

'Indigestion,' responded Tilden. 'Nothing more.' He motioned for his wife to get up.

'You mustn't worry,' said Mrs Tilden, rising to her feet, 'he's as strong as a circus horse. Aren't you, Henry?'

He grimaced, his teeth clenched behind his lips. He allowed his wife to put her arm round him.

'Is there anything I can do?' I asked.

'It's all right,' said Tilden, 'just . . . a patrol.' His wife helped him to his feet.

As they left the mess I glanced towards Clara. Although we sat across from one another she'd studiously avoided looking at me. I thought she might stay until Stanislav and Sasha had left but she chose to leave with Mrs Jackson. She saw me looking as she rose from the table, but gave no sign of familiarity or friendship.

17

I joined Stanislav in the common room for a whisky. It was a cold night and the prospect of a midnight walk in the desert didn't fill me with joy. I needed a nightcap to lift my spirits and, as Tilden didn't approve of anyone drinking after supper, my intention was to have just the one before I finished sorting out the darkroom. Bateman's photographs still needed cataloguing. I'd found two large envelopes in which he'd kept his photographic record of what had been unearthed and had merely glanced at the pictures. What I'd seen had been reassuring. They were sharp, the objects suitably framed, but not beyond the wit of any photographer worth his salt.

Yet Stanislav wouldn't hear of me staying for just one. 'First you'll tell me about yourself and then I will tell my story. One whisky for your story and one for mine; two whiskies to fly, otherwise our friendship will never take off.'

119

'We'll see,' I said. 'But your motor's running. You start.'

'All right,' agreed Stanislav, wiping his spectacles. 'My father died when I was eight and at the age of twelve I worked as a farmhand on the estates of nobles.' He put his spectacles back on. 'You left school at what, thirteen?'

'Fourteen.'

'By fourteen I was working at the local iron foundry and was involved in revolutionary politics. After witnessing the terror of the Tsarist regime I joined the anarchists, and by eighteen I'd been arrested three times.' He smiled and ran a hand over his shaven head. 'The third arrest came when an infiltrator was able to testify against me. I was sentenced to death by hanging, but the sentence was commuted to life imprisonment and I was sent to Butyrskaya prison in Moscow. During the revolution I fought with the Black Army. We fought the White and the Red. Do you understand so far?'

'Perfectly.'

'We drove the White Army from the Ukraine to Romania, from Romania to Slovakia.'

'And that's where you met Sasha.'

'That's where I met Sasha,' agreed Stanislav. He lifted the bottle and pointed its neck towards me, but I shook my head. 'She is my rose plucked from the dunghill.' He paused as he topped up his glass. 'Can I tell you what the world really is?'

'As opposed to what I imagine it to be?'

He smiled again and took a sip of whisky. 'It's a shoddy

120

contraption of deserts, barren seas and stinking towns. Tilden thinks of the world as Cambridge, grouse moors and pikes in glass cases. I see slaughter, prisons, a London slum. Can anyone seriously worship a god of such injustice and filth? You've heard, I presume, of your Welsh miners, of negroes in the lynching states of America, slaves in Africa, untouchables in India. Brothels, poverty, prisoners, cruelty, and dirty factories all over; and clean factories, too, which keep their slaves alive longer and persuade fools into thinking they're better. Do you think that such a world is the creation of a reasoning creator? That all the stench and cruelty are meant to endure? I say they're not.'

'And what do you propose?'

'I will speak the truth. I am an apostle of a combative creed and believe in none of your toyshop idols.'

'You must believe in something.'

'Anarchism, birth control and bathos,' he replied firmly. 'The more taboo the topic of conversation the more I want to discuss it. But we are merely skimming the surface,' he protested as I waved my hand for him to stop.

'Your ideas intrigue me,' I said, putting down my glass, 'but I have work to do.'

'You're not going to desert me?'

'It's late, and there are photographs to sort out.'

'But I want to get to know you, at least as well as you think you know yourself. You seem bright, but ill informed.'

I thanked him for his candour.

'Your feelings aren't hurt are they?' he asked.

'Not in the slightest. In fact I find your attitude refreshing.'

'To a man who feels, the world is a tragedy; to the man who thinks, it is a farce. Think about it, Mr Ward.'

'I'll try, Mr Stanislav.'

'Call me Victor; there is no need for this formality between friends.'

'Then you must call me Harry.'

He nodded in approval.

We left the common room in good spirits and said goodnight outside the studio. Stanislav didn't want to remain drinking alone. Instead he would return to the warm bosom of his wife; a bosom where he could hide himself. 'They are my blinkers,' he exclaimed loudly, 'her breasts are my blinkers, though unlike your servant class I choose to wear them.'

I congratulated him on his good fortune. We shook hands and he started out across the courtyard.

It was cold in the studio and I rubbed my hands together. The two envelopes that contained pictures of the dig were kept in a locked drawer beneath the workbench. On the bench, beside the gooseneck lamp, was a pile of twenty or so discarded photographs. Tilden had dismissed them as Bateman's unofficial record.

After glancing at a dozen or so I could see why Tilden had no interest in them. They were casual, impromptu shots, nearly always the poor relation to one kept in an envelope and thus frequently marred by something: a flash of sun, the blink of an eye. But I was curious to see those he'd discarded, to find out whether there was anything worth salvaging.

I was halfway through the pile, shaking my head at how much time and photographic paper he'd wasted, when I came across something that struck me as rather odd.

It was an external photograph of the chamber at the top of the ziggurat. The picture was merely a record of their discovery, their anticipated grand entrance, with Tilden and Suarez standing on the roof of the second chamber. Tilden had taken off his homburg and held it, by its brim, at his waist. With one hand he shaded his eyes against the setting sun. Bateman's shadow was squarely between the men's feet. Suarez was gazing back at the hole they'd made in the brickwork. Yet what had caught my eye was something on the wall behind the men. It was a diagonal shadow. A casual glance and it was their shadow: a broad, black ribbon thrown over Tilden's shoulder. Yet it couldn't be. Theirs would have fallen directly behind.

I peered at the picture, stared into the dark, inky band. And as I did so everything around me – the cold evening, the yellow light of the lamp, the familiar objects that lay on the bench – fell away; everything but the grainy image in my hand. My thoughts, my limbs, my gaze became momentarily trapped in time. From the grainy shadow there seemed to emerge a sunken face, a

123

distorted, tortured face of grey and black. A screaming spectre rolling out from the yawning hole behind the two men.

I shivered, and cast the picture aside.

A trick of the light, a chemical distortion? I picked up the remaining photographs. I searched for another taken outside the temple, but there was nothing else. The rest I could dismiss with a momentary glance.

I looked again at the picture. It must have been one of the last photographs Bateman had taken. I put it directly beneath the lamp and tried angling the image one way and then another. The misshapen face was still there, caught with its hollow mouth open in anguish, hurtling towards the sky as though escaping from the blackest pit imaginable. Its suffering eyes were dark hollows, staring out without pupils, as though blinded by pain and grief, as though its eyes had been burnished by the sight of countless horrors. I rubbed my brow. It was late. Too late to be dealing with shadows, trying to make sense of something so fantastical.

Outside a dog began barking. I looked behind me. There was no one there. The wings of a moth tapped gently on the glass. I was alone in the room. And yet I felt uneasy, as if I was being watched, as if something had been alerted to my presence; aware that I knew of it at the very moment that I had registered its existence. I slid the photograph into my jacket pocket and walked across to the door. Except for the muffled drone of the generator all was quiet in the courtyard. I stepped outside. There was a light on in the guard's room beside the gate, but otherwise everyone else appeared to have turned in.

I looked at my watch. It was just before midnight, but I was in no mood to walk across to the dig in the pitch black. It was a reluctance that had once been all too familiar, a fear I'd tasted when wading through the marshes towards the canal. I cursed myself for having agreed to check on the two workmen, yet there were no shells outside, no machine-gun post between me and the dig. Was I becoming afraid of the dark?

From the doorway of the studio I could see that the gate was locked. The guard's light was on and he was waiting for me to go and look. Did I want to cross the yard and venture out into the night? Pushing the door wide open, allowing the yellow light to spill out, I stayed beside the wall on my way back to the common room.

I put my hand inside the door and flicked the switch. For some reason I couldn't look into the darkness; in my mind there was something in the shadows, the same face hiding; watching and waiting.

I picked up Tilden's torch from the divan where I'd left it. I was arguing with myself, telling myself to get a grip. It was only a photograph, a trick of the light.

At the gate I tapped on the guard's door and a sleepy figure, with a blanket round his shoulders, emerged with a bunch of keys. Coughing and spitting, as if to make some sort of protest, he unlocked the padlock and then proceeded to noisily haul the chain through the bars. He pulled one of the gates towards him. It opened with a groan that was so hideous it was almost comical.

He waited.

I shone the torch ahead into the blackness. The guard said something in Arabic – a curse probably. I turned and looked at him. His skin was dark; there were heavy creases round his eyes, eyes that appeared to be struggling to stay open. I thought of ordering him to accompany me, but knew he'd refuse to understand; knew he couldn't leave his post, that he would be locking the gates behind me. He waved me forward, mimed locking the padlock and passing a key through the bars to me on the other side.

Hesitantly, I advanced a yard into the night. The gate clanged behind me. I listened: the slow, metallic drumming of the chain, the clunk of the lock, an urgent whisper. I pocketed the key.

A dog barked again in the distance. Was there any need to go any further? I shook my head and dragged myself away from the gates, shining the torch down on the path. My line of sight was blinkered by the dark. A school hymn entered my head, one that had given me comfort on the battlefield, and later at the sanatorium. I began to stumble through the words as I walked towards the ziggurat. 'Day is over, night is drawing nigh; shadows of the evening steal across the sky.' It was a five-minute walk at most. A wind gusted fitfully across the desolate plain. My voice trembled, but I continued with the miserable hymn. 'The darkness gathers, stars begin to peep, birds and beasts and flowers, soon will be asleep.' The words were childish and I berated myself for being so foolish. I tried not to think about the photograph. A camel-spider scuttled across my path. 'Comfort every sufferer, watching late in pain; those who plan some evil from their sin restrain.' This was a test, a test of my resolve, my nerves. Why should I be scared out here in the desert? 'Through the long night-watches angels spread their white wings above me, watching round my bed.' The floor beneath my feet was made of cracked mud, changing in colour from tawny to a dark brown. Insects, drawn by the light, fluttered beneath the beam. 'When the morning wakens, then may I arise, pure and fresh and sinless in thy holy eyes.'

I shone the torch ahead and could just make out the top of the ziggurat sitting in its cradle. To one side there were the glowing embers of a dying fire. The dismal wind continued to gust, but otherwise all was silent.

I continued with another verse as I crept towards the fire. I couldn't see the two Arabs. I called out, expecting them to surface from beneath their blankets. Nothing stirred. From twenty yards away I called again and brought the beam of the torch to bear on where I expected to see them lying. Their blankets were there, tossed aside, but otherwise I could make out no sign of the men. The fire was fluttering, dying. I scanned the ground around me. Nothing. At first I was annoyed rather than alarmed that they were nowhere to be seen. Was this something I had to report back to Tilden – would he really want to be woken in the middle of the night? Cupping my hands round my mouth I shouted away from the house and into the blackness. There was no response. Not immediately.

I half turned to stare at the ziggurat. It was standing closer than I recollected, as though the edifice had silently crept forward. Had there been an echo from inside? The entrance was just a dozen or so yards away. I was reluctant to shine the torch towards it. 'Is there anybody there?' I called. Annoyance had faded from my voice. Would they have been so foolish as to climb into the temple? I approached the earthen ramp that led up to the chamber.

Something just within the mouth of the ziggurat was moving. I could hear it clawing at the wall. I couldn't tell whether or not it was looking at me. The torch felt heavy in my hand. I didn't have the strength to lift it, to direct its beam towards the increasingly frantic scratching. Instinctively, almost mechanically, I moved backwards, while my eyes remained fixed on the entrance to the chamber. I felt a blanket beneath my heel, saw the embers out of the corner of my eye. I turned and started to retreat down the hill, hurriedly walking back to the path, trying hard not to let my imagination get the better of me. Yet what I'd seen in the photograph was becoming more than just an anomaly, much more than a chemical smudge.

It was then that I tripped and fell. At first I thought it was a sandbag, though it stank like a latrine, even in the cold night air. The torch was on the ground, shining at my feet. Cursing, I lifted my head and saw what it was, what had been half covered with earth. With no one having come to claim the drowned boy, he'd been buried close to where Tilden had left him. Only the jackals had found him, had dragged him halfway out of his makeshift grave. In the torchlight I could see where they'd chewed at his nose and lips. But they'd been disturbed, or had found his flesh too sullied even for their taste.

I scrambled back to my feet. I'd seen bodies like his before, half buried in the desert, in worse shape than his, though never smelling as bad. There was almost the feeling of relief, peculiar as that may sound. This was something I could deal with, something that was too familiar to frighten me. The men had chased the jackals away – they would be returning soon. Whether I believed that or not didn't matter; it was the most rational explanation, and the one I could handle.

18

'Ward,' the voice kept calling. 'Ward, are you all right? Are you up?'

Light was streaming through the yellow curtain. 'I'm fine,' I answered, the words slurred across the pillow as I tried to gather my senses. 'I'm fine,' I repeated, trying to make myself understood. 'I'll be there in a minute.' Tilden had come to rouse me. He wasn't the sort to make any concession.

It'd been after one when I'd crawled into bed, another hour or two before I'd banished the thoughts that had kept my mind turning over. But sleep had given me little succour. It had been a restless night filled with strange sensations; what was left was a blur, ghostly pictures of coloured cloth, golden jewellery, and plaited beards as black as liquorice. I knew that something had been hiding in the dark, that its presence had infiltrated my thoughts. I'd heard it breathing: a slow and languorous undulation, its scaly hide expanding and contracting, bellows-like, breathing, waiting, a flash of yellow claws in the moonlight.

From out of the darkness the figure had uttered a strange, soft mocking sound. There was a woman's laugh: the peal of a bell, an unabashed joyful note. She'd been coming towards me; her laughter overtaking the breathing of the creature that had been waiting in the dark. Her mouth was against my ear, coarse black hair covering my face, her warm limbs rubbing against my own. Her weight was upon me, her suffocating, pendulous breasts sliding over me, filling my mouth with soft, smooth flesh.

Then, for a moment, a newsreel had played out to an audience as quiet as any congregation. The projected soldier, bruised by failure, was gazing up at the sky like some demented character from a Goya painting. In the grey flickering light she straddled him, held his mouth open and spat between his teeth. He swallowed. She looked into the camera and her eyes were staring into mine, eyes of copper, eyes pearlescent and black; eyes in which my face was reflected, eyes that held the world and understood everything.

Another lurid dream, nothing more. That was what I told myself. To give in to the suspicion that it was anything other than a hideous conjuration would have meant sinking back into madness. I rubbed a hand across my face. Tilden had gone. The room was cold. I climbed out of bed and went across to my jacket which was hanging

132

on the back of the door. I felt in each pocket in turn before glancing down at the floor. The picture wasn't there. I knelt down and looked beneath the iron bed-frame. It had vanished. I'd seen something in the picture, a spectre that had momentarily threatened to unhinge me, and now it had disappeared. Had I imagined it all? I'd been rattled by the sounds and visions that had floated through my mind during the night. I could have allowed myself the comfort of doubt, but back then I could still tell truth and illusion apart. In my head were the cold facts. The photograph had been no figment.

Mrs Tilden was the only one left at the breakfast table. There was no smile as I entered, just the merest flicker of resentment. I stood across from her and poured myself some coffee. She sat, in her brown woollen jumper and cotton dress, one hand cradling her china cup against her bosom, the other lost in her red hair. Her thin shoulders were hunched over the table. 'I thought I was the last to breakfast,' she said glumly. Then, with a sullen flick of her pale hand, she gestured behind her. 'There's some toast on the side.'

My first impulse was to tell her about what I'd seen, to share the intensity of what I'd felt. I couldn't of course. Instead I watched her while she continued to look down at her plate. It was the first time I'd seen her at the breakfast table; the first time I'd seen her vacant gaze, her listless appearance. Sitting before me was the miserable husk of a woman.

'You do know the rest of the party's left for the dig?'

'I slept badly.'

She glanced up at me. 'That's not uncommon.' There was an air of intense weariness about her. She had a tight, suspicious mouth and yet there was something vulnerable about her, almost forlorn. 'You look washed out.'

'It was a rough night.' I could have told her everything, but chose instead to ask her about her husband.

'Unwell,' she replied, her voice flat and cold. She paused. 'Bateman found it difficult to sleep. I guess you've been having bad dreams?'

I nodded.

For a second there was the faint glimmer of recognition in her face, a softening of her features. Yet it faded as quickly as it had appeared. 'Henry won't be happy if you're late.'

'Bateman found it difficult to sleep?'

'Rarely slept a wink.'

'Why was that?'

'Troubles hurt most when they're self-inflicted, wouldn't you agree?'

'If you say so.'

'You mean you don't know?'

I shook my head. 'What do you think happened to Bateman?' I asked, too tired to be anything other than bold.

'In the end he crawled into a bottle.' There was another pause as she sipped her tea. 'Hadn't you better be running along?'

'Is that all?'

'My husband's unwell. He needs your help.'

'You think it had something to do with the ziggurat?'

'Carter died because of a mysterious force, or do you think Tutankhamen's curse is all gibberish, Mr Ward?'

'You think Tilden's in danger?'

'In Carter's tomb there was a room filled to the top with dried mud. It's hardly coincidental.' She gave me a long appraising look. 'I know what you're thinking. You think I'm highly strung. You're wrong. I'm not the sort of girl who bolts from a party, who imagines things.' Her voice was becoming increasingly taut. 'But I'll be frank, Mr Ward, I dread the night, I dread it with my whole being.'

'Why?' I asked. I placed a hand on the table and leaned towards her. 'What is it that you fear?' I wanted her to confess, to acknowledge that she shared my malaise.

'Don't pretend you don't understand. The dead are everywhere. We're sitting on mounds of the dead.'

'And there are things that you hear?'

She waved the question away.

'Why do you dread the night?'

She was trembling. Unsteady fingers returned her cup to its saucer. She called over her shoulder for Amuda.

'Why did Bateman leave?'

Her pale face suddenly became pinched with suspicion.

'You mean they haven't told you?'

I shook my head, and she laughed. It was a hollow, mocking laugh. 'And you can't cut out the picture without a pair of scissors?' She stared at me with utter contempt. 'Well, you'll find out soon enough.'

19

It was a blustery morning and my jacket flapped incessantly in the wind. The sky was a strange milky white, tinting the landscape and everyone in it with a pale luminescence. I looked down at the dusty earth and tried to retrace last night's path. The boy's body had disappeared. Reburied, or taken by his family. There was no sign of the two guards. Only a windblown circle of ash remained. I breathed a sigh of relief. Everything appeared to be in order.

I saw Tilden standing by the entrance to the ziggurat. I wanted to tell him about the photograph I'd seen, about the brittle conversation I'd had with his wife, but I didn't want to worry him. I couldn't face the questions that would follow, the quizzical look, the apprehensive manner it was impossible to disguise. And what was I to say? That I'd seen a photograph with an inexplicable shadow.

I would have shown it to you, but it's disappeared. Oh, and by the way, I had a nocturnal emission last night, the first since school, and when I was searching for the guards I thought I heard something inside the ziggurat, but I was too afraid to look. It was easier to blame it on the lack of sleep, or the drink; or to see them as symptoms of a delusional fancy.

Tilden impatiently beckoned me towards him. I expected him to be angry, but he was simply in a hurry. He didn't even ask me about the men who were supposed to be guarding the temple.

'I want to show you something,' he said, although without the gusto, the authority of yesterday. His eyes were dark and, though the morning was still cold, there were beads of perspiration across his brow. I followed him into the ziggurat. I was apprehensive, but Bilal's son was ushering me forward. The three of us slowly descended on wooden ladders to the chamber that had been flooded. It still stank like a sewer and I was hoping that whatever Tilden wanted to show me wouldn't take too long. 'Here,' he said, pointing to the floor. 'The same design, Lamashtu. It's a stone portal to the next chamber, another plug in another floor. We're opening it up as soon as you've taken a picture. And here,' he said, pointing the beam up to the ceiling. 'It's Pazuzu.'

'Pazuzu?'

'Ask Suarez.' He winced again and pressed a hand against his stomach. 'There are inscriptions in each corner. I'd like a picture of each.' He handed me the torch and started to climb out of the chamber. The boy was waiting for me by the ladder. In his hand was a paraffin lamp, its yellow light dancing across the walls. It was cold in the poisonous chamber and the stench was almost overpowering. I hurriedly took the necessary photographs and left as quickly as I could.

It was still and silent in the ziggurat, yet as I climbed to the entrance I could hear the wind howling past the walls. Outside Tilden was nowhere to be seen. Sand was swirling around the building. I narrowed my eyes and made my way over to Suarez who was shouting at Bilal. The foreman had his hood over his head, the hem of his camel-hair robe flapping at his old Turkish cavalry boots. There was the look of forbearance on his leathery face. Or maybe he too was tired, too old to go on fighting. There was some discussion about how many were needed inside the chamber and how much they were to be paid. Finally a deal was struck and the foreman called down to several workmen who were digging beneath the rim we were standing on.

'We'll be running out of rupees soon,' said Suarez, turning to me. 'Such a damn waste.' He'd raised his voice in order to be heard over the wind. 'At least it's only four floors. Hardly the great ziggurat Tilden was hoping for.'

'I've finished inside. I'm heading back.'

'When it's found to be empty we can all go back.'

'There are some carvings.'

'Another Lamashtu,' he exclaimed dismissively.

'And on the ceiling, with its dog head and scorpion tail?'

139

'You mean Pazuzu? That was unexpected, though it's almost impossible to remove.'

'And Pazuzu was . . .'

'An Assyrian spirit; one of the most feared. It defeated Lamashtu.'

'How?'

'In battle. When the Assyrian empire collapsed, before the city of Nineveh was ransacked by its enemies.'

'It's not simply a temple to Lilith?'

Suarez shrugged his shoulders.

'What do you think it is?' I asked.

'An unfinished affair. It's been robbed, if it ever had anything worth stealing. But you're missing the point: we shouldn't be digging here.'

'What makes you think it's unfinished?'

'They were in a hurry,' he said, 'anyone can see that.'

I watched him as, with his back to the wind, he tried to roll himself another cigarette. We stood in silence.

Several Arabs with pickaxes and lamps had gathered at the entrance to the tomb. Suarez, having finished rolling his cigarette, glanced up. He was annoyed to see the Arabs waiting for him and ordered them into the ziggurat. He shouted at Bilal and told him to accompany the workmen. With a hand cupped over one side of his mouth he managed to light his cigarette. 'You want to know why they were in a hurry?' he asked, exhaling smoke in one short, quick breath. 'Why there are few carvings, no decorated walls?'

'I'd like to know, if you can spare the time.' He glanced

at me quizzically. He wasn't in any rush to join the workmen inside.

'It must have been one of the last things they built,' he said, drawing on his cigarette between each sentence. 'Forced to build outside the walls, and with the Babylonians already gathering their armies. One last temple built in vain, to curry favour with their gods.'

Suarez turned to me, the collar of his jacket lifting in the wind. 'You know this whole place was razed to the ground? These vassal states hated the Assyrians. They'd seen their kings flayed alive, their skins and heads displayed. This was revenge for centuries of tyranny. Long before your druids built their stone circles, even before your prehistoric mounds appeared. This is where Assyria ends in the history books.' He stamped his foot in a theatrical gesture.

'You think they abandoned the ziggurat before it was finished?'

'It's the only explanation that makes any sense.'

'What happened to them?'

'Assyrians? What do you think? Massacred, annihilated. Other empires disappeared, but the people lived on. Not with the Assyrians. The land was sacked and pillaged. It was genocide. The ancient Greeks found nothing but ruins.' Suarez paused to relight his cigarette. 'How long do you think your empire will last?'

I looked back at him, but didn't answer.

'It's already dying,' he said. 'Way I see it, it's nothing more than a syphilitic whore. I've been to London, seen its heart. And this King Faisal's just another British puppet.'

'Didn't we liberate them from the Ottomans?'

'You created a country and bombed them into submission when they refused to play ball.'

'And you don't want their cooperation, their oilfields? This place is crawling with American geologists.'

'We're just trying to catch up. You're much quicker at getting into bed with people, I'll give you that, but we're learning fast.'

He flicked his cigarette away and started towards the entrance, but stopped. 'Hey,' he shouted, 'ever thought of a moustache?' He pointed unnecessarily to his top lip. 'A Clark Gable affair ought to do it.'

'Makes it look worse,' I answered, 'draws attention—' He'd raised his hand. He'd heard enough. I watched him disappear into the dark and wondered if his little rant had anything to do with Clara. Was he telling me he already knew? That I was angry rather than troubled surprised me. That I could stand and have a civil conversation with a man I'd cuckolded seems hard to believe. Unless what was hidden was already corrupting our thoughts, changing the way we saw one another? Was it seeping into our blood, the yearning for the sly caress, the hidden corner? It makes it easier to understand, easier to excuse.

I shook like a dog and decided to get back to work, to take a few photographs of those uncovering the last remaining wall at the base of the ziggurat. Standing above them I took care not to let my shadow fall across their heads. The air was warm and the wind that had been blowing all morning had unexpectedly dropped to a gentle breeze. The smell of sweat from those carrying the dirt in buckets was almost palpable. A hush fell around me as I peered through the viewfinder. Initially I thought it was the camera that had caused them to fall silent. Yet as the chatter died away they started to clamber up from the trench. Men were pointing towards the east. I turned and, with a hand shielding my eyes against the sun, I surveyed the horizon. There was a brown, undulating band stretched across it. The band was surging forward, increasing in thickness, increasing in height. The land suddenly appeared to be reaching up towards the sky, rolling higher, toppling, then inexorably climbing again.

The wind was suddenly shoving hard against my face, my chest. I staggered away from the rim, bracing myself against the gale, a hand covering the lens of the camera. A dark tidal wave of sand came churning towards me. It was a biblical vision: day turning into night. It flew at us, obscuring the sky, blocking the sun. Bilal reappeared and was shouting something. Shovels and buckets were being thrown down, the workmen scattering away towards what light was left, or scrambling into the ziggurat.

I started to lift my leaden feet. I was stumbling back towards the expedition house. The ground was stirring; small eddies at first, then larger and larger ripples racing over one another. I could taste the dust in my mouth and I remember the sucking, yielding silence that descended before it hit, the howling wind momentarily holding its breath. I had the presence of mind to shove the camera back into its case. Then, within a hundred yards, a soft hissing sound began to surface as the first grains being carried in the air were scattered, cast against stone, cloth and skin. We were running now, though others were crouching down, huddling together, murmuring indecipherable prayers. The flying sand was stinging my face, blinding me. I ran, bent double, one hand shielding my eyes, the other outstretched in front. I was fighting my way through a whirling, shifting mass of sand. Every so often a muffled call was carried by the wind, though it was impossible to say where it was coming from or what was being said.

For what felt like hours I staggered away from the ziggurat, my skin chafing, my hands and face stinging. Finally I stumbled against the wall of the expedition house, crawled round to the gate and then, with my head bowed, ran across the swirling courtyard to the studio.

The studio was dark, the heat almost unbearable. The sand was ricocheting off the glass, sweeping in under the door, spreading in scalloped sheets across the floor. I flicked the switch, but the generator wasn't running. The atmosphere was stifling yet I knew I had to block every gap if I was to stop the sand. There were periodicals that Bateman had thrown beneath the bench. I knelt down and started to tear out pages. My face felt like it was on fire. Droplets of sweat dripped onto the paper. Sand was raining against the glass.

Then there was another sound, the tread of bare feet crossing the studio. When I heard her step towards me I didn't turn. Instead I glanced at the shaving mirror that was hanging by the door. Behind me a figure swept through the darkness with a delicacy of movement I'd seen before. Outside the sandstorm continued to howl and shove its way around the house. I couldn't see her face, but her touch was familiar. Bare arms encircled me, mouth nuzzling into my neck, lips kissing the burnished skin. She stood naked and silent in the dark, pressing herself into my back. When I tried to speak a hand brushed across my mouth. There was no need to say anything. She ran a finger from the bridge to the tip of my nose, and then softly traced my parted lips.

20

When I awoke she was gone. It had been a short, brutal interlude, made all the more absurd by having fallen asleep on the floor. I climbed to my feet and rubbed the back of my neck. The window had stopped rattling and the palm tree had grown tired of self-flagellation. I was brushing myself down when the pages beneath the door scratched across the floor. Stanislav stood there. He smiled and picked up my crumpled jacket. It wasn't the first sandstorm the Russian had suffered, though such storms were rare in November. 'Have you taken pictures of the inscriptions?' he asked, twisting the gooseneck lamp upwards and peering at yesterday's negatives.

'Hasn't Mrs Jackson made copies?'

'She hasn't left the common room. The women sat it out together. How long will your pictures take to develop?'

'A little over an hour. Longer if you want them enlarged, but that will have to wait till the morning.'

'Why not tonight?'

'You need sunlight to enlarge.'

Stanislav nodded as though this was something he'd forgotten. He took off his spectacles, pulled out the tail of his shirt and wiped them clean at his waist. It was a habitual act, and usually indicated a change of subject. 'This is a strange dig.'

'Suarez thinks it's a waste of time.'

'Tom's a fool. Americans are only interested in keeping their sponsors happy, filling their museum cabinets.'

'And his wife?' I asked.

'She's smarter than him, plays chess better than him. And pretty, kulak pretty, though her body is soft.' Stanislav leaned towards me. 'You know what I think?'

I shook my head.

'I think Tilden could be right.'

'About what?'

'About Lamashtu, or Lilith as he prefers to call her. There must be a sign, a revelation in the final chamber.'

'What do you mean?'

'Well, the warnings we've seen.'

'You mean the storm?'

Stanislav smiled. 'The carvings, the inscriptions. Perhaps we'll find something to do with the Garden. Something that gives us a better understanding, something that adds to the myth. You know the Bible is just a collection of other people's stories.'

'And that's why Suarez is reluctant to continue?'

'For him to admit that the Flood is taken from a Sumerian legend hurts. Just imagine him faced with an early account that challenges his understanding of Adam and Eve. Imagine Christianity having to explain away Adam's mistress, or Adam the rapist.'

'The rapist?' I exclaimed. 'Isn't that a rather far-fetched idea?'

'Is it? You should read the Talmud, or the Alpha Bet of Ben Sirah; Hebrew texts which speak of Lilith refusing to lie beneath Adam. Lilith, made of the same dust as Adam, rejecting his advance, him pushing her to the ground. What you English call the missionary. Adam tries to force her, she utters the magical name of God and is borne away.'

'I thought she was cast out?'

'Cast out, borne away.' Stanislav waved his hand in a dismissive gesture. 'Early accounts contradict one another, though they all agree in other ways; that she went to a cave and consorted with demons, that she returned to lie with Adam for a hundred and thirty years, that she seduced other men and created her own legion of followers from man's seed. God tried to destroy her children and Lilith took revenge: strangling babies, destroying the unborn, spreading sickness.'

'And the biblical Lilith is our Assyrian Lamashtu?'

'And the Sumerian Lillake, and Greek Lamia; goddesses punished for their behaviour. But their daughters take revenge. The Lamiae seduce sleeping men, suck their

149

blood, eat their flesh. In Athens, according to Mrs Jackson, there's a relief that shows a naked Lamia straddling a traveller asleep on his back. A sign of rebellion, a sign of wickedness in a world where women were treated as chattels, were forced to lie on their back. Greek witches refused to be submissive, they always wanted to ride their mate.'

'Like vampires and Fabians,' I uttered casually; suppressing any thought of the dreams I'd had, the alarming idea that the shadowy figures weren't just the product of a febrile imagination.

'To any man who fears a woman's sexuality they're a threat. In Greece they were also known as *Empusae*, "forcers-in", and in the north as "Children of Hecate".'

'But you don't believe in such tales?' I asked, searching for reassurance.

'Of course I don't. But everything has its origin. You know the word Eden comes from the Akkadian word *edinu*, and the Assyrian legend comes from the Sumerian?' Stanislav turned towards the table and began idly looking through the pictures Bateman had left.

'For you there's only the physical world to contend with?'

'Isn't that enough?' he asked. 'You don't really think the storm was some sort of sign?'

'It isn't that. It's just . . .' It was hard for me to share what I'd seen, or thought I had. Yet Stanislav was a man of logic, someone I could trust. 'I was sorting through those last night.' Feeling as though I was incriminating

150

myself I pointed at the pictures he held in his hands. 'One was taken just outside the entrance to the ziggurat. There was something strange about it. There was a shadow. It didn't fit, shouldn't have been there.'

'A reflection?'

'No, it wasn't that. The shadow appeared at the wrong angle. Bateman was careless, I could see his shadow at the foot of the picture. This other one went off at an angle, cut diagonally behind Tilden and Suarez.'

'It wasn't theirs?'

'It couldn't have been.'

'Headlamps from the lorry?'

'Not in broad daylight. Besides, there was something else.'

'What?'

'This shadow appeared to have a mouth, eyes. It appeared to be screaming.'

Stanislav snorted dismissively. 'Where is it?' he asked, glancing back at the discarded pile on the bench.

'It's not amongst those. It was in my jacket pocket, but it's gone.'

'What do you mean?'

'This morning it wasn't there.'

'You've lost it?'

'I think it was taken.'

'At an excavation things are always disappearing. It doesn't mean anything. The shadow was a trick of the light, or something went wrong when Bateman developed the photograph.' His look of concern was one I'd seen before; the muted sympathy for those suffering with sunstroke or prone to hallucinations. 'If you think about it rationally I am sure you can come up with a dozen reasons.' He put his arm round my shoulder. 'Come on,' he said, his voice urging me out of my stupor. 'You've been cooped up in here for too long. Why don't we have a drink before supper?'

21

The next morning the cook and houseboy continued to sweep out the sand while at the ziggurat Suarez oversaw the work gang. He'd been complaining about the number of Yazidis arriving each morning. Every day there seemed to be more of them wanting to work on the dig. They were easy to recognise with their shirts buttoned up to the neck, and their loose white trousers and white cloaks. Their turbans, like their greasy ringlets, were black and away from the dig they usually carried long rifles in their hands, or pistols in their belts. In appearance they were an imposing, manly race: tall or of medium stature, with fine noses, and clear brown eyes. Their strong voices were audible from afar: frank and confident, or fierce and angry. Their complexion was usually dark and they sometimes shaved their heads, leaving only a long, thin forelock.

The Yazidi women were rarely seen beyond the foothills,

though they were also easy to recognise. The married women would dress entirely in white, while the girls wore white skirts and drawers with long coloured dresses. The girls would bind fancy kerchiefs round their heads and adorn themselves with coins as well as with glass and amber beads. They were also prettier, according to Stanislav, than your Kurd and were reputed to have better manners.

Through necessity Suarez was forced to employ Yazidis, but he refused to have them working with him. That morning he'd taken five Arabs inside to prise up the limestone portal; paying them more than the Yazidis had asked to work in the foul-smelling chamber.

By lunchtime they'd managed to break through to the chamber below, but what they'd found dismayed everyone. It was full of sand. Not from yesterday's storm. There was no mistaking that this hadn't happened by accident. The sand was too fine, too pure to have simply poured in through some fault in the brickwork. And what had become obvious was that the chamber above had been flooded on purpose. Its floor was sealed with bitumen and was thicker than any other; strengthened to withhold the weight of the water. The reason why it had been filled was unclear, but I started to feel increasingly uneasy as I watched each bucket of sand being carried out of the ziggurat.

Tilden, who'd gone back to his bed after trying to eat a little lunch, didn't appear at the supper table. He was looking pale and drawn and, though Suarez had kept him informed of the day's progress, was apparently in no fit state to share his thoughts. O'Neil had visited him and had prescribed bed rest and something to settle the stomach. In his opinion Tilden must have swallowed some of the stagnant water. He didn't think it was too serious and expected his patient to be a little better within a week or two.

At supper Stanislav read out his translation of one of the inscriptions found in the flooded chamber. Clara was the last to arrive, and as soon as she entered the Russian stood up. Again there was the customary warning that the translation was simply a rough interpretation of what had been written three thousand years ago. Those at the table listened attentively, although I could see Suarez was impatient to hear what Stanislav had to share. 'This better be worth a day's labour,' he warned as he stubbed out his cigarette.

'Oh it is,' Stanislav reassured his audience. He took out his notebook from the inside pocket of his jacket and with the finger he'd licked he worked his way through several pages before clearing his throat. His voice was solemn and steady; fit for the pulpit. '"And he will stretch out his hand against her and destroy her. Here she resides in desert and in river, in desolation, and in wilderness. Flocks shall lie down in the midst of her, all the beasts of the nations: both the cormorant and the owl shall sing at the window; desolation shall be in the threshold. Every one that passes by shall hiss and wag his finger. This is the rejoicing demon that dwelt without care, who said in her heart: I am, and there is none besides me".'

Silence followed. Suarez asked Stanislav to read out the translation again.

Once he'd finished repeating it Mrs Jackson declared that it was Lamashtu. 'And the "he" . . .'

'Is Pazuzu,' said Suarez authoritatively.

'It certainly sounds biblical,' I said.

'There must be something like it in the Old Testament,' agreed Stanislav.

'Nonsense,' snapped Suarez. He was sitting in Tilden's seat and impatiently beckoned Amuda forward before turning to face Stanislav. 'And I wish you'd stop trying to link what we have here, which is an Assyrian folly, with the Bible. Yes, I know Sumerian tablets speak of a flood. Yes, I know Lilith surfaces in Hebrew texts, but what we have here is a godless monstrosity. Nothing more.'

'This is more than just a folly,' countered Stanislav. 'It's Lamashtu's temple – or a kind of mausoleum. I've started to translate the second inscription and it's a register of names, of Lamashtu's children, and a warning, a warning which forbids anyone from entering the temple.'

Suarez shook his head.

'If there's a warning then perhaps there's something worth uncovering,' said Clara, 'have you thought of that?'

'You mean a crock of gold?' said Suarez. His tone was mocking, but after a moment's reflection I could see how her suggestion appealed to him.

'After the Assyrians were slaughtered,' said Mrs Jackson, 'after the city was razed to the ground, we know that this whole area was abandoned for over five hundred years. Why? Does it have something to do with Lamashtu's temple?'

'The whole of Assyria was crushed,' replied Suarez. 'Nineveh wasn't the only place to suffer, other places were left uninhabited for centuries.'

'But nowhere else was left so devastated. And what about the *Lament of Nineveh*? It speaks of a curse.'

'Like every other clay tablet from the king's library.'

I turned to look at Mrs Tilden. She sat passively focusing on the plate in front of her. 'What does your husband think?' I asked.

'He's sleeping,' she replied, hardly above a whisper. There was an awkward silence, a hope that she'd elaborate, but she didn't say anything else, just kept on staring at her plate.

'It's goat curry,' said Mrs Jackson. 'You like it.'

In response to her prompting, Mrs Tilden picked up her fork, though her face remained expressionless. She continued to gaze at the plate as if she were afraid of catching anybody's eye.

'When will you finish translating the inscriptions?' asked Suarez.

'Tomorrow,' replied Stanislav.

'And this *Lament of Nineveh*?' I asked.

Stanislav smiled. 'I'll lend you a copy.'

22

'O city, the lament is bitter, the lament made for you. How long will your bitter lament grieve Lamashtu who weeps? O city, your name exists but you have been destroyed. O city, your wall rises high but your land has perished. O city, your rites have been taken from you, your powers are cursed. How long will your bitter lament last? How long will your bitter lament grieve Lamashtu who sleeps?'

The feeble light of the bare bulb lit the bed on which I was lying. Resting against the pillow was the slim volume that Stanislav had lent me. I had finished copying out the *Lament* into my notebook and had started to read the footnote at the bottom of the page. It spoke of Lamashtu as the demon lover of Adam, able to snare men with her soft kisses. She was referred to as the Sumerian goddess of desolation, the destroyer of newborn infants and Satan's consort. In the same sentence they called her a snake, a giant bat, a hyena. Certain stories suggested wings, others focused on her ability to take on many shapes. A daughter of hers, it was once recorded, presided over the Temple of Bel, kept there to entertain their god. I had begun to make notes when there was a faint tapping at my door. Before I had time to say anything Clara entered. She waited, quivering with nervous excitement, as I closed the door.

'I've dirty linen to wash,' she declared, with an impudent smile. She was holding her stockings in one hand and a box of Lux was lodged beneath her arm. 'You know you've been ignoring me.'

'Hardly, it's just I've been . . .'

'What? Too busy or feeling guilty? Or too busy feeling guilty?'

She turned and draped her stockings over the door handle and placed her Lux on the chest of drawers. With her back to me she quickly started to unbutton her blouse. It was all so methodical, so taken for granted. Her lack of guilt was infectious. 'Do you think we should?' I asked; a half-hearted attempt to stop what seemed to be unfurling.

She turned round. 'We won't get caught. Not if you can keep quiet.' She lifted her short slip above her head, and then shook her short black hair. Her breasts gently swayed in front of me.

I picked up my pen and books from the bed. 'Is this some sort of habit of yours?'

'What?' she asked as if I'd insulted her. Her hands were on one side of her hips, and she was looking down at the buttons on her skirt. 'Creeping into your room in the dead of night?'

I nodded, but she ignored the question she'd set herself. Instead she started to unbuckle my belt.

After it was over we simply lay there, slippery with sweat, her head resting on my chest. I asked her if she'd be visiting again.

'Perhaps,' she replied.

'Outside normal visiting hours?'

'When I've stockings to wash.'

'You don't feel guilty?'

'Why should I? I was born in a barnyard and brought up to play kiss-in-the-ring. Besides, musical beds is the party game here. Or hadn't you noticed?'

'You don't mean that.'

'Well, it's not for everyone.'

'Tom?'

'Let's not talk about him.' She paused. 'Will you do me a favour? If Tom ever asks you to go into town with him, please don't. And don't ask me why.'

'All right, I won't.'

'Do you have a cigarette?'

'No, it's not a habit . . .'

'I didn't ask . . .' Clara didn't finish her sentence, but pushed herself away. She wiped her glistening belly with the sheet and then climbed out of bed.

161

'You do know Susan and Bateman were lovers?'

'The thought had occurred to me.'

'Bateman was in love with her. Does that surprise you?'

'Why should it?'

'Don't you think she's a little crazy?' she asked, stepping into her skirt.

'A little aloof, perhaps.'

'That's the Limey's way of putting it. You know most men seem to find her aloofness stimulating, though I guess she's yet to ply you with one of her confessionals.'

I shook my head.

She straightened her skirt and then ran her fingers through her hair. 'Shall I tell you one?'

'If you're not in any hurry.'

'When she was a girl she was involved with a games mistress who liked nothing more than smacking her pert little backside. A sadistic Mrs Brady bent on kissing her better.'

'How do you know this?'

'How do you think? She told me, one warm afternoon when the boys were digging sandcastles. We drank whisky and told each other our little secrets, opened up to one another, if you catch my drift. Susan's a wanton creature. In my limited experience the sons and daughters of ministers are always the most shameless, wouldn't you agree?'

'Personally, I've only ever had tea with a vicar's daughter. Does Tilden know about Bateman?'

'Tilden's all beard and bedroom slippers. He's gravy-stained and perversely puritanical, but he's not stupid, at least when it comes to some things.' She paused after she'd finished buttoning her blouse. 'But Bateman wasn't running away from Tilden, if that's what you're thinking.' One hand was resting on the door handle, the other held her stockings and washing powder. 'But you're not going to run away, are you?'

'Don't worry. I'll be here for the month.'

Clara folded her arms over the packet of Lux and smiled. It was a wide smile, yet at the same I saw the rubbing of her thumb and forefinger as though remembering her want of a cigarette. It was an absent-minded gesture, but for a moment it betrayed her face. She stepped towards me, still with her arms crossed, and gently kissed my cheek.

23

A rather solemn-looking O'Neil sat flicking through a magazine in the common room. As soon as he saw me he stood up. 'You've just missed lunch,' I told him, 'but if you're looking for Susan she's just gone back to her room.'

'It's not Susan I've come to see, though this is bound to upset her. I'm here with Captain Fowler on what he's keen to label as official business.'

'It sounds serious.'

'Serious and regrettable, but unavoidable I'm afraid. A man's body has been discovered on the banks of the Tigris. Captain Fowler brought what remained of the corpse to the consulate. It's the body, as far as I can tell, of a white male, though I'm not certain about its age or how long it's been in the river.'

'You think it's Bateman?'

'That's a possibility,' answered O'Neil. 'I've asked

Suarez to gather the others together in the mess.' He paused. 'How's Susan?'

'Finding it hard to sleep. Worried about her husband.'

'You know this is unlikely to help the poor woman? If you can . . .'

Amuda appeared in the doorway. He told the doctor that the others were waiting for him. O'Neil sighed and nodded at the boy.

In the mess there was an atmosphere of curiosity and unease. Captain Fowler, a tall, grey-haired man with a thick moustache, waited for us all to settle. I sat down at the table, while the captain remained standing. It was the straight-backed, hands-behind-the-back posture that had obviously served him well, and in short, plain sentences he told us about the grisly discovery and how the body was like no other he'd ever seen.

O'Neil, who'd taken a chair to the right of the captain, faced those gathered in the mess. At the end of Fowler's speech he felt he needed to clarify a point or two. He remained seated, with his mottled hands clasped together as through in prayer. 'Normally, a drowned corpse expands,' he explained, his knuckles rocking backwards and forwards. 'The skin swells. The body brought to the consulate this morning was similar to a deflated football. The skin is in loose folds, it's the flesh that's contracted. If anything it appears to be devoid of liquid, other than a little river water in the lungs.'

'You say the body was found on the banks of the Tigris?' asked Suarez.

'It was,' responded the captain. 'We believe the fellow drowned, though he may have met his end in several ways. With such a poor corpse it's hard to tell.'

'It's more or less desiccated,' added O'Neil. 'The face is impossible to identify, though there's still hair attached to the skull.'

'Colour?' asked Suarez.

'Light brown.'

'It's Bateman, isn't it?' said Mrs Tilden, echoing what everyone else was thinking.

'I'm afraid he seems to be the most obvious candidate.'

'And his eyes?' she asked, her voice betraying her anguish.

'We can't say for certain,' answered O'Neil, 'possibly blue.'

Mrs Tilden bit her bottom lip.

'Face is like a bulldog's,' added Fowler. 'An ugly sight. The tongue, for example, is quite—'

'Oh God,' exclaimed Mrs Tilden, suddenly rising to her feet. 'I think I'm going to be sick.' She staggered a few yards into the courtyard before she was overtaken by a nausea that caused her to double up.

O'Neil stood up, though it was Clara who went to help the poor woman. For a moment we quietly sat and listened to Mrs Tilden retching outside.

'What I meant,' began Fowler, who felt he needed to explain his description of the corpse, 'is we can't say for certain. However, we'll endeavour to contact Bateman's family in England. Hopefully they'll have heard from him by now, and this is simply a matter of mistaken identity.'

'You say you're not sure how he died?' prompted Suarez.

O'Neil wiped his brow with his handkerchief. 'It's impossible to tell. In all my years as a medical practitioner I've never seen a corpse like it. In some ways it's like a mummified body. Whether it was poison or something in the river that made its flesh contract is hard to say. The lack of fluid in the tissue is frankly inexplicable.'

'We may be looking at an accidental death, possibly a suicide, but we can't rule out murder. First, however, we need to ascertain who it was. I'd like a volunteer to try and identify the body. Though Dr O'Neil met Bateman on several occasions, it'd be better if someone closer to him, as it were, was able to verify a likeness.'

'I'll go,' said Suarez, 'unless Tilden objects.'

'I doubt he will,' replied Mrs Jackson.

'What we need,' said Fowler, picking up his cap from the table, 'is for all of you to be vigilant. We can't rule out the Kurds or some Arab chief wanting to avenge some imaginary slight.'

'Or the Yazidis,' said Suarez.

'Quite,' answered Fowler. 'As a result of former persecutions they've lost large amounts of land. In one or two places feelings are running high.'

'There's also talk of a woman being stoned,' added Suarez.

'Yes,' admitted Fowler cautiously, 'there's been talk of a woman being stoned for adultery and our need to intervene.'

'And a man as well I assume,' said Mrs Jackson.

'Sorry?' said Fowler.

'I imagine she couldn't have committed adultery by herself.'

'I see your point,' acknowledged Fowler. 'Anyway,' he continued, his brow lifting as he picked up the thread of his customary warning, 'they've been quiet for a while, but you never know what they're plotting. Their promises can shift with the sands, as anybody who's served out here can testify.' He glanced at me as though expecting some sort of unspoken communion. I didn't give him the satisfaction and met his gaze with impassivity.

'And this woman,' said Suarez, 'this adulteress, don't they bury them up to their waist, before stoning them?'

'Yes,' answered Fowler, somewhat reluctantly.

'And the man?' asked Mrs Jackson.

'They put them in a black sack before the stoning begins.'

'I mean you'll try and save him as well.'

'Of course, though there very often isn't a man. By your question I'm assuming you want me to acknowledge that the men often get away and it's the women who are punished?'

'I just want you to reassure me that you'll do your best to save them both,' answered Mrs Jackson.

'Well, we'll do our best, though you know as well as I do that sometimes it's not prudent to interfere. Now I really think we need to identify this body as soon as possible.'

Suarez left with O'Neil and Fowler. I made some sort of an excuse to Mrs Jackson and returned to the studio. It was hard to say whether Suarez had simply been stoking trouble for the Yazidis or wanting to warn me off. I was glad Clara hadn't been there. As I closed the studio door I began to wonder if it was wise for me to stay. The dreams that had plagued me, my involvement with a married woman, the suspected death of Bateman; none of it made my remaining a sensible proposition. I'd been shattered before by what I'd seen and the last thing I wanted was to fall apart again. I thought of leaving, of ditching the shards of pottery and cuneiform inscriptions and returning to the daily grind of weddings and catalogues. A railway ticket would have taken the consulate no more than a couple of days to sort out. And yet I paused at the thought of those dull, drab streets. In England there was nothing but despair. I was dead, or indifferent; immersed in the routine of my existence, ploughing through the days and months like some soulless worker. In Iraq everything seemed sharper: emotions, conversations, even the outline of a face. And how would Clara feel if I just disappeared? Even though conflict was inevitable, she deserved some show of loyalty. The naked intimacy we'd enjoyed had been wrong, but it had also been wonderful. The lust she had fanned was hideous, but I couldn't escape from wanting her.

24

That afternoon Clara suggested we take a stroll down to the ancient city. It was quiet in the house. Suarez wasn't back and I had just finished photographing a collection of bronze figures. The suggestion of a walk wasn't driven by anything untoward, just a need to get things straight. The furnace-like heat had started to fade, and the idea of getting some air was perfectly acceptable.

We left the courtyard and Clara lit a cigarette in the shade of the house. The Tigris was still shrouded in mist and the leaves of the palm trees along its banks appeared to float like dead starfish. I asked her about Susan. Clara said she was sleeping. Apparently something similar had happened to her in England. One summer Susan had spent a weekend with her piano teacher in a hotel in Brighton. He was a married man, and when he returned home he committed suicide. 'Sounds like an episode from some pot-boiler for *jeunes filles*, doesn't it?' said Clara, shaking her head, though I couldn't tell whether it was in sympathy or disbelief.

As we started towards the river she stopped talking about Susan and began to tell me her own story. She was the youngest of five and her childhood had consisted of an unromantic migration north, fuelled by dry cornbread and turnip greens. Her father, a man driven to drink, had owned a farm in Texas until boll weevils had devastated his cotton crop. Before they'd reached Detroit he'd disappeared, but her mother managed to find work in one of the many factories. Clara liked the city, but preferred Chicago. Before Suarez she'd been seeing a Lithuanian who'd been working in a stockyard cutting up cattle. She was young and in love, and had given him what he had wanted. Then one day he told her that he'd married his cousin, a fifteen year old who'd just arrived with her family. He was the most handsome man she'd ever met, broad and strong. Physically I wasn't her type, but there was something about me that had caught her imagination. She spoke in her matter-of-fact style about how people are attracted to those whose state of consciousness is related to their own. In the past she'd made the mistake of crediting others with a sense of decency which she didn't have and this was something she felt I might understand. Clara talked to me as if she was thinking aloud, although I can now only recall the mood, rather than her exact words. I remember the warmth, the serenity that surrounded us. She asked me if I'd ever been to the

States. I told her I hadn't, though it was a place I'd always wanted to visit.

'You must come,' she said, but didn't say any more about it.

Near the river we clambered round inlets filled with rushes and stagnant pools of brown water. The mist moved in slow, humid currents across the reed beds. The only sound was the lulling of the river as it lapped against the reeds. She asked me about my childhood and I told her my own tale of genteel poverty and quiet desperation. How my father had been a tailor until the recruiting sergeant had taken away most of his best customers. How my sister had been a stenographer until she got married. For a year she'd lived with her husband in Battersea. She was pregnant when she died of influenza in the winter of 1918. Neither my ignominious return from Mesopotamia nor her death had shaken my parents' faith. 'They believed that God was in charge of our destiny and that he had it all mapped out.'

'Then it's hard to think he loves us,' said Clara.

'I imagine watching your son being crucified makes it hard to forgive. When I saw men crawling through mud, trailing blood and shattered limbs, I thought he must hate us, or we hate ourselves, which more or less means the same thing.'

In the distance I heard the Ford lorry. She must have heard it too, but it didn't seem to bother her. Instead of turning round she slipped her arm through mine. I didn't know whether she was being brave or foolish, but the guileless act brought with it an intimacy stronger than anything else.

Following an old irrigation channel we made our way into the city. We walked past a scorched heap of sand and black earth and she told me it was what was left of Nabu's temple. Nabu, she explained as I wondered whether it was worth taking a photograph, was the Assyrians' god of writing and the son of Marduk. The larger mound to the right was Jonah's tomb. She pointed out where the botanical gardens were thought to have been. We strolled past the armoury, the zoo, the library. The whole site was marked by mounds and lumps, dusty heaps of brick and crumbling masonry. A sluggish tributary, which meanders through the centre of Nineveh, stopped us from going any further. The mist on this narrow river had all but evaporated and standing on its rotten bank I could see a foul-looking bloom gently rolling with the water below. Flies skated above the green mantle, zigzagging through the thin cloud.

On the other side of the river was the palace of Sennacherib, the largest mound in the city and pockmarked with stone-vaulted tunnels and exposed brick. Clara turned towards me. 'Do you think much about the war?' she asked quietly.

'I try not to.'

'Mrs Jackson said she thought she heard you crying in the night.'

I shrugged. 'It's not the first time. Sometimes it haunts me. The things I saw, the things that happened.'

'You know when you're at the table, and you've finished eating, you always sit with your thumb beneath your chin, your fingers crooked beneath your nose. It's a habit of yours, isn't it, to hide your lips when you're listening.'

'I wasn't aware I was doing it, though I'm flattered you're taking such an interest.'

'I just want you to know you don't have to hide your scars from me.'

I nodded. 'I'll remember that.' I looked up at the half-hidden palace. A black and white crow was skulking at the entrance of one of the tunnels. 'Didn't you say this place was haunted?'

She smiled faintly, thinking that I was changing the subject. 'Tilden hasn't told you about the underground galleries?' she asked.

I shook my head.

'It's a story he likes to tell, about the hidden cells beneath the palace. Of course it's full of scorpions and spiders and there's nothing in it now of any value. But in one of the temple rooms, screened by a wall once plastered and painted, there are stone steps descending deep into the earth. The story goes that about a hundred years ago an archaeologist and a French doctor heard the rattle of chains, as well as something else: low murmurings, a noise unlike anything human. With their lamps out in front of them the two men descended and ventured into a narrow passageway.' Clara paused as though trying to recall what Tilden had told her. She held out an imaginary lamp and lowered her voice. 'The first few cells were empty, but as they shuffled forward the savage cries grew louder. The archaeologist covered his nose with his handkerchief. The French doctor was to liken the setting to the ape house in the Menagerie du Jardin. A clamour arose like that at feeding time.

'The men were horrified by what they discovered. In the first inhabited cell the filthy prisoner, head bowed, crawled sobbing towards the light. A thin arm reached through the bars, fingers grasping at the lamp's rays. The archaeologist stepped back,' as Clara did, 'only to feel the tips of another man's fingers brush against his shirt. The two men, keeping to the middle of the passage, continued on their hellish journey. There were more than a dozen solitary prisoners, each one manacled and chained to the wall. They tried to question them, but if any prisoner had ever had the ability to speak it had long been forgotten. The doctor soon declared that each man was mad, stark staring crazy. At the end of the passage there were three young mothers suckling infants of a disturbingly strange appearance. These infants died soon after their exposure to the light; a circumstance which the doctor thought most merciful. The archaeologist believed that they were slaves, though to whom or to which tribe they belonged was never discovered.' She stopped, as though she was expecting me to applaud. 'What do you think?'

'A travelling theatre couldn't have done it any better.'

'Why thank you.' She smiled and held the hem of her dress as though she was about to curtsy.

'Any truth in it?' I asked.

'Well, it's a story Tilden likes to tell. I think it's apocryphal, or straight out of *Weird Tales*. Lovecraft's my favourite for that kind of thing. Where do you want to go now?'

I glanced back at the mound of curiously pale earth with its tunnels and charred bricks. 'Away from here,' I said.

'How about the library?'

'You've got some overdue books?'

'Don't you mean tablets? There ain't no such thing as books.'

I smiled. 'Anywhere out of the sun.'

'It's cooler in the library,' she said, 'and there's less chance of being disturbed.'

25

By the end of the following day they'd cleared half of the fourth chamber and had found nothing. At the start of supper there was a subdued atmosphere, though this had more to do with the workmen's failure to find anything than with the news of Bateman's death. Yet when we sat down to hear what Stanislav had deciphered there was the same eagerness to understand what had been carved into stone centuries ago. The discovery of Bateman's body, for that's what Suarez had eventually identified, had somehow failed to eclipse the argument surrounding the building's purpose and its theological significance. It sounds callous, but the only one still grieving for the photographer was Mrs Tilden. At supper it was obvious that she'd been crying. Her eyes were bloodshot and she seemed oblivious to those around her. However, when Stanislav climbed to his feet, she, like the rest of us, lifted her head and listened attentively as he explained what he'd discovered.

'The second inscription is, as I stated last night, a list of names and a warning.' The Russian sounded uncharacteristically nervous. 'The third and fourth again act as warnings, but, if I'm correct, this isn't a temple or a tomb.'

'What else can it be?' Suarez asked.

'I'm not sure, perhaps some sort of prison for a high priestess.'

'That's ridiculous,' exclaimed Suarez.

'Why?' I asked.

'A jail for a priestess? There's nothing that even suggests such a folly.'

'That doesn't mean it doesn't exist,' countered Mrs Jackson. 'You should know better. What was hell but a prison built for Lucifer.'

'But that's an abstract concept,' said Stanislav.

'Is it?' I asked. 'Can't it be man-made?'

'Thanks for the philosophical insight, Ward,' said Suarez.

'Circles of ash beside the Dead Sea proving the existence of Sodom, balls of brimstone fallen from heaven. Your words, not mine,' I replied.

'There's a difference.'

'For some, Tom,' said Mrs Jackson.

'What makes you believe it's a jail?' asked Clara.

'All right,' answered Stanislav, 'just wait until you've heard what I have to say.' He opened his notebook, cleared his throat and began to read. '"Here is the first: she who

182

slithers like a snake, immortal monster, daughter of the sky god, killer of crib and the womb, snatcher from crib and womb, seductress and demoness, mother of night demons. Scattered are her sons and daughters. Immortal corrupter, she dwells among the desolate ruins where owls, jackals, arrow-snakes and kites keep her company".'

'It sounds like a temple,' said Suarez dismissively.

'It's the fourth inscription that spells it out,' answered Stanislav with a trace of annoyance. He turned another page and started to read again. '"Her daughters hide in corners, her daughters shriek in despair. Pazuzu has defeated Lamashtu. Pazuzu has buried Lamashtu. Her spirit is alive and they bide their time. Reader flee. Look not around, return to the light. They are here in the shade, they are here in the shadows, they reign in the night".'

'Pazuzu has *buried*,' echoed Suarez.

'Alive,' asserted Stanislav, 'and immortal.'

'Her spirit,' said Suarez, shaking his head, 'and if you're determined to see her as a biblical figure, then how can she be immortal? She would have died with Adam and Eve. Remember, they brought death down upon us all when they disobeyed God, when they bit into the apple.'

'But by then Lilith had long been banished from Eden,' said Mrs Jackson. 'She escaped the curse which overtook Adam. She'd fled from him long before the Fall.' Suarez continued to shake his head, but Mrs Jackson carried on. 'For some she's Sheba and Helen, for some she's the demoness who destroyed Job's sons.'

'You seem to know an awful lot about her,' said Suarez.

'And you seem to be forgetting I'm a theologian, not an archaeologist. I've studied the women within the Old Testament, tried to make sense of the patriarchal world, the papist, misogynistic realm of half-truths and marginalised women.'

'Is this an attack on Christianity or the Catholic Church in particular?'

'Neither, Tom. It's a desire to understand, to piece it all together. Lilith, like Mary Magdalene, was pushed out. Don't you see,' with her eyes she appealed to those seated round the table, 'they represent the free-thinking woman, the sexual woman. Lilith typifies the Assyrian women, women encouraged to have sex before marriage. And it wasn't just the Assyrians. The prophets denounced Israelite women for following these Assyrian practices, for indulging in pre-nuptial promiscuity. And what happened to the fees they'd charge? Why, they were given to the priests. Reread Deuteronomy and you'll see I'm right.'

At the mention of Assyrian practices Clara glanced across at me. There was a flicker of a smile, a smug 'I told you so'. I tried hard not to express any emotion. I sat and listened to the others, averting my eyes from her for fear of arousing suspicion. I felt again the need to say something. In these theological discussions I had little to offer, other than the occasional question. 'And these shadows, the repeated mention of *they* . . .?' I stumbled with my sentence, but Mrs Jackson understood. Suarez just stared at me as if I'd spoken out of turn.

'The "they" must be her daughters. In the Talmud Lilith's daughters are the Lilim, in the Greek they're the Lamiae. Those that thought they'd trapped Lamashtu must have feared her daughters.'

'Why?' I asked.

'They not only strangled infants, but also seduced men.'

'Seduced men . . .' I uttered.

'For a hundred and thirty years Lilith milked Adam of his seed and through her nocturnal visits gave birth to her legion of demons.'

'And they continued to multiply?'

'God would destroy a hundred a day, but still they increased in number. She was punished for wanting her independence.'

'Mina,' said Suarez, 'you seem to have some sympathy for Lilith, some sort of sisterly love for this demoness.'

'The victim becomes the villain, at least that's often what happens to women.'

'And tomorrow, what do you and Stanislav propose we do?'

'Continue to clear the chamber,' replied the Russian without a moment's hesitation. 'See if anything is buried there.'

'But you're not afraid of what we might unleash?' asked Suarez mockingly.

'I doubt there's anything there that'll trouble me.'

'Does your husband know of this?' I asked Mrs Tilden.

'He's asleep,' she replied after a moment's hesitation. I

185

suspect I startled her. Throughout supper she hadn't said a word. 'He sleeps a lot.'

'But surely you've told him about what's been happening?' asked Stanislav. 'I've given you copies of each translation.'

Mrs Tilden, as if she hadn't heard the Russian's question, picked up her spoon and stirred her bowl of peaches and condensed milk. Her head was bowed and she suddenly seemed absorbed by the swirling pattern in front of her.

'Susan,' said Mrs Jackson gently, 'Henry's getting better isn't he?'

'He's just sleeping.'

'Perhaps someone should look in on him,' suggested Suarez.

'I saw him yesterday,' said Clara, 'after I returned Susan to her room.'

'Check on him again. Susan, do you want to accompany Clara?'

Without answering Mrs Tilden pushed her chair back and followed her towards the door. Before she went out into the courtyard Mrs Tilden turned and faced the table. 'It's in our dreams,' she cried, although her voice was barely above a whisper. 'He has them. They come to him. I've heard them.' She leaned towards Mrs Jackson. 'You know what they are. You understand.'

'Please,' said Suarez, 'just get her out of here?'

Clara put a hand on Susan's shoulder and gently steered her towards the door.

'You see them too,' said Susan.

186

'See what?' asked Clara.

'I heard you in the studio, above the storm, I heard you.'

'Don't be silly,' said Clara as she guided her out of the mess, 'it couldn't have been me.'

'She needs looking after,' said Mrs Jackson, after they'd left. 'O'Neil needs to see her.'

'I agree,' said Stanislav. 'Since Bateman's disappearance . . . and now with her husband ill, and Bateman's body having been discovered . . .'

'O'Neil's concerned,' I added. 'He asked me to keep an eye on her.'

'To spy on her?' asked Suarez.

'No, just to watch her. She's having trouble sleeping.'

'Unlike her husband,' he quipped. 'And were you asked to keep an eye on anybody else?'

'No.'

'Well, I find that hard to believe,' he declared, looking straight into my eyes, 'but I'll give you some advice: don't be fooled into pitying her. Crocodile tears is all she'll give you.'

'And what about her nightmares?' asked Mrs Jackson. 'Did O'Neil say anything about what she's been hearing?'

'She's delirious,' said Suarez dismissively.

'Has anybody else heard anything?' I asked.

'Why, are you compiling a report?'

'No, I just thought . . .' I couldn't ignore what Susan had been saying and I had an answer; it waited on my tongue. It was another chance for me to speak, to tell

187

them that I'd been suffering: the creeping nightmares, my growing fear of the dark. But I held the sentence in my head, and found myself thinking about Clara. I wasn't losing my grip, it was just that I couldn't say anything. Chin resting in the palm of my hand, knuckles hiding my lips. A fly landed on the rim of my bowl. I watched it crawl towards the condensed milk.

The conversation had left me in its wake. Instead of sharing my tormented nights I was back at the canal, walking between bullets that fizzed past my ears, seeing men falling around me. Facing forward and not daring to flinch, not allowing anything other than my own sense of what was right, what was expected from me to dictate my actions, my behaviour. Until it was too late, until I couldn't keep pretending that it was me. I was sleep-walking into hell. *Are you OK? Are you all right? You look a bit pasty, you look as if you've seen a . . .* a shake of the head, a flick of the chin and we fall back in line. The fly was crawling out of its crater.

26

I thought I'd bolted the door. Half asleep, I felt her sliding between the sheets. Her nakedness didn't surprise me, her smooth skin warm against the cotton, her dark hair grazing my cheek. Her mouth was hot and moist; kisses bursting like Very lights across my neck and face, pushing into the flesh, weighted with bestial desire. A soft finger lay against my lips – ushering silence. Her warm body slid over mine, limbs intertwining. There was the absurd smell of damp fur and incense. A determined hand reached down and caressed, assessed and guided me in. Her breathing sank, snagged in the mouth, harnessed itself to the thrust, the rhythm of her hips. Her breath was tethered: rising, grinding, groaning; louder than before. 'Shhh,' I whispered, and tried to remind her that others might hear.

She caught my hand as I reached out to feel for her

mouth. Somewhere in the blackness my wrist was being held tightly in her grasp; held then thrust back into the pillow. There was an urgency, a wetness which was spreading from between our thighs, slippery and moist, sliding over me, gliding together. Glistening, sweaty, greasy. She was pushing against me; shoving, thrusting. The bed was scraping, inching its way across the floor. It was knocking against the wall, dashing itself against the bedside cabinet. Her unbridled lust was chiselling into wood and brick. Then, through the crashing and scraping, there was a knocking, a knocking at the door. Someone must have heard.

Was it Suarez? Was he looking for his wife?

I tried to shake my hand free, tried to lift her from me, but her legs tightened around mine. I was being held, drawn in, I had the strangest feeling that I was being lifted away from the mattress. 'Did you lock the door?' I was struggling to get out from beneath. 'Did you lock the door?' I whispered urgently as the knocking resurfaced. There was no answer from above, just a grinding of hips, a determination to finish what she'd started. I tried to sway to one side, to throw her from me, but she pinned my shoulders down, her nails digging into my flesh. 'Clara,' I cried, 'Clara,' I hissed again, wanting her to stop.

I heard the handle turning, saw the door inching open, the grey night widening across the floor. She was riding me, thumping down urgently. Caught in flagrante, she'd lost even the decency to desist. 'Clara,' I cried, a

190

bitter angry shout, an attempt to bring her back to her senses.

An answer came from beside the door. 'Harry?' she said. It was Clara, her voice I'd heard, her figure in the darkness by the chest of drawers, standing over us. I turned my eyes away and tried to focus on the face above me, the face that was screaming in frustration. With her lips curled back I saw what looked like teeth, felt her breath: warm and sickly sweet. Fear was rising in my chest. It was impossible to see who or what it was that was thumping down upon me, but it already knew its chance had been lost, it could sense the panic coursing through my veins, the horror it had generated. Clara, standing motionless, was staring into darkness, listening to its panting, its cries of anguish and frustration. I heard her stifle a sob as it lifted its weight from me, the body shifting like a retreating wave across my limbs. She turned and stumbled out of the room. The disturbed sham crawled from beneath the sheet and appeared to scuttle after her retreating figure.

I sprang from the mattress, but could only stagger behind whatever had crept into my bed. There was nothing in the courtyard, nothing that lingered out of the shadows.

A fleeting figure. The slam of a door.

I listened. My limbs were shaking, head reeling. I listened, one hand pressed against the cold brick, my legs feeling as if they were about to give way.

There were no raised voices, no angry husband. All was still. The truck was gone. Had Suarez driven into town, or was he comforting her, calming her down? I became conscious of the muffled drone of the generator. It must have been before ten. I went back a step and flicked the switch in the room. The bedclothes were in disarray, but there was nothing else. No sign of the seductress, no sign of a struggle. I lifted the sheet from the mattress and saw the smudges left by her limbs; powdery marks as though a thousand moths had brushed their wings against it.

I stood listening, thinking. The bulb was casting its sallow light. A moth fluttered into the room. I tried to remember how it had begun, but felt nauseous as I recalled its warmth, its smooth, damp limbs. What had Clara seen, and where was Suarez? I lit the paraffin lamp; another light to protect me against whatever was lurking in the dark. What was it: a harpy, Lilith, one of her daughters? Whatever it was, the foul creature had seduced me. It was degrading, debilitating to think of such a thing. I wanted to wash, to scrub away her scent of decay. Yet I couldn't face walking to the washroom. The thought of stepping out into the darkness caused me to tremble uncontrollably. Could it still be out there, hiding in some dark corner?

I bolted the door and collapsed beneath the glaring light. The lamp's wick was burning. It was only a matter of time before the generator would be turned off. I covered myself with the soiled sheet and sat waiting for something else to happen, for a scream or the sound of Suarez hammering on the door; but nothing stirred. If Clara had

192

cried out I would have gone to her. I waited, almost wishing for some sort of confrontation to occur. It was only when the noise of the lorry's engine filled the courtyard that my head fell back onto the pillow. There was a lingering trace of incense, the smell of a damp, decaying cellar. I had the feeling we were being punished for trespassing, for being part of a myth we didn't understand. From that moment on her scent became synonymous with the night.

27

Someone was rapping a knuckle against the door. Light was showing beneath the curtain. It was Suarez's voice; he wasn't accusing me of anything; he was rousing the party. My mind was stumbling over what had happened. There was a patchwork of awful shadows, and the grotesque suspicion that I'd irredeemably sinned, that I'd unwittingly thrust myself beyond redemption. I desperately wanted to dismiss it as some sort of crushing nightmare, yet there was the desire to make sense of what had crept in, the warmth and weight of what I'd felt. It unnerved me to think, to try and reason. What if it wasn't a figment of my own overwrought imagination, what if Clara was able to confirm my unspoken fear? Was I mad, or had she seen something; a figure straddling me, thumping itself against me? Had she cried out, had she been there at all?

I should have escaped, grabbed what was mine and

fled back to Mosul, but I was numb, reeling from the nightmare that I couldn't dispel, from the shock of what I could recall. I was struggling with the idea that it couldn't have been another woman, yet the memory, the feel of her flesh against mine, was lodged in the mind. I pulled back the sheet; it was covered in brown dust, shapes coalesced into shoulders, arms, legs. I needed to immerse myself in the morning's routine to safeguard my sanity. I needed to speak to Clara, to establish what she'd seen, whether or not she'd even entered the room.

I opened my door onto a cold, grey dawn. Mrs Jackson was crossing the courtyard towards the *antika* room. Following in her wake was Clara, her green cardigan wrapped tightly around her. She was staring down at the dusty ground. I started to shake uncontrollably and suddenly felt as though I was about to collapse. The sight of her had catapulted the scene back into my mind. I heard again the demented shrieking, smelled the stink of grease and sweat. It was a suffocating, oppressive sensation. The courtyard was pitching me towards her. Leaning against the doorframe I heard Mrs Jackson say, 'Are you all right?' I managed to nod in acknowledgement, managed to wipe the cold sweat from my brow. I came forward. Clara was standing some thirty yards away, her head and shoulders visible beyond the oxblood bonnet of the lorry. She stood in silence behind Mrs Jackson, waiting for the woman to unlock the *antika* room. I stared at the back of her head, her black hair an inch above the woollen

196

cardigan. My mouth was dry. I tried to speak, but couldn't; a hoarse whisper, nothing more. She turned her head and glanced in my direction. I stared back at her. I could hear the key turning in the lock, saw the door pushed open behind her shoulder. There was no expression on her face, no recognition, no acknowledgement that I was standing there staring at her. Her lips may have parted, but that was all.

I wanted to follow her into the room, but her husband was calling me. I turned to see him beckoning. 'If you want coffee . . .' he was saying. I heard the *antika* door swing shut. I shook my head. I needed to wash. Tracing the wall with my fingers I stumbled towards the washroom. I needed to speak to Clara, but my legs had almost given way at the sight of her. My mind was throbbing, my thoughts grotesque. I couldn't speak to her while she was with Mrs Jackson, I couldn't draw attention to myself. Routine was what I craved, at least a morning for my mind to settle, to put some distance between us and what had happened, to scrub away the filth.

In the grey dawn I saw Suarez and Stanislav standing together. I left the dusty track and crossed towards them. They were staring at a pile of stones. Stanislav turned and nodded. Suarez was putting his tobacco away. I stood beside the Russian, my arms tightly crossed, my hands clapped against my sides. I too stared down at the pyramid. It was about a foot tall, made of stones that were smooth and grey.

'There's another pile over here,' said Stanislav, pointing towards the ziggurat. 'And one more on the other side of the track.'

'What do you think it is?' asked Suarez, taking his unlit cigarette from between his lips.

'Perhaps it has something to do with the Jewish custom, leaving a pebble at a grave. It shows a visit's been made.' He muttered something that sounded like Yiddish.

'You think someone's been paying their respects?' said Suarez.

'Possibly. They must have brought them up from the river.'

'The boy that drowned?' I suggested, trying to radiate an aura of easy cohesion, but the brittleness was there, the fragility. It was there in the thickening voice, the flushed face. No one acknowledged what I had to say.

'Why are there three piles?' asked Suarez, flicking his match against the stones.

'Perhaps they're Lilith's children,' said Stanislav.

'Cut the crap,' said Suarez.

'So who is it?'

'It's the Yazidis,' he said firmly. 'They're trying to mess with the excavation.' He took a long drag on his cigarette and then pushed the toe of his boot into the nearest pyramid. We watched the stones sliding, its shape collapsing. I tried to stop myself from thinking about what had happened, yet the link was being forged as the stones slid to the ground: the irrepressible idea that one of her daughters had crept into my bed and then added

198

her stone to the pyramid. I had to speak to Clara, to see her before anything else unnerved me.

'Bilal,' Suarez shouted over his shoulder. 'How long will it take you to finish emptying the chamber?'

The foreman trudged towards us.

'How long?' demanded Suarez.

'Sand very heavy.'

'How long?'

'Maybe tomorrow.'

'Empty it by the end of today and I'll double the pay of each man. You understand?'

Bilal nodded and then started back to the workmen who'd gathered round the ziggurat.

'The sooner you all see there's nothing there, the sooner we can get away.' He turned towards me. 'Take a few photographs of the workers and the other piles. Remember you're here to document the work, not just the artefacts. I'm heading back.'

'OK,' I replied, although too late for him to hear. I was acting as if everything was all right. I wanted to return to the house, to the exposed prints, the clay shards, and copper bowls.

I watched as he made his way down to the expedition house. There was a brief backward glance, but nothing else to indicate an interest in me. I turned and made for the ziggurat. Bilal had already organised a line of men. It was time to expunge the tormenting feelings, to focus on the work ahead. Buckets were being used inside the ziggurat to empty the chamber. Outside the sand was tipped into a pile from where it was passed from shovel to shovel to a larger pile that stood some thirty yards away from the exposed walls of the temple.

I took out my Leica and framed three men in the line. As soon as they saw the camera pointing in their direction they grinned sheepishly. I shouted and signalled to them to look away. Reluctantly they carried on with their work. I was framing a photograph. The sun was warming the ground. I was trying not to think about what had happened. What did it matter if it had been a nightmare, a brief reoccurrence of what I'd already suffered? In the sanatorium things had taken me by surprise. In the sanatorium I'd seen shadowy figures darting like ghouls through the thick, malevolent night, and I'd found myself crawling towards sandbags, the tiled floor shaking from falling shells; hands trying to restrain me while I ran with fixed bayonet, through the smoke, the smell of burning horseflesh. I'd seen the wounded crawling out from beneath the beds, the dying, and the delirious, damaged and bandaged and bloody. In the cold glimmering corridors I'd seen soldiers being ripped apart, heard their piteous screams, felt their warm blood trickling across my cheeks. I would try and wipe them away, but interfering hands would hold my wrists. The nurse was there to pull me backwards. Through the cacophony of shells, the thud of bullets, the thumping and knocking of our guns, I'd heard her soft entreaties, her tender words. Behind the mechanised sound of slaughter was a lullaby for a grown man. A lullaby coaxing me back to bed.

In the sanatorium I was not merely mistaken, I was delusional. And so what did I fear the most: that I was falling into a filthy stupor, a world created by my own corrupted imagination, or that something had actually entered my room, rested itself against my flesh, sported across my body?

I cast around for another chance, another shot. Apart from the shuffling of feet, and the occasional word, it was a quiet morning. They'd yet to start their chanting, and there was an urgency which I hadn't seen before. The incentive Suarez had offered was working. Holding the viewfinder to my eye I tried to focus on the line, but the frame was shaking. I was beginning to have trouble holding the camera. The more I considered the ordeal I'd suffered the more I trembled. Nothing remained steady. I put away the Leica in its leather case. I turned to go back down to the house and saw Stanislav was heading towards me. 'There's breakfast,' he called. 'Are you OK?'

I acknowledged his question with an apologetic wave of the hand. Stanislav, with his hands on his hips, stood waiting for me. 'You look pale,' he said.

'I'm not sleeping well.'

'Tom's gone to fetch O'Neil.'

'How long will he be gone?' I asked as we started for the house.

'They'll be back before lunch. They'll also pick up the wages for the workmen.'

'They?'

'Clara's gone with him.'

201

It took a second to sink in, but I didn't let it throw me. 'Tilden's getting better?'

'He is,' confirmed Stanislav. 'It's Susan he's worried about. With Bateman's death . . .' He glanced across. 'She was the only one who had any time for him.'

'You didn't like him?'

'No. He was a prig.'

'And Susan?' The conversation had a cold, bracing effect and I didn't want it to stop.

'She's been of some assistance, but she's no archaeologist. My guess is there's some sordid history waiting to be uncovered. Before Bateman disappeared she always found the misfortunes of others quite amusing. She was, as the French would say, an *allumeuse*.' Again he glanced at me. 'And now Bateman's not the only one to have disappeared.'

'What do you mean?'

'Two Arabs have vanished. Their families were here this morning.'

'Two Arabs . . .' I echoed.

'The pair who were guarding the ziggurat the other night. You know, I've never known a dig as cursed as this one.'

28

'Clara's staying in town with a nurse,' Suarez explained to Mrs Jackson. 'It's her choice.' He smiled at those round the table. I nodded as though it was a matter of little consequence, though my mind was in a maelstrom of its own making. She was trying to avoid me, to prolong my crippling unease. Outwardly I remained calm, appeared unperturbed as I listened to Suarez's explanation. Silently I damned her for not returning; she was being cruel and unfair. I could hardly make out what Suarez was saying: a spate of deaths in a suburb near the Tigris. Clara was to help the nurse with the task of comforting and reassuring those who were flocking with their sick children to the consulate's surgery. O'Neil was to visit as soon as he could get away.

While Suarez spoke to Stanislav about what had been happening in Mosul I tried to dismiss her, but I was out of patience, tired of trying to hide my agitation. 'When will she be back?' I asked. 'Is she coming b-back?'

Suarez smiled. It was a broad smile, a triumphant tilt of the head. 'Why do you want to know?'

My face flushed, semaphored in scarlet the scale of my shame. 'Isn't there cataloguing?' I stammered. 'With Susan ill . . .' I looked towards Stanislav, imploring him to step in. 'When will your wife return?'

'That's hard to say,' said Suarez, watching me squirm. 'She'll probably be needed tomorrow. Clara's quite safe. She's sharing a room above the consulate with the nurse. Quite safe,' he repeated as he brought out his tobacco and started to roll one of his infernal cigarettes. 'I don't blame her,' he continued. 'Allah loves the compassionate. Isn't that right, Mr Ward?'

'Of c-course,' I stuttered. 'You agree, don't you, Mrs Jackson?' I was saying anything just to deflect their gaze. *Why was he so desperate to know*, that's what they were all thinking. *What was Clara to Mr Ward, what had she done to him?* I knew Suarez was onto me. This was some sort of game he was playing. Was it too late to extricate myself, to make amends, to show I was no gigolo? There was talk of paying the Arabs, a conversation that drifted away from the Judas in their midst. I had to grab the first opportunity to speak to her, to elicit an answer, an explanation. But what had she seen? As the hideous memory of the night receded I was becoming more confused, more uncertain about what had happened.

* * *

204

It was dusk when O'Neil drove his Mercedes into the courtyard. He greeted me cordially and gave a bottle of wine to Amuda. He visited Susan and her husband; a gentle tap at each door, the hat waving in front of his face, a whispered greeting. I'd watched him from my doorway; a fruitless wait to see if he wanted to ask me about Susan, to ask him about Clara.

After he'd seen his patients he joined us for supper in the mess. Tilden's health was gradually improving, but Susan was a worry. He'd given her something to help her sleep and asked Sasha to return to her, to watch over her until something could be done. We talked about whether or not that meant a proper nurse here or moving Susan to Mosul. There was, as I sat there drinking, the temptation to declare myself equally unfit. I'd done it before, why shouldn't I do it again? I'd spent a wretched afternoon, enlarging several photographs in the courtyard, while continually vacillating over whether to stay or to make the journey to Mosul by foot. As the afternoon had worn on the inclination to leave had faded with the dying of the light. Now it was dark and I'd resolved to stay, to wait for her to return. I was still hoping that mine was a temporary malaise, an affliction of the mind that would soon right itself.

I continued to drink as I listened to Mrs Jackson giving her opinion on Susan: there was no point in her staying at the house. She had no interest in knowledge, only in gain or what a thing was worth. Her education had started and finished with cigarette cards. Mrs Jackson was adamant, she rapped her knuckles against the table; her hands medieval, all knobs and knuckles, skin like parchment.

'Bateman's death seems to have knocked her for six,' said Stanislav. I sat there, far from sober but not quite as drunk as I would have liked, admiring his use of the idiom, his desire to defend Susan.

'Bateman,' echoed Mrs Jackson dismissively.

'You never like him,' observed Sasha in a rare burst of English.

'Bateman couldn't accept any woman whose interest in life went beyond coitus.'

'You're such a romantic,' said Suarez.

'I know,' Mrs Jackson replied, 'too much granite and not enough rainbow.'

Amuda opened another bottle. We were drinking in the midst of adversity, drinking to raise our spirits so we could go on fighting, ploughing, digging. At the dig matters were faring no better. The fourth chamber had been more or less cleared of sand, but nothing had been found. Suarez wanted to abandon the temple, but it was a decision he couldn't make without Tilden's approval.

Clara's chair was empty. O'Neil was sitting in Tilden's place. He proved a welcome distraction, willing to feign an interest in what Stanislav had to say. The Russian was explaining that Akkadian shared its grammar with Hebrew and Arabic.

'Sumerian's harder,' snarled Suarez. 'Akkadian isn't too difficult. Their writing isn't too hard to translate, not if you're any good.'

'And how did it evolve?' asked O'Neil. 'What made the scribe press his stylus into the clay?'

'Bookkeeping,' answered Suarez. 'The exchange of sheep, grain, cloth, though your anarchist finds it hard to swallow.'

'It is a rather prosaic start,' added Mrs Jackson, 'but trade was the catalyst.'

'The important thing,' said Stanislav, tapping the table, 'was that it allowed us to express ourselves, to reject slavery, the social order that forces man to exploit his fellow man.'

'Spare me the politics,' said O'Neil. 'I want to know more about these scratches you see in the tablets.'

'Cuneiform,' said Mrs Jackson.

'Cuneiform,' repeated O'Neil.

'These scratches,' said Stanislav, '*were* used to count produce, but they soon evolved. They soon came to represent cities and individuals, to warn others, to communicate ideas. On their tablets and walls you can see their ideas, understandings that have since been endlessly repeated.'

'An understanding about what?' asked O'Neil.

'Everything,' replied Stanislav with an expansive gesture which embraced everyone seated at the table. 'What we were, what we wanted to believe. Listen.' He reached inside his jacket and took out his notebook.

'There's nothing the Assyrians can teach us,' said Suarez.

'Then why are you here?' I asked.

'I'm here to uncover the truth, Harry. To see how cruel the godless were. How the amoral behaved.'

Stanislav, having flicked through the pages, grunted in

satisfaction and started to read. '"Marduk splits the night into two halves, like an oyster. The upper part forms the sky, the heavens, the lower part becomes Earth. And God created Heaven and Earth".' Stanislav looked up. 'He then creates rivers and mountains and mankind.'

'As it is in the Bible,' observed O'Neil.

'Not as it is in the Bible,' protested Suarez, but Stanislav ignored him. 'Marduk is the Hebrew god; your God, Doctor.'

'Then you've nicely covered politics and religion,' said O'Neil. Suarez said something, but nobody was listening to him. 'What about the birds and the bees? Do your Assyrian friends have anything to say on that matter?'

'Of course,' said Stanislav.

'One can't work as an archaeologist in Mesopotamia if one's prudish about such things,' declared Mrs Jackson, 'though they're like the English, they speak in metaphors.'

'They mingle their waters; their sweet and salty waters; which needs no explanation,' said Stanislav. 'The female body is likened to the earth, the damp areas of the marshes used to symbolise female genitals. The little swamp drying up refers to a neglected vulva. The whirlwind is often invoked as a sign of potency, and a trapped raven, the most useless bird to be caught, is a reference to an impotent phallus.' He paused. 'As you so quaintly put it: the birds and the bees.'

'But let's not be bashful,' said Suarez. 'A womb can be glutted with shiny semen, or it's poured across a woman's backside, making it glisten like the moon.'

O'Neil, who'd sat forward, shook his head in disbelief.

'You'll have to forgive him,' said Mrs Jackson, 'he seems to take delight in the most indelicate of translations.'

'If *you're* not offended, then there's nothing to forgive,' replied O'Neil.

'Far from it, though I must explain that this isn't just a prurient interest in the past, it's how the Assyrians treated women and what the Hebrews had to say.'

'You mean what's in the Bible,' I said, 'such as The Song of Solomon.'

'That sort of thing,' replied Mrs Jackson. 'What we have here is something to do with Lilith, the archetypal femme fatale, the sexually voracious woman. You only have to look at the way Lot's daughters behave.'

'"And the woman was arrayed in purple and scarlet",' said Stanislav, reading from his notebook, '"and decked with gold and precious stones and pearls, having a golden cup in her hand full of abominations and filthiness of her fornication. And upon her forehead was a name written, Mystery, Babylon the Great, the Mother of all Harlots and Abominations of the Earth".'

'Another tablet?' asked O'Neil.

'No,' I answered, 'the Book of Revelations.' Suarez was frowning. 'A misspent youth,' I explained to the table, 'or at least I once thought it was.'

'Like Babylon,' began Mrs Jackson, 'they associated Nineveh with depravity and fornication. In the Bible this was a sinful land of suffering and tears. And the Jews who were taken as slaves by the Babylonians are still here; in

Baghdad and Mosul, they've been here for over two thousand years. They wrote the Old Testament, judged the women of Nineveh and Babylon and labelled them whores.'

'Ha,' said Suarez. A hollow laugh, but one I understood. He was about to say something else, but Mrs Jackson hadn't quite finished.

29

The wine and the conversation had had a lulling effect upon me, but I was no hurry to sleep. Sleep was something I faced with trepidation. The night had become an ordeal and I was glad to delay confronting it for as long as possible. It was a cold evening and I returned to my room to pick up my woollen jersey. I flicked the switch by the door and saw my room in the feeble light of the bulb. I caught sight of myself in the small mirror above the chest of drawers. There were dark half-moons under my eyes, which were wide, almost vacant. My mouth was a thin, corrugated line. It was a tired, haggard look. There was nothing comforting in the mirror, no sign of my Arabian adventure; all enchantment, all pleasure had vanished from my face. I silently said her name and watched how my lips moved. She'd once looked at herself in the same mirror, made a neat adjustment here and there.

I walked into the common room and found Stanislav kneeling in front of the brick fireplace and lighting some kindling. 'I think we deserve a fire,' he said, getting back onto his feet. 'Why don't you pour the whisky. Suarez won't be joining us.'

I went over to the sideboard. When I turned round he was sitting in the middle of the divan, his arms spread out along the back. I sat opposite him and placed the bottle and two tumblers on the small table between us. 'Those stones we found this morning,' I remarked quietly, courageously, 'who do you think left them?'

Stanislav dismissed the question with a wave of his hand. There was the snap of dry wood in the fireplace. 'Let's not talk about the dig. Strange things can happen. That the fourth chamber is empty makes no sense. Why was it filled with sand? Perhaps we'll never know.'

'And Bateman?'

'It's not healthy to dwell on the inexplicable. Let science figure it out.' He sat forward. 'Tell me about photography.'

I shrugged my shoulders. 'What do you want to know?'

'Is it a passion?'

'I think it's a passion, a longing to capture everything that appeals to me.'

'And you feel the same passion for photography as you would feel for a beautiful woman?'

'Does she have to be beautiful?'

'Of course, but beauty can be anything, a thought, an accent, the way she puts her hand across her brow to

212

protect her eyes from the sun. And you would take a photo? Clara, for instance, standing like this?' He mimicked her stance in the only photograph I'd taken of her.

I didn't reply, and I believe he took pity on my discomfort.

He sat back and spread his arms again along the back of the divan. 'Perhaps there was once a quiet, awkward English girl who allowed herself to be ravished?'

'Perhaps there was, before the war . . . before . . .'

Stanislav nodded sympathetically. 'Well, their beauty also fades, and we crave variety: it is always the same act, the same sounds, softer, louder, protesting, demanding, the same ending.' He sipped his whisky and looked into the fire. 'Euphoria, comfort, warmth, pissing in the same pot.'

'But you still find Sasha attractive?'

A smile played across his lips. 'A drunken priest once told me that the best lover is not the man who can make love to a thousand women and satisfy each one, but the man who can satisfy the same woman a thousand times over.'

'That's a very touching sentiment.'

'He was supposed to be celibate. What did he know? It's a trick to keep people married, to promote a sense of loyalty above your own pursuit of pleasure. Nothing more. I just happen to be with a woman who makes me happy, and for that I am willing to suffer. For what they call love there is always a sacrifice to be made.'

'I'm sure the fairer sex . . .'

'No, don't make this mistake. There's nothing fair about them.'

'But Sasha . . .'

'Believe me, women will do anything to win your heart. She'll play the goddess, the mother, the whore, the sister; whatever it takes. Winning is everything to a woman. To me or you it is how we play, how we fight – we take comfort from being a gallant loser. But it's not the same for women.' Stanislav tutted to himself. 'Women live to win – what you have to do is turn yourself into the prize worth winning, allow the woman to compete for you. Overwhelm her with attention and then turn the tap off. Love is war, it's a game of chess, and we Russians know how to play, how to fight.'

'How to fight? And how to lose.'

'Are you still talking about chess?'

'You mentioned chess.'

The Russian stroked his shaven head. 'I know what you're thinking. We never lose at chess. But as for war . . .' He shook his head.

An awkward silence descended. He was inviting me to agree, to say that the Russians had let us down in Mesopotamia, had failed to push the Ottomans back.

'I served in Kurdistan and every morning I cursed the Tsar.'

'And that's why you left the front.'

'We turned our backs and fought for justice; stopped fighting for imperialists.'

214

'But you're not a Bolshevik.'

'No, I'm an anarchist. A disciple of Kropotkin and Bakunin, not Marx. I fought with the Soviets and then was foolish enough to criticise the new order.'

'So your civil war achieved nothing?'

'At least, at the start, I was fighting for something I believed in. Trust me, nothing beats fighting for a better world.' His voice wavered, his eyes appeared to shine momentarily in the firelight. 'And what were you fighting for? Here in Mesopotamia. What do you remember of your war against the Turk, against the Ottoman Empire?'

'What do I remember?' I asked, as though I hadn't quite heard the question.

'Yes. How bad was it for you? Was it worse for the Turk, for the Arab?'

'In some ways as bad, in others . . .' I had the feeling he knew there was something I was trying to avoid, something that I didn't want to relive. 'You want to know how we suffered? Is that what you'd like to hear?'

'Don't hide behind the collective, tell me what happened to you. How you endured. I want to hear your story.'

I drained my whisky and put the glass down. 'We were wading through shallow water.'

'Why do you speak of others, this *we* again?'

'The *we* was an infantry battalion, part of the Norfolks.'

'The collective doesn't interest me. I want your part, how you suffered.' He refilled my glass. 'It was hot in the summer, yes?'

'It was like marching in a furnace; in the shade it was

215

over a hundred and ten degrees.' I sipped the whisky, the spreading warmth on my tongue carrying with it an affinity, a physical memory seared into flesh and bone. It was a familiar story, an old story, one I was primed to tell. I didn't want them to think that I'd deserted. Some of the inmates had been mad with fright, fearing that they'd be shot for desertion as soon as they'd recovered their wits. It was a madness, a fear that was self-perpetuating. Yet I was ready with my little speech. I was reciting from memory, giving the account I'd rehearsed in my head while steaming back towards the grey skies and grey corridors. I stretched out a hand towards the fire. 'In the shade it was over a hundred and ten degrees,' I repeated, the needle of the phonograph placed back into its groove. 'A line of date palms indicated where the river had been, before it had burst its banks and flooded the land. In places the water was up to my waist. Our boots sinking into the mud. We ended up paddling bellums, local canoes, in deep water.'

I looked across at Stanislav. He had tutted once or twice but my story was holding his attention, and I was ready for the occasion.

'Then we were punting or dragging them through the shallows. Our kit was brought along in paddle steamers. Behind were sloops, tugs and barges. Before long we were under fire from Turkish artillery, and on the sandhills, through tall reeds, marsh Arabs began firing at us with muskets and rifles looted from our camp. Bellums and men were constantly being hit.'

216

'Do you remember seeing your first?'

'My first?' I asked, unperturbed.

'Your first casualty.'

'Of course.' I paused, but Stanislav's face invited me to continue. 'It was unexpected.'

'Few men awake in the morning believing they're going to die.'

'What about the deserter?'

'It was an execution?' he asked.

'No. It was a pilot.'

'British?'

'Turkish.'

'What happened?'

'His plane had appeared overhead; spying on our advance. We heard the guns firing, saw it tremble. It began to lose height. Slowly at first, then silently it started to revolve, spiralling like a sycamore seed. We stood and watched, some cheered when it hit the ground.'

'And at the front?'

I shifted uncomfortably. It was something I'd spoken about before, but there had always been a price to pay. For many years the scene had haunted me; now it was like exhuming a corpse, knowing it was better to leave it buried. 'You don't need me to tell you what it's like to see someone fall.'

'Are you afraid to tell me how you felt?'

'I'm not afraid,' I said. 'It was a horrible fluke, that's all.'

'Then describe it to me,' said Stanislav. His manner was

217

gentle, albeit authoritative, as if he wanted to hear the truth, and wouldn't be satisfied with a sanitised account of what I'd seen.

'All right.' I finished the tumbler in front of me. 'It was as we advanced towards Kut. There was cover down by the river: palm trees, bushes. We were waiting for the order to charge. Our shell fire was deafening, ears singing for days afterwards. Private Sinclair was lying down, holding his rifle, bayonet fixed. He had his eyes closed and looked to be half asleep. The chime of a bullet, his rifle suddenly shifts beneath his fingers, and the sergeant kneeling beside him topples backwards.' I illustrated the incident with my hands. 'The bayonet struck, deflects the bullet, the bullet hits the sergeant's forehead; smack between the eyes. Sergeant Houghton, father of three, falls back, stone dead.'

Stanislav shook his head. 'How did you feel?'

'Dazed. Then Sinclair started crying – Oh, my God, Oh, my God – over and over again. Giving the sniper time to reload. We'd scattered, but we called to him to get down. He just sat there on his haunches, his pith helmet by his side, staring into the sergeant's face. I wanted to knock him flat, we all did, but there just wasn't time. When the truce came, for the Red Cross and the Red Crescent to tend to the wounded and bury the dead, they were carted off together.'

'And why were you there?'

'Why were we there?' I thought for a moment, derailed by such a question. 'We were there to try and relieve those

218

besieged at Kut. When we left England I thought we were heading for Flanders, but we sailed to Basra.'

'You weren't there to defend the Persian oilfields, to protect the oil pipeline, British oil interests?'

'We were there to fight the Turks.'

'It's not as simple as that. You were there to fight, to replace the Ottoman Empire with your own.' Stanislav refilled my glass. 'You want to believe that Iraq will be self-governed one day. King Faisal's on the throne, and he's someone the Anglo-Persian Oil Company can trust.'

'It was a war,' I muttered. The Arabs were better off under the British than they were the Turks, or the French in Syria, or the Germans, had the Kaiser won. 'At the beginning, when Germany had persuaded Turkey to side with it against the Allies, they'd made a great play of harbouring sympathy for the Muslim world. The Germans had encouraged a holy war, had urged the Arabs to side with the Turks, even tried to spread unrest against the British as far as the Indian frontier. There were Turks who were convinced that the Kaiser was going to embrace the Mohammedan faith.'

'It was a war, like all wars, fought for gain, economic and political.'

'This began as a war to defend Belgium, a just cause . . .'

'An excuse. One that had been brewing for years. It's always the same. The victor benefits: plunders the defeated, influences decisions; always for profit. Look around Nineveh. Where are the huge winged bulls and the walls which were decorated with the exploits of Assyrian kings?

Are they still here? Of course not. When you defeated the Turks what did you find at Babylon, at Ur? Crates packed for Germany, for the Berlin museum. And what happened to those crates, those antiquities? I'll tell you. They were taken as war booty, as the spoils of war, and shipped to your British and American museums. You won the war, you keep the spoils.'

'That's as may be, though I never saw such crates. But attitudes are changing. Baghdad has its own museum; Miss Bell wants to see it well stocked.'

'And you now believe all artefacts will remain in Iraq?' Stanislav smiled. 'It's true. The British spinster has given Iraq a museum. But don't forget that it suits you to establish a national identity, to create a country where there was none, and so you allow them to keep a share of what we uncover, a few insignificant cylinder seals, cuneiform tablets. The imperialist thinks a museum, a flag, a king, and an anthem will give a people a cultural identity, a unity that didn't exist before. Soon the rupee will be replaced with a different currency; one, no doubt, with King Faisal's head on one side. And this will bring all those different tribes together: the Yazidis, the Kurds, the Chaldean Christians. At least until you've finished your business.'

There was no way of winning with Stanislav. Bell hadn't intended her museum in Baghdad to be an instrument of oppression or exploitation, or whatever the anarchist believed was its true purpose.

'I know what you're thinking,' he said, 'but it's the

220

mark of an educated mind to be able to consider a thought without accepting it.'

'You think I'm well educated?'

'Quite the contrary, I'm suggesting you have the ability to think beyond what you've been taught to believe.'

'And you share this ability?'

'Perhaps.'

'Even when it comes to matters beyond our comprehension?'

'Are there such things?'

'I think there are . . .'

'Well,' he said, 'you're entitled to your beliefs, no matter how misguided.' He smiled and I tried to mirror his levity.

It was almost midnight when Stanislav left. I tried to detain him. We disagreed about the war, but there was never any ill feeling. With the strength of his convictions there was something dependable. Like all disciples, there was a predictable certainty, a fixed way of viewing events. I didn't want him to leave, but Sasha was waiting for him.

The common room was warm. I crossed over to the divan and stretched out. I thought about what we'd said, what I'd always found hard to convey. We were all carrying snapshots, revolving spools of slaughter projected in the mind's picture-house, burned into the retina, imperishable negatives. There were statues, gargoyles lurking in the dark corners. They stand in silence, their last moment carved in sandstone. My mind is cluttered with such statues, flickering in the shadows as the spools of film play. Some are weatherworn, names fading or running into one another. The shelling that reduces men to blood and bone, soldiers without knees, scalps taken by shrapnel. Other incidents remain sharp, are too deeply chiselled to forget. Like the young corporal, shot as we turned back; the entry wound: a dark bloody hole just beneath his shoulder. Thought it a cushy one at first, and told him so to his face. A chalky-white face fills the screen, sweat sits on his brow. He looks up at me, at the camera, eyes like those of a bloodhound, grateful for the diagnosis; a mere flesh wound. But I'm wrong. The bullet has hit the shoulder bone, has been deflected down into the intestines. The lad is in agony and soon becomes delirious. He is a dying man. Pitifully crying out for water, for his mother – after an hour I can hardly recognise his voice, but we're at the talkies now. A young Arab boy sings softly while he writhes in agony. I hear them, can see them still.

Those that survived are still in the nightmare, and for a while the passing seasons remained faceless. There are countless gruesome tales told and untold. I had to deal with the lack of self-worth, the knowledge that I had survived while better men, stronger men had died. Feeling guilty doesn't help, nor does spending nocturnal hours standing at the edge of a cliff or beneath a bough strong enough to take the weight of a man.

I didn't want to go back to my room. I was comfortable where I was. The fire was dying. I dragged myself up and placed a log on the embers. I took a blanket from the back of the armchair and lay down on the divan. The whisky and the talking had had a cathartic effect, had performed some sort of provisional exorcism, soothing the ghosts and orphaned voices that had troubled me in the past. It was a momentary break, a short-lived rest from the horror that was gathering, for the dead travel faster than the living.

30

Loud voices outside the common room, some sort of a commotion. Suarez's voice repeating the same question. An Arab was answering, hurriedly explaining what he'd seen. It was Bilal, telling Suarez that he'd found the doctor's car; abandoned this side of the bridge, left at the side of the road, the driver's door hanging open.

Stanislav would stay behind and organise the men who were waiting at the gates of the expedition house. Suarez saw me standing at the door and told me to get into the lorry.

It was cold in the cab and he struggled to get the thing started. Eventually the engine laboured into life and, with a thrumming clatter and a crunch of gears, we reversed out of the courtyard.

In silence we forged our way against the slow tide of

workmen. Suarez was bent over the wheel, staring ahead through the dust-encrusted windscreen, ignoring the water boys who waved at the cab.

When we arrived at the car there were twenty or so Arabs standing beside it, their gowns lit by the rising sun. Suarez sounded the horn and they retreated a yard or two. He climbed out of the lorry and barked at them, ordering them to move away. They turned and looked, muttering between them, shuffling their dusty feet. Most started reluctantly towards the expedition house, though several simply moved a few paces back.

Suarez walked round the abandoned vehicle, shoving the occasional Arab out of the way. I put my head inside. The interior was as cold as the lorry, and there was the familiar smell of leather from the upholstered seats. The Mercedes' key was still in the dashboard. I pulled out the choke and tried the engine. There was a short whirr from beneath the bonnet, but nothing else happened. The switch for headlights was up. They must have been on all night. For a moment we stood with our backs to the car, eyes searching between the heads, searching as though this was our last opportunity to spot O'Neil.

Suarez turned to me. 'I'm going to drive into town. You'd better get back. Ask if anyone's seen the doctor.'

'I should come with you. One of the workmen can take a note.' I felt for my notebook and pen.

'No,' said Suarez. 'Go back to the house.'

'He's been taken, hasn't he?'

'What do you mean?'

'You know what's happened. He's been taken, just like Bateman.'

'Listen, just go back to the house and tell the others I've gone to see if he's at the consulate.'

He didn't want me to see Clara. I understood why. My job was to warn the others, and after warning them I'd walk into Mosul with my things and try and find her. I stood back and watched him climb into the cab. With the horn blaring, the lorry pulled round the Mercedes and headed across the bridge. I took a last look at the abandoned car and closed its gaping door. As I did so I glanced briefly at the handle. My hand recoiled from the snaking scratches beneath it. There were four parallel lines and the bare metal gleamed in the sun. The savage marks were about six inches in length, indented, waving their way towards the desiccated earth. Plucking up the courage, I ran a finger down one of them, tracing whatever had scratched its way into the metal.

A shiver ran through me as I turned and started back to the house. Each step was taking me away from the safety of the town. I struggled to ignore my instinct. I wanted to do what was expected, to see it through, to warn the others. Yet I couldn't stop thinking about what was happening: a sinister evolution beyond my comprehension. The undisturbed sleep of last night had given me the chance to weigh up the situation rationally. I knew what had happened to O'Neil, knew he wouldn't be found at his clinic. He'd disappeared, snatched by whatever had taken Bateman and the two Arabs.

* * *

227

Susan was sitting in the common room. She sat flicking through a copy of *The London Illustrated* and failed to look up. I stood a yard or two in front. Her hair hadn't been brushed and her dress was creased. I crouched down on the faded rug. She had a slightly feverish look and her thin lips, which were very red, stood out against her pale, freckled face. I looked at her green eyes. They were staring at the page. Not scanning a line, but stationary, as if concentrating on a single word. 'Susan,' I said softly.

Her head jerked an inch to one side at the sound of her name, but she continued to stare at the printed word.

'Are you all right?' I asked; the curiosity of a fellow sufferer.

She ignored my question.

'Susan,' I repeated and reached out to hold her wrist, 'we have to leave.' Seeing my hand, she thrust herself back into the divan, her startled eyes lifting to meet mine.

'Don't you dare,' she exclaimed. 'Don't you dare touch me!'

'It's not safe here.' I tried to warn her, but she continued to rail against anyone touching her.

'I don't want it,' she cried. 'It mustn't be uncovered. Leave it, I told him. Don't touch. Don't touch.' With her head bowed she started to sob in front of me. I tried to comfort her, but she became increasingly distraught. She lifted her hands and brushed her hair away from her glistening cheeks. Her watery eyes appeared to see me for the first time. 'He wants the floor taken up. He knows it's caught.'

'It's all right,' I said calmly. 'Nothing's going to hurt you.'

'You don't know that. He knows it's there, trapped beneath the floor.'

'There's nothing beneath the floor.'

Susan replied with a mocking laugh. 'You don't know. But I've seen it. It's caught and screaming to get out. I hear it at night, hear it groaning. It's hungry and he'll let it escape.'

'We need to escape.'

'She will,' cried Susan, thumping her knees with clenched fists, 'she will!'

I heard footsteps behind me and turned to see Sasha hurriedly coming towards us. 'Hush now, hush now,' the young Slovak was saying.

Susan retreated into herself; pulling her knees up to her chest and cradling her bare shins in her crossed arms. 'I'm tired of the whispering, tired of fighting it.' She was rocking backwards and forwards, her red hair swaying in front of her face. 'It's not just kiss-chase he wants to play.'

'Go, Mr Ward,' said Sasha. 'I help.'

'We have to leave.'

'You leave. Go.'

I shook my head, but she was waving me away. 'Please,' she said. 'Go see Victor.'

'Scram,' shouted Susan with a sudden vehemence. 'Run away. You don't want to get caught, you don't want people to know?'

'Hush now,' Sasha was saying, her hands gripping Susan's wrists. Susan was struggling to get free, spitting her bitter words at my face. She'd turned into a foul-mouthed fiend and I was the target of her fury. It didn't make sense to hang around. Shaken by her assault, I rose to my feet and left the common room. I thought of hammering on Tilden's door; his wife was hysterical, we all needed to leave the site. I hesitated in the yard. What madness was I going to share? Was he in any fit state to take action? Better to speak to Stanislav, let him know what had happened, explain to him why we had to leave.

Stanislav was standing at the edge of the dig. 'Have you found the doctor?' he shouted as he saw me coming towards him.

'No,' I called back across the undulating sand. He waited for me to approach, arms folded over his flannel shirt. From the bowels of the ziggurat I could hear a chorus of hammers and chisels. Above the muffled ring of metal on stone I hurriedly described what we'd found, told him that Suarez had driven into town.

'I expect he's made his way back to the consulate by now,' said Stanislav, sounding more exasperated than worried.

I stood in front of him, shaking my head. 'He's gone, just like Bateman. There were scratches on the door . . . around the handle.'

'Keys,' said Stanislav, 'drinking, a dark night.' He

uncrossed his arms and with one hand fenced with an imaginary key.

'They were claw marks.'

'Then it was a hyena or a fox.' He turned away.

'We need to leave,' I said. 'Right now. I need to see Clara.'

'I can't just walk away.' There was bafflement and irritation. 'We're so close to seeing if Tilden's right. We can't just abandon the site.'

'Susan needs to be seen. She's hysterical. O'Neil is gone.'

'O'Neil will be back. There are no monsters here, just damaged people. People who drink too much, or dream too much.' He paused, his annoyance subsiding. 'Listen, Susan will calm down, she always does. As for O'Neil, let's say he's been snatched by some tribal leader. There'll be a ransom to pay, and that's it.'

'And so work continues?'

'Of course. O'Neil will turn up, he always does.' Stanislav lowered his voice. 'He likes to drink. Perhaps he has a woman, like Suarez, a woman he visits.'

'Suarez has a woman?'

'In Mosul. What the Germans call a *Zeitfrau*.'

'Suarez has a woman?'

'Perhaps O'Neil has one too; perhaps he's still in his bed with her.'

'Why didn't you tell me?'

Stanislav shook his head. 'Why should I have told you? Because you want to excuse your own behaviour, to alleviate your guilt?'

231

I flinched as he spoke. I was too ashamed to answer. 'Does Clara know?'

'Of course. A woman always knows how far she can trust her husband. Why, you don't think her affair was simply driven by some uncontrollable passion? She's unhappy and sought pleasure, as you did, with the feverish appetite of those disillusioned by love. In many ways you're well suited and I suggest you wait until she returns. Now, if you'll excuse me, I must return to the chamber.'

My ability to think was almost overwhelmed by anger and humiliation, but I couldn't afford to falter. 'You can't go back inside,' I said in a tone which surprised him. 'We have to leave, to look for O'Neil.'

'There's little we can do.'

'Stop being so bloody callous. O'Neil's disappeared, taken by something . . .'

'You mean someone.'

'. . . and you don't seem to give a damn!'

Stanislav shrugged. 'When you live next to the cemetery, you can't weep for everyone.'

'Please, no more cheery Russian proverbs. They're no better than catchpenny slogans and I'm sick of them, sick of your revolutionary doctrine, sick of you thinking you know everything.'

Stanislav snorted in amusement. 'All right,' he said. 'No more anarchism, no more superstitious nonsense. What do you suggest we do?'

'We get out while we still can.'

'Why don't we wait, at least for Suarez to return? Wait

until this afternoon.' He went to put his arm round my shoulders, but I raised a hand, not quite a fist, and he stayed a foot or two away. 'A drink's what you need, a shot of whisky before lunch to banish these thoughts. We're on the verge of making an important discovery. Stay at least until they find O'Neil. You'll see there's nothing to be afraid of, nothing that could frighten a couple of veterans like us.' He paused to take stock of the effect he was having. 'And if Suarez returns and O'Neil is still missing, I'll go with you to Mosul and we'll visit your *Zeitfrau* together. All right?'

I didn't respond. I couldn't stop myself from thinking about her for any longer, from silently unpicking what he'd said. There was no reason why she had to stay with Suarez. I could explain to her what had happened. Why we had to leave.

'You had a better night's sleep I think,' continued Stanislav. 'No screaming or crying. And you know we've finished clearing the fourth chamber? There was nothing in it, other than sand. Not even an inscription.'

'So why are you carrying on?'

'Tilden's convinced there's something beneath the chamber. He wants the floor pulled up.'

'He thinks there's something underneath?'

'This is what we're here for: to find out. If there's a chamber beneath, then it's smaller than the one above. The outer wall of the fourth chamber has nothing directly beneath it. That's why we're taking the bricks up in the middle. If it's a tomb then perhaps there's a hidden chamber.

You wouldn't want to risk missing out on photographing something as big as Carter's discovery, would you?'

'A hidden chamber for what?'

'A priestess. For someone who's been dead for a very long time.' Stanislav was staring at me, still trying to gauge my mood. I know I was beginning to behave oddly. 'Look, if the doctor hasn't been found by this afternoon, then we'll speak to Tilden.'

I didn't want to desert them, to leave them to their fate, and in the warmth of the morning sun my fears suddenly seemed so far-fetched as to be ridiculous.

'Now why don't you take some photographs of these tiny pyramids?' said Stanislav. 'Some crazy Arab's gone to a lot of trouble to decorate the site.'

I looked round. There were more stones in amongst the barrows of sand and dirt. Most of them were lying in a heap, kicked over by the workmen. Stones carried by God knows what? Piles scattered now beneath the sun, but gathered together for some strange purpose. Was Stanislav testing my resolve? Why wasn't he alarmed that more had appeared during the night? I laughed to hide my distress. What else could I do to defuse the unsettling sight around me but laugh until I'd convinced myself that it would be madness to do otherwise?

31

Suarez returned just before lunch. There was no sign of O'Neil, but he'd seen Clara. He was going back to get her. Fowler was coming and wanted to speak to us. 'It pains me to say it,' said Suarez, smiling, 'but there's no chance of you leaving here. Fowler wouldn't allow it.'

I sat down and Amuda placed a bowl of soup in front of me.

I would wait for Clara to return. I looked for a distraction and found it in Tilden. He had joined us at the table. His face was gaunt and unshaven, his movements slow. He barely had enough strength to lift the soup spoon to his lips. For more than a minute we watched in silence. Spoon, in slightly unsteady hand, chipped bowl: ascending and descending. Halfway through he sat back and pushed the bowl away. We waited for him to speak. He wasn't worried about O'Neil. He wanted to share his thoughts about our progress, how it was imperative for me to stay for at least a few more days. Suarez listened patiently, yet his sullen expression made it obvious that he thought it a waste of time trying to dig under the ziggurat. Tilden, however, saw the double layer of limestone slabs in the floor not as a dead end, but as a sign that they were finally onto something. 'It's my opinion,' he said, his voice scarcely above a whisper, 'that the whole edifice is shaped like a cedar tree.' With his elbows on the table he created a triangle with his thumbs and fingers pressed together.

'A cedar tree,' echoed Suarez scornfully, unable to contain his frustration any longer. 'It's a ruin. Nothing more.'

Tilden, in a weary motion, shook his head. 'A tree,' he said as convincingly as he could, 'with a trunk we've yet to see.'

Suarez tried to interrupt, but Tilden continued. 'The trunk is the cellar, hidden under the floor, hidden under water and sand.'

'This isn't the Valley of the Kings. There's no hidden chamber. You're just wasting time.'

Tilden waved away Suarez's attack.

'If Stanislav's right,' said Mrs Jackson, 'and it is a tomb, then this must be where her priestess is buried.'

'Is it her?' taunted Suarez. 'Is she the one who visits you at night?'

Tilden, his eyes moist, shook his head.

'Look at you,' continued Suarez, 'you're not fit to lead this expedition.'

236

'I've never been ill before.'

'And where's your wife? Is she the helpmate you wished for? You want to impress her, only a find as big as Woolley's will do, isn't that right? That's why you've undertaken this stupid dig?'

'Susan's unwell,' uttered Tilden, 'delirium. If O'Neil—'

'She has no interest in the dig, all this talk of Assyria bores her. She'd rather be shopping at Lipton's or getting ploughed at some Lambeth party.'

'I think you've gone far enough,' cried Mrs Jackson.

Tilden, who'd let his head fall into his hands, uttered a dry curse. Yet he was more wounded than angry; crushed at having his dreams, his marriage, so publicly ridiculed. It had sapped his willingness, his ability to fight. You could only feel sympathy for the man as he sat bent over his soup bowl. Even Suarez sat back from the table, as if his work was done, as if he was aware of what the others were feeling. However, it wasn't just sympathy that I felt. I wanted to ask Tilden about his visions, to share what I'd suffered. Were they the same nightmares, was he prey to the same abominations? Mrs Jackson had risen from the table and was helping him out of his chair. 'You don't know when to stop. You really don't,' she stormed at Suarez, her cheeks flushed in anger.

Suarez, like a hound that's caught its quarry, watched the two of them as they shuffled towards the door. 'Can anyone tell me why we're wasting our time?'

Stanislav looked across at Suarez. 'That was cruel, and unnecessary.'

'It needed to be said. Drugstore dreams, that's all he has. We can't waste any more time. There are some graves, just inside the wall. There's probably not much, but hopefully enough to keep Chicago off our backs for a while.'

'That's not going to happen,' said Stanislav. 'Tilden's in charge of this dig and you're certainly not about to change his mind.'

'But there's nothing in his damn folly,' exclaimed Suarez. 'Except for the inscriptions we've found.'

'Inscriptions that make no sense, inscriptions you can find on any half-baked tablet. Face it, it's empty.'

32

After lunch Suarez drove into town to bring Clara back. He'd made it clear that he wanted to play no further part in the dig. If Tilden didn't agree to return to within the city walls and to continue excavating where they'd begun the season then he was going to quit. They'd pack and say their goodbyes, and leave Mosul as soon as Fowler was through. I wanted to go with him into town, but Suarez wouldn't hear of it, and Stanislav wanted me to be there when they uncovered whatever was beneath the last chamber.

Suarez visited Tilden briefly just before leaving in the lorry. I don't know what Tilden said to Suarez, whether or not some sort of deal was struck, but the lack of raised voices led me to believe he'd reappear with Clara that afternoon. Perhaps it was foolish to have so much faith. Looking around I could see the whole expedition was falling apart. Susan was delirious with some sort of brain fever. Stanislav had carried her back to her room; the cook repeatedly saying *fanti*, a Hindustani word I hadn't heard for a while, but meaning the same as doolally. Sasha had resorted to keeping her under sedation in order to allow her troubled mind to rest. She desperately wanted to see O'Neil. According to Suarez, Fowler was certain he'd been abducted. It had been a while since they'd had any trouble from the Kurds, but his instinct told him that they were to blame; either the Kurds or the Yazidis, it didn't really matter. Apparently it was time to teach them a lesson. They'd been bombed into submission before; it was time to remind them who was in charge. His advice was to be cautious. As a precaution he was going to send two of his men to the house while the search continued. Whether or not it was the work of some other Arab faction was impossible to say. Without a body there was certainly the hope that he'd simply been taken and would be returned when whatever was troubling the kidnappers was resolved. Yet why hadn't they taken his car? If it was a matter of money then the car was a prize worth having.

As I walked back towards the ziggurat I heard the familiar sound of hammers and chisels resounding inside. With most of the workers having been dismissed there was nobody outside. It was a cloudy, still afternoon and the jagged building, squatting in the soft banks of sand and dirt, looked disturbingly sullen against the grey sky. I crossed the earth ramp to the entrance but instead of entering the ziggurat I stepped onto the ledge and, with the camera tucked safely behind my back, managed to pull myself up to the roof. When I reached the flat top, which was no more than three or four yards square, I stood up, with some trepidation, and gazed westward towards Mosul. Despite the height of the building I was merely a few feet above the ground which rose up five yards or so away from its uppermost wall. Yet I could see the date palms that fringed the Tigris and, narrowing my eyes, houses and minarets stretching into the distance. Closer still was the ancient city with its gates and its circling wall of baked bricks and mud. Everything within its walls appeared to have been built on a grand scale. Its wide avenues, halls and temples: an Assyrian declaration of power. I'd seen pictures of the friezes that had decorated the corridors of the king's palace, the hunting of lions, the destruction of other cities, other cultures. It was hard to believe that such a ruthless and warlike kingdom could have been defeated, that the city was ransacked and then left buried for centuries.

Yet the Assyrians, as Suarez never tired of telling me, had been cruel masters and had become hated by everyone. Like the Turks, with their gipsy executioners, they'd believed in their deity, believed in their divine right to rule, to punish, to purge. So many lives lost to topple gods and monarchs merely to replace them with their own impotent deities and demons. How arrogant, how presumptuous we were to think that anything could last forever. I'd always wanted to live a life that would stand up to examination, yet the horrors I'd witnessed at the

241

front had unhinged my mind. The hideous interlude in the sanatorium had shaken my sense of self, had undone every opinion worth having. By digging, by being here, they'd either unleashed something from within the ziggurat or there was something still lurking within me. I was certain of this, convinced that there were demons to be slain, shadows which hadn't been buried deep enough. But this time it would be different. This time I thought my grip would be tighter, my resolve firmer.

The rhythmic chiselling beneath my feet had started to falter. I took a final look around and then carefully sat down. Turning on my hands, I slid out, swung my feet behind and lowered myself back to the ledge.

I shuddered involuntarily as I stepped into the chamber. There was a faint light burning below, but I picked up the remaining paraffin lamp standing in a corner and lit its wick. Taking hold of the ladder propped against the wall I started my descent. Inside there was the smell of stagnant water, and the air was humid. The lamp I held illuminated my hand, stirred the shadows around me; otherwise darkness held sway in the subterranean mausoleum. Below me I could hear the reassuring sound of Stanislav speaking to the workmen. What sounded like several voices answered him in Arabic. Their speech was garbled, an animated clucking and clearing of throats.

'Here comes our brave Mr Ward,' Stanislav cried when my feet appeared in the fourth chamber. He was tying a lamp to the end of a frayed rope. 'Tilden was right,' he said excitedly. 'Come and have a look.'

I crossed the sandy floor and squeezed between Mrs Jackson and the Arabs who were crowded around a space no larger than a small porthole. They'd broken through and had discovered another chamber. The limestone they'd prised away lay under their feet. Beneath the stone they'd found a layer of glazed tiles, tiled in such a manner, said Stanislav, that they'd found it a struggle to punch their way through. Looking down there was nothing to see but blackness, as though it led to a bottomless void.

Mrs Jackson told Bilal's son to go and find Tilden. It was unlikely that he would have the strength to make the journey, yet it was only proper that he should know that they'd found something, that his hunch had been right.

After tying the lamp Stanislav started lowering it down into the dark well. The first thing I saw was a brick column, just inches to the side of the descending lamp. Other heads were peering down, nudging against mine, jostling to see. I could smell the workmen's sweat, their hot breath on my neck. The anxiety, the panic I'd felt that morning had been replaced by curiosity, by the thrill of the treasure hunt. The lamp continued to descend. Stanislav pushed a head away and uttered something in Arabic. At a depth of about twenty feet a dusty floor appeared with three broken tiles lying directly beneath where they'd forced their way through. We strained to see if there was anything else.

Again Stanislav snapped in Arabic and heads reluctantly retreated into darkness. 'I'll swing the lamp,' he said to me. 'Tell me if you see anything.'

Mrs Jackson stepped back. 'Your sight's better than mine. Take a good look.'

'OK,' I replied, my eyes fixed on the dimly lit square. I was leaning forward on my knees, peering down into the chamber. Slowly Stanislav started to swing the rope in his hand. He was swinging it backwards and forwards, taking care to miss the brick pillar. Beyond a yard and the lamp disappeared; along its path shadows appeared to be dancing, running backwards and forwards as the light raced across the dusty floor.

'Nothing?' asked Stanislav.

'There's something – it glinted. A spearhead, then a wall, perhaps a sarcophagus.'

'Anything else?'

I strained my eyes, stared into the tidal darkness. 'The edge of a sarcophagus: stone, possibly granite.'

Stanislav had stopped swinging the lamp. 'We need to take up more bricks. To get down there.' He slowly started to coil the rope round his arm.

I climbed to my feet and brushed the sand from my trousers. 'What do you think it is?'

'A burial chamber,' said Mrs Jackson, 'probably for Lilith's high priestess, though I've never seen a cell hidden beneath a ziggurat before. She must have been feared or loathed.'

Stanislav glanced across at me. 'Or the chamber predates the ziggurat, and they just happened to build on top.'

'Seems unlikely.'

'It happens. Anyway, the chamber could have been robbed a long time ago. We'll have to wait and see.'

'How long will it take to widen the hole?'

'No more than an hour. I'll lower Bilal's son down as soon as we can. Do you want to go and tell Tilden what you've seen?'

'All right, though I want to be here when the boy's lowered down.'

'Of course,' agreed Stanislav. He turned away and spoke to Bilal. The men were picking up their hammers and chisels. I left the fetid chamber and started to climb back to the entrance.

Halfway to the top of the ziggurat I could hear the rain. I could hear it falling through the walls, the drumming hiss increasing as I climbed towards the final chamber. As I stood up in the topmost chamber, I realised it wasn't simply a shower, but a torrential downpour. Angry drops were being sprayed like bullets, dashing themselves against the ancient brickwork, drilling into the ledge. I put out the paraffin lamp and stared at the rain from just inside the opening. Dark clouds stretched as far as the horizon and I could hear thunder rumbling in the distance. The air was losing its heat and a cold spray was hitting my face and shirt. I stepped back. Should I wait for it to stop, or should I return to Stanislav? I stood there wondering how long it had been since the ziggurat had felt rain falling on its walls, its stone roof. The sound was such that I couldn't tell whether they had started chiselling again. It was spitting around the mouth in the brickwork. I turned away to see a faint glow coming from the hole in the floor. The chamber was no larger than a backyard yet its corners were now cellar-dark.

I peered into the gloom. There was a sound, a shuffling of cloth and claw. It was impossible to say whether it was inside the chamber and yet I suddenly felt that there was something watching me. It was hidden in the darkness, staring back from one of the corners. There was a peculiar sensation, a wave of revulsion. I knew that I was in the presence of something indescribably evil. A cold chill ran down the back of my head and I cursed myself for putting out the lamp. The excitement I'd felt only moments ago had fled. Fear was flowing through me. I began to shiver. I wanted to clamber outside, to run towards the house, yet I couldn't turn away from the far wall. I put a hand behind me and felt for the brickwork. It was cold and wet. I could feel the rain hitting my fingers, stinging my knuckles, the back of my neck. My eyes switched from one corner to the next. Was there just the one? How many were hiding in the dark?

As if in answer a pearl-like pebble rolled out from the far corner on the right. I watched it traverse the pitted floor, staring down at it in disbelief. It was shining, wet. It stopped just short of the ladder that led down to the next chamber. A primeval fear was growing inside me, stealing away any attempt to think straight. From the opposite corner a grey pebble appeared. It slowly rolled towards the ladder, gently rocking on its axis. My back was against the wall, my heart pounding against my chest. I remember biting my lip, tasting the blood on my tongue. This was not a dream. A faint, bitter odour floated across the chamber: the smell of burning incense. It grew in strength until the air was thick with it, until it became a choking, indescribable stench. Out of the darkness a face drifted towards me, a face as pale as alabaster, an angelic, seraphic face, though one straight from the charnel house; statue-like at first yet full of a sullen, unearthly pride. I stared in horror as trembling, living wires appeared to pull at its fixed mouth. It was sucking in the foul air, filling its lungs. A heavy, voluptuous mass of flesh, feathers and scales seemed to break the stagnant surface. A pregnant silence, a stillness, the lull before the storm, and then a shrieking, a screeching into the night; a demented, high-pitched wail, loud enough to herald the awakening of the dead.

A cold hand grabbed my shoulder, pulling me backwards. I cried out and my legs gave way. I was staring up, cowering on the stone floor. There was no sound, no trace of incense. The grisly smile had vanished. He looked concerned, his dark face dripping onto mine. It was Bilal's son. The boy stretched out a hand, helped me to my feet. He said something I couldn't understand, and smiled again. I had no words to explain what had happened, nothing I could share. There was only the instinctive need to escape. Without a backward glance, without seeing whether or not the face was still there, I hurriedly climbed through the wall and out into the thundering rain.

33

In summer it's too hot for your Indian, in winter too cold even for your Scot; in the south there was too little water for the sailors, too much for the soldiers. In the north the rain had washed away cities and civilisations. It's no coincidence that Noah's story came from Nineveh. There was no end to the rain. It was hammering down on the roof, rattling the window panes, gathering in the court-yard. Water was dripping from my hair, dripping into my eyes. I stood in my room and started to pack. I couldn't give an explanation. I was running away yet this had nothing to do with feeble minds, or jerry-built brains. Such notions were peddled at Napsbury: a jerry-built brain collapsing under its own weight. No, I'd made the adjustment, I'd recovered, rejoined the social machine, a little impaired perhaps, a little less efficient, but rejoined nevertheless. They'd applied the self-serving argument that those who'd suffered because of what they'd seen at the front would recover and be cured within a few weeks. Soldiers were enfeebled by a mental trauma that was temporary, with recovery taking place relatively quickly. Those who persisted and became chronic must have had innate instabilities.

My collapse had been because of the war, what I'd been through, the horrors I'd witnessed. I was not unstable. Before coming to Nineveh I'd slept well, wasn't prone to ghoulish visions, erratic behaviour or uncontrollable shaking. I'd been through their hardening centre, the whey-faced coward had been turned back into the functioning citizen.

There were hotels in Mosul, there'd be a train. There was the Ottoman Bank. I scribbled a message to Clara. Sasha would see that she got it. I needed to safeguard my sanity, to get away from the site. I'd stumbled into a waking terror and I had to escape the madness that surrounded me before it was too late. My pack was ready. I'd walk into town. I was already soaked to the skin, so what did it matter if I made my way again in the driving rain?

The gate was still open. I started to walk hurriedly across the muddy courtyard. Lights slid across the gate-house wall. Through the incessant hissing came the growl of a motor, the clipped whine of brakes. A car was pulling into the courtyard. It lurched towards me, yellow headlights pinning me to the wall, the shining bonnet sliding to a stop inches away. I narrowed my eyes against the

250

glare and saw Suarez leaping out of the car. He was shouting, but it was lost in the falling rain. My eyes were searching for Clara when he collided with me, grabbing my arms, his fingers digging into the cold sleeves. He was shoving me back into my room, cursing me. I tried to dig my heels in, but it was too late. Behind him came Fowler and two soldiers, their turbans appearing momentarily monstrous. I struggled against them until a rifle butt thumped into my stomach. A fist landed clumsily across my mouth.

'Damn you,' Suarez was saying, endlessly repeating the line as he pushed me roughly towards the bed. 'You're not getting away.'

I was winded. My pack fell to the floor and I couldn't stop myself from being shoved back. I was outnumbered and there was little fight left in me. Fowler and his men followed Suarez into my room. There was no space for me to stand, even if they'd allowed me to. My knees folded and I fell back onto the mattress, my haversack swinging from one shoulder. I stared up at the American. His vicious, ugly face loomed inches away from mine. His knuckles were bleeding and he was shouting, 'Where is she? What have you done with her?' He caught hold of the front of my shirt and was pulling and pushing, trying to shake out an answer. Then Fowler, with his hands restraining Suarez, was saying something about Clara. Clara had disappeared and her husband was blaming me.

'Is she waiting for you? Were you planning to run away?'

I suddenly felt as if I was going to be sick. I wanted to say yes, I do know where she is. I tried to say something, to tell them the truth, but Suarez wasn't listening. He was hoping it had something to do with me, that she hadn't simply disappeared like Bateman and O'Neil.

Fowler wanted to know why I was leaving. I told him it had nothing to do with Clara. I wanted to know when she disappeared. Didn't Suarez see her that morning? But they weren't there to answer my questions. I told them that the dig was cursed, that we had to get away, we had to find her.

Suarez was mocking what I was saying, damning my words as so much junk. Fowler looked unconvinced. I didn't expect either of them to understand. Fowler told me that I couldn't leave the site. An argument ensued, which did little to alleviate the American's suspicion that I was mixed up in Clara's disappearance. Fowler wasn't going to arrest me, but until O'Neil and Clara were found then I had to stay here. The two soldiers were for our protection, but if I tried to escape they had orders to detain me. 'Where are the others?' asked Fowler.

'When did she disappear?' I asked in answer to his question. I was persistent, if nothing else.

'This morning,' said Fowler. 'She left the consulate around dawn.'

'This morning,' I repeated. I stared at Suarez. Had he lied about seeing her?

'The nurse she was bunking with heard her leave the room this morning. At first it didn't concern her, then after O'Neil was reported missing we thought Clara might have returned here. When Suarez came back to the consulate it was obvious that there was something wrong.'

If she had disappeared during the day then there was a chance that she'd simply fled. The more I thought about it, the less likely it was that she'd been taken. Had she had the courage to run away? Did Suarez deserve to be told?

'Where are the others?' asked Fowler again.

'They're here.'

'Where?'

'Stanislav's inside the ziggurat.' I looked at Suarez. 'Tilden was right. There's a chamber, a tomb under the building.' His expression was contemptuous, that of a man convinced I was trying to distract him. 'The others are somewhere in the house.'

'We need to get them together,' snapped Fowler. He clicked his fingers at the two Indians who were waiting by the door. The sergeant was told to bring back Stanislav, the other was to knock on every door. They nodded in unison and shuffled out of the room. Fowler asked Suarez to go and see if any of his wife's things were missing. After his search he was to wait with the others in the mess.

If she was sensible she would have taken the pay book, or anything that would have given her access to the funds held by the Ottoman Bank.

Suarez was unwilling to leave.

'Look,' said Fowler, 'do as I say and we'll get to the bottom of this.'

'Make sure the son of a bitch doesn't give you the slip.'

'He's not going anywhere, believe me.'

'OK,' he replied, though hardly mollified. 'I just don't want you making some sort of Limey pact behind my back.'

'Are you saying I'd wilfully fail to discharge my obligation?' asked Fowler, 'because if you are, if you're accusing me of dereliction of duty, I'll have you arrested, do you understand?'

'He's in a heap of trouble, and he damn well knows it. That's all I'm saying.'

'Mr Suarez, your wife is missing. I suggest you concentrate on finding out what you can, rather than wildly accusing people of all sorts of things.' Fowler turned to face me. 'Put your haversack on the floor, Mr Ward.'

I glanced at Suarez. He was seething, but there was nothing he could do. He cursed me again and then, after thumping the door in a melodramatic show of frustration, he stormed out into the courtyard.

Fowler sat down next to me on the bed. A polished holster, which was strapped to his hip, reared up in an ugly fashion against his thigh. He took out a packet of Craven cigarettes from inside his mackintosh and offered me one. 'Is there anything you want to tell me, now our friend has gone?'

I took a cigarette, but didn't reply.

'You were with him when he found the Mercedes?'

254

'Yes.'

'You wouldn't happen to know where O'Neil is?'

'No.'

'Then you think he's been abducted?'

I took hold of the match; fingers trembling a little, lips tight around the cigarette.

'He told me you fought in Mesopotamia.'

'For a while.'

'Which regiment?'

'The Norfolks.'

'You were at the siege of Kut?'

'Yes.'

'Baghdad?'

'No.'

There was a pause. He was wondering why I'd missed the triumphant march into the capital. Fowler was easy to read.

'You know I saw it all on the Western Front. Had a friend, a fellow like you, in the Army Cyclist Corps. The gas-pipe cavalry, that's what we called them.' He was playing the avuncular officer. A thin smile slid out from beneath his moustache. 'There was a certain type within the corps, a different kind. In the Royal Engineers there was little trouble. Too busy mining under their trenches for any of that sort of nonsense.'

This was his cue, the prelude before he exercised his God-given right to share his well-worn reminiscences. His war, his victory; one only hindered by the weak and degenerate. Fowler trotted it out through the cigarette smoke while Clara's face shone like the burnished face of winged victory. She'd gone and it was just starting to dawn on me. The shock of being accused replaced by the sense of loss. She had escaped, I was certain of it, but death was still stalking me. My grave had been too shallow. There were those who should have died, and those who should have lived. I was neither one thing nor the other; neither dead nor alive. There were others like me. This is what they'd discovered. Even as far back as Bateman. He'd photographed an empty grave, something that had been lying in wait, ready to drag him down. The nightmares I'd been having weren't imaginary. I'd seen its face, felt its weight. I'd seen the undead passing through the shadows.

'Ward,' said Fowler. He'd realised I wasn't listening. 'Ward,' he kept repeating. I turned and looked at him. He brushed some ash from his knee. 'Did you sleep with his wife?'

I ignored his question. He had to appreciate what was happening. 'It's not that simple.'

'It's a perfectly straightforward question.'

I shook my head, avoided his eyes. 'There are things hiding in the shadows, dealing in lust, lecherous thoughts, preying upon men, snatching others.'

'The Yazidis?' he suggested, trying to make sense of what I was saying. 'You think they're involved in O'Neil's disappearance.'

'It's not the Yazidis.'

'It's a damn peculiar religion, but they're wholehearted supporters of the British.'

'It's not the Yazidis.'

'During the war they sheltered many . . .'

I couldn't stand him rambling on about the war again. 'Have you heard of Lilith, or her daughters? Terrible things are happening because of what we're uncovering, what we're about to uncover. Bateman knew he had to get away. There are demons, monsters, older than the Bible. They'll seduce us and then they'll kill us.'

I glanced sideways. Fowler's face had a look I'd seen before: the look of officialdom's incredulity. There was that mocking jerk of the head, the tilt of the chin. 'I've never heard such rot. What are you trying to sell?'

'I'm not trying to—'

'Did you sleep with Mrs Suarez?' He was becoming irritable. He'd tried to wheedle a confession out of me and now his patience was at an end.

'You don't understand.'

'Just answer the question, Mr Ward.'

'Are you trying to build a case against me?'

'It's simply an informal line of inquiry, that's all. I'm not taking notes, am I?' Fowler leaned towards me, the smell of tobacco on his stale breath. He asked me again if I'd slept with Clara.

I nodded. There was no point in lying. What was another mark of dishonour in the eyes of this foul and no doubt hypocritical inquisitor?

'How could you?'

'It wasn't difficult. It's where we are, what we're doing.'

'Another fellow's wife?'

'It's happening. Her daughters are coming.'

'Do you know where she is?'

I snorted.

He repeated the question.

'Of course I don't!'

'All right,' said Fowler. He didn't believe me, and he wasn't listening to what I was saying. If O'Neil and Bateman hadn't disappeared it would have been worse. 'All right,' he said, trying to soften his tone. I was angry and he didn't want any more trouble. 'Is there anything else you want to tell me?'

I could have told him that I was scared, terrified of the demons that were congregating as we sat talking. Others were going to disappear, but he wouldn't believe me. The thoughts in my head would only get me into trouble, undermine what faith, if any, he had in my testimony.

'All right,' repeated Fowler. 'You need to pull yourself together. Don't go wandering off.' He paused before turning another inch towards me. 'Try not to annoy Suarez. Keep out of his way.'

'He won't be here for much longer.'

'That's not quite true. I want you all to remain at the site. If the Kurds are taking people then you're better off here, under guard. It's for your own safety.' He smiled again. 'Last thing, before we go, I'd like you to tell me what you think of Suarez.' He patted my hand as if this brief show of physical contact could forge some sort of alliance.

The cigarette was back between my lips. I took a drag.

Fowler flicked his ash onto the floor. It drifted like dirty snow towards my boots. 'I don't know,' I said. 'What do you want to hear?'

34

Our entrance was greeted with silence. Tilden, Mrs Jackson and Sasha were seated at the table. Suarez was leaning against the far wall, his arms crossed. Susan had been left in her room. The faces round the table were expressionless; ready to hear what Fowler had to say. The atmosphere was tense and I wondered if Suarez had told them what had happened. I looked at each one in turn, trying to detect a change in their opinion, the sort of change I'd seen after I'd been released from the sanatorium. I concluded adultery was a kind of madness, a madness which caused the same kind of revulsion in right-minded people.

'We'll just wait for the Russian,' said Fowler. He'd placed himself at the end of the table, his hands resting lightly on the back of a chair. I stood by the door, facing Suarez. We were listening for the sound of footsteps in the courtyard. Tilden, unable to observe the solemnity of the moment, asked me about the progress we'd made, wanting me to describe what I'd seen from the floor of the fourth chamber.

'There's a brick pillar, a dusty floor,' I replied impassively, not wanting to dwell on what had been lurking in the shadows. 'What looked like a spearhead or dagger, and a low wall. I think it's the side of a sarcophagus.' I could feel Fowler studying me, wondering if there was to be a repeat of the irrational outburst that he felt he'd successfully managed to rein in.

Tilden nodded. 'And how high would you say the tomb is?'

'About twenty feet.'

'And the size?'

'I can't say.'

'You can't say,' muttered Tilden.

'Stanislav should know,' said Mrs Jackson, reaching across to clasp Tilden's hand. 'He'll tell you when he gets here.'

'But this is her chamber, isn't it? This is Lilith's temple?'

Fowler turned towards Tilden. 'Who's this Lilith character?'

'Adam's first mate, cast out of Eden for rebelling.'

'For not kowtowing to her husband,' corrected Mrs Jackson. 'She's an Assyrian goddess, the Hebrew queen of the night. Read your Bible, you'll find her there.'

'I see,' said Fowler, one finger idly stroking his moustache. I doubt he understood, or even cared.

'What we've discovered is a temple dedicated to Lilith, the first of its kind,' said Tilden, glancing at Suarez.

'Fascinating,' said Fowler. Above the sound of the rain we'd heard footsteps crossing the muddy courtyard. The captain looked relieved to see Stanislav. 'You'd better take a seat,' he said.

With his shirt dripping onto the stone floor, Stanislav smiled broadly at Tilden. It was clear that he'd found something else. He ran a hand over his shaven head, and shook the water from his fingers. Suarez was looking intently at the pair. He'd uncrossed his arms and was quietly rapping his knuckles against the wall behind him. I'm not sure if Stanislav knew that Clara had disappeared, or that the doctor had yet to be found, though as Fowler began to tell us what had happened his smile quickly faded. There was no news about O'Neil. Like Bateman, he'd simply disappeared. Clara had been staying in the nurse's room above the consulate. The nurse had a vague recollection of her getting up at dawn. At first it was thought that she'd returned to the expedition house, but when the nurse heard about O'Neil she reported her missing. Stanislav glanced at me, then Suarez.

I stood anxiously listening to Fowler's little speech, expecting Suarez at any moment to publicly accuse me of being involved with his wife's disappearance. But he remained silent. Out of the corner of my eye I watched him roll and light a cigarette. I shouldn't have slept with Clara, I shouldn't have succumbed so easily to the allure of another man's wife, but I didn't know anything about her

263

disappearance. I had my suspicion that she was already making her way back to Chicago, that it wouldn't take them too long to work it out. While Fowler was talking I occasionally met Suarez's gaze, stared into his hooded brown eyes, appraised his grim, brutish face. I stared long enough to show that I wasn't scared, that I had nothing left to hide.

'It is imperative,' Fowler concluded, 'that none of you stray beyond the site.'

'Is that for our own safety or are we being kept as suspects?' asked Mrs Jackson.

'Keeping you safe is my main concern. We could be dealing with disgruntled Arabs. Abductions in this part of the world are not uncommon. As some of you know, ever since the Germans tried to whip up a holy war against the British there have been sheiks keen to unsettle things. And I don't think we can trust the Kurds.'

'Or anyone else for that matter,' added Suarez, staring at me from beneath his brow.

'We've always got on well with our workforce,' protested Tilden.

'Even the Yazidis?' asked Fowler.

'Even the Yazidis,' confirmed Tilden.

Suarez muttered Bateman's name.

'Well that's as may be,' continued Fowler, 'but until I have something to go on it's best to be cautious. I'm leaving a sergeant and a man for your protection. I assume you have no objection to them lodging here?'

Tilden shrugged his shoulders as though he had no choice in the matter.

Fowler had finished and those sitting round the table turned and uttered some perfunctory words of sympathy to Suarez. He didn't say anything in response. He held his head still and continued to draw languidly on his cigarette. His eyes remained fixed on me. At the table the conversation had moved on. They were talking about letting the two Indians sleep on the cook's floor. Satisfied with Tilden's arrangements, Fowler said he needed to speak to his men. Suarez wanted to accompany him back into Mosul, but the captain motioned at him to remain where he was.

'My wife's disappeared,' said Suarez coldly. 'I need to find her, to find where she's hiding.'

'You think she's hiding?' asked Mrs Jackson.

'Hiding, waiting for someone. He knows where she is,' said Suarez casually waving his cigarette in my direction.

'I don't,' I replied.

'Then why were you running away?'

'It wasn't because of Clara.'

'Harry's got nothing to do with this,' said Mrs Jackson.

Suarez switched his attention to her, his face a mix of contempt and incredulity. 'Don't pretend you don't know. It's just like Bateman all over again. I was the only one then who had the guts to speak out.'

'I think you should stop there,' said Tilden.

'Why, are you afraid of what the others will think? We're all suspects. That's why you want to keep us cooped up, isn't it?'

'You're safer here,' replied Fowler, 'that's all. There's

265

nothing you can do. I've spoken to Mr Ward and he's explained why his bags were packed.'

'And why were you leaving, Mr Ward?' asked Tilden.

'Because of the things I've seen.'

'Don't you mean the things you've done,' said Suarez.

'What we've all been doing,' I said, with sufficient venom to let him know I wasn't the only one who carried an ill-kept secret. 'The trouble is you don't understand what's been happening here. I was just trying to keep what's left of my sanity. That's why I was trying to get away.'

'But now it's understood; nobody's going anywhere,' said Fowler, picking up his peaked cap and gloves from the table.

'So we all just stay and fester?'

'Tom, you're forgetting why we're here,' said Tilden.

'Of course, we're on the trail of Woolley's gold.'

'Whether or not you continue to work on this dig of yours is up to you,' said Fowler, keen to brook any argument. 'So long as you stay on the site.'

'I think you should hear what I have to say,' said Stanislav.

'Does it have anything to do with Mrs Suarez's disappearance?'

'No, it's about the dig.'

'Then it will have to keep,' said Fowler. 'If I've any news I'll return in the morning. In the meantime don't do anything foolish.' He straightened his cap, the light from the bulb dancing across the peak. 'We'll find Mrs

Suarez, I'm certain it's only a matter of time before we hear something.'

I watched Fowler leave. It was raining and it was dark.

'Do you want to stay and listen?' asked Tilden.

'Do I have a choice?' replied Suarez.

'Of course you do. I just thought with your wife . . .'

'Perhaps we should have a drink first,' said Stanislav. He said a few words in Slovak and Sasha walked out of the mess.

'I'm not forcing you to stay. Are any of Clara's things missing?'

'I've already looked. Nothing's been taken.'

'Well why don't you have a lie-down?'

'Are you trying to get rid of me?'

Tilden shook his head. 'Come and sit at the table.'

Suarez remained leaning against the wall.

Sasha reappeared carrying a whisky bottle and glasses. Her blouse was spotted with rain.

'I won't,' said Tilden, moving the glass away from him.

'I think you'll need it,' answered Stanislav.

Sasha poured us all a glass. She filled Suarez's last, and left it on the table.

'You should sit down,' said Tilden, gesturing towards me. I acknowledged the invitation with a brief nod. Seeing me sit, Suarez dropped his cigarette butt to the floor and stubbed it out underfoot. He pulled out a chair, dragging the legs across the brick floor. Water had begun to drip down the chimney and into the hearth. Suarez sat with his head in his hands, his glass in front of him. It was

267

hard to tell what he was thinking, what he genuinely felt for Clara. When they were together I'd only ever witnessed indifference. He had shown no wish to please her, but rather seemed to take delight in contradicting her in front of others. Stanislav had started to speak and my thoughts drifted back to the table.

'Ward was there when we first broke through to the tomb below. It took us an hour or so to widen the hole.'

'You haven't been down there yet?' asked Tilden.

'I was preparing to lower the boy down when Fowler's man arrived.'

'A pity. It will have to wait till morning. You've left guards?'

'Bilal and his son are there.'

'Describe what you've seen.'

Stanislav paused. Suarez had lifted his head and was gazing miserably in his direction. 'It's a large, tall chamber. There's an open sarcophagus which looks like it's made of granite.'

'Has it been robbed?' asked Tilden.

'I don't think so,' replied Stanislav. 'Beside the sarcophagus there's what looks like a necklace, and around the chamber we've also the remains of those who were entombed: bones, a sword, a spearhead. One was a musician, if what I've seen is a lyre.'

'And within the sarcophagus?'

'There doesn't appear to be anything, though the high walls make it impossible to say for certain.'

'The lid to the sarcophagus?' I asked.

'It's lying on the floor. Again it appears to be made of stone, but it's broken, split down the middle.'

'That's curious,' exclaimed Tilden.

'Is it really?' I asked.

'It's been robbed,' said Suarez. 'That's why the lid's broken.'

'No, it hasn't.' I couldn't stop myself. 'This isn't a temple or a tomb.'

'What do you mean?' said Suarez.

'Do you believe what Fowler was saying, that Bateman and O'Neil were abducted by Arabs?' I shook my head. 'Bateman's body was drained of all fluid. This has nothing to do with the natives squabbling.'

'And Clara?' asked Suarez.

'What Harry is saying is the ziggurat was a prison,' said Mrs Jackson, 'and we've discovered the cell beneath. The cell we were warned not to open.'

Suarez was unimpressed. 'You're trying to tell me Clara's been taken prisoner?'

'Lilith was its prisoner,' I said. 'She was trapped, but not any more.'

'That's damned nonsense,' cried Suarez. 'Your raving on about Lilith isn't fooling me.'

'What's happening is all linked to what we've found. The nightmares Tilden's been having, Susan's behaviour . . .'

'Is she alive?' demanded Suarez, refusing to listen.

Tilden was rubbing his eyes with the palms of his hands. 'It's true. I've heard things whispering, hazy images. Not

269

nightmares. Nightmares have a climax of sorts. She drifts in and out.'

'I've shared the same dream. She visits at night, creeps into my bed.' I gazed at those round the table. Mrs Jackson was looking on sympathetically. Suarez had given up on his question. He started to say something else, but didn't finish his sentence.

'Nightmares are not the same as a stalking demon. How can a mythical creature visit anyone?' demanded Stanislav.

Mrs Jackson leaned forward. 'But what if she isn't a mythical creature? What if the Assyrians had her trapped within her cell?' Stanislav was shaking his head, but Mrs Jackson held sway. 'What if her daughters were being drawn to her? Is this Lilith visiting Henry, or is it her daughters; are they the ones that have been leaving pebbles by the site?'

'You think Clara's been snatched by one of these demons?' asked Suarez.

'No, I don't,' I said.

'If you believe in Jesus, or guardian angels, then why not demons?' asked Mrs Jackson. 'I can't explain why she's vanished, or where she's gone, yet I'm certain it has nothing to do with Mr Ward.'

Suarez thumped the table. The glasses rattled. 'You don't have a clue,' he cried. 'You're just spinning your own fantasy, asking me to believe in a myth. Lilith and her spawn, her litter, they've nothing to do with what's been happening here.'

'Tom,' replied Mrs Jackson, calmly but authoritatively, 'Genesis is built upon Assyrian events, stories that existed long before the Hebrews arrived. This is something you can't deny.'

'If the nightmares are real, and the others have been taken, then we need to be vigilant,' I warned.

'You're crazy,' exclaimed Suarez. 'Are you going to listen to him? My wife's gone, and you think she's been snatched, stolen by some Assyrian she-devil. Why, it should be obvious to anyone, even to a chump like me.'

'Your sarcasm's not going to help,' said Mrs Jackson.

'You know, I thought you were just a harmless old dame, but I guess I was wrong.' Suarez turned towards Stanislav. 'Tell me you don't believe any of this bull.'

'No, I believe in what I can see, what I can understand. But if what we uncover contradicts your beliefs then that's something you have to deal with, at least until your God starts slaying your enemies.'

'I've had enough of this,' cried Suarez. 'I want nothing more to do with this crazy expedition. When Fowler comes back in the morning I'll tell him I want a room in Mosul. I'm not staying in this madhouse, I can tell you that.'

Mrs Jackson tried to calm him down, but he wouldn't listen. For the second time that evening he started to square up to me. I stood up, expecting to take a punch. I noticed which knuckles were grazed and was ready for him to lead with his right. He called me a pug-ugly hick, but I didn't let it distract me. When he threw his punch

I managed to swerve and the intended blow whistled past my face. I grabbed hold of his wrist and drew back my fist, but Stanislav knocked Suarez backwards before he'd had a chance to throw another. The American fell against the table, yet managed to stay on his feet. Humiliated, he wrestled himself free and stormed out of the mess, cursing us all as he left.

'Let him go,' said Tilden.

'Someone should watch him,' said Mrs Jackson. 'Has he got a revolver?'

'No,' replied Tilden, 'not as far as I know. What is it with you photographers?'

'It isn't just me, or Bateman. We're all affected by what's happening here.'

'Well, whatever it is you think is going on here, it won't stop us.' Tilden pulled a hand over his tired face. 'Tomorrow we'll continue to excavate the tomb, and once this is over, once Fowler's finished his investigation, I want you out of here.'

35

All I had was the smell of dust and decay. At first I wasn't sure where I was. I couldn't see anything in the blackness, but I knew the room wasn't mine. It was Bateman's, and the same thing that had taken him was coming for me. I was certain it was somewhere nearby. It had flown into the yard, landed outside my door, and dragged itself into a dark corner. It was crouching in the room, hunched on its hind legs, waiting in the dark, watching from less than a yard away. A low, soft chuckle floated in the air.

My head fell back against the pillow. I pressed myself into the mattress, one ear straining to catch the slightest sound.

Silence. We were both holding our breath.

A gentle breeze brushed against my face. My eyes were closed, but I could feel it staring at me, floating above me. They fall like dead leaves; fall with a lightness, a

273

grace that is slow and sombre. And with their arrival comes a cold, blank smell, like the smell of a church. It is the smell of the dead and buried. Falling through the night, leaving the flavour of their graves behind. The cotton sheet, twisted across my chest, started to shift, to unravel. It glided over my limbs, a soft, delicate movement. Then the sheet was ascending, lifted by an unseen hand.

I lay motionless. My hands beside me, my face turned to the wall. The sheet fell beside the bed, the cotton making a soft sound as it crumpled to the floor. I felt the air shift.

What was it that hovered above me? I only had the echo of a nightmare to guide me, but I knew what it wanted. I had always known. I fought to keep them on, grabbing at the waistband. There was a struggle, I was wrestling, yet it was a match I couldn't win. From the very beginning I knew I was merely delaying the inevitable.

Was it a nightmare? Was it another wet dream? Not since boarding school. In the mirror there were crocodile purses under my eyes – a wet dream, an emission in the night . . . the heat, the whisky . . . the sight of the bruised flesh stopped me believing. Something had been in my room, had taken possession of me, milked me – for want of a better word. I could hear it raining outside. I had woken with a jolt from the nightmare which had followed me into the conscious world. But I wasn't in my room, or Bateman's. I was in the common room, stretched out

274

on the settee. The fire had died, no ember glowed, no spark of light.

Tilden found me at dawn. I'd relit the fire and was sitting with a blanket round me, my hands spread out in front of the flames.

I looked up and saw dark rings under his eyes. I thought he'd still be angry with me for having slept with Clara, but it wasn't anger that he was carrying. It was more a bitter disappointment, a feeling that he'd been betrayed. 'You're going to continue to work?' he asked, or ordered. His voice was worn out, hard to interpret.

I sat still. All I wanted to do was to board a train and get as far away from Mosul as possible. I stared back at the grate. Was there a choice? Weren't we all prisoners? At least the fire had afforded me some protection. I'd managed to keep the nightmare inside my head, to fend off any physical manifestation.

'I expect you to help,' said Tilden. 'At least to earn your keep.'

'All right,' I said, unwilling to argue or to point out the futility of the venture.

'Good,' he said. My agreeing with him allowed him to relax. 'We'll gather in the mess.'

'Is Suarez coming?'

'I don't think so.' Tilden slowly stroked his cheek. 'I don't approve of your behaviour, Mr Ward. What you've done to Suarez. It's a despicable way to treat someone.' There was a pause, an invitation to respond.

'I never intended it to happen.'

'If I had my way, you wouldn't still be here.'

'If I had my way, neither would I.'

'It's not that I'm disappointed with your work . . .'

'There's no need to explain.'

'To explain?' said Tilden. 'How do you explain . . .?' His voice trailed away. I noticed he was staring down at the well-thumbed copy of the *Town Tattle* which lay on the floor. Tilden picked up the magazine. On the cover was a German actress: high cheekbones, thin, pinched lips. The face wasn't dissimilar to Susan's. He glanced at me and then looked back at the cover, his hands trembling a little. 'If she'd been herself she wouldn't have done it,' he muttered, his words barely audible. 'Perhaps you're right. Perhaps there's something in what you've been saying. The desert brings out a sickness in the blood, stirs it up.' He lifted his head and focused his eyes on me again. 'They have a tendency to misbehave.' He grimaced. 'Sasha's looking after her. This sort of thing's bound to take its toll.'

I nodded.

He cast aside the magazine and rubbed his face. When his spectacles fell back over his eyes he was blinking, trying to keep me in focus. 'Have you a mackintosh?'

'No,' I replied.

'Pity. It's still raining.'

36

The cook had placed a tin pail in one corner of the mess to catch the water that was dripping through a crack in the ceiling. 'This rain can't carry on for much longer,' said Mrs Jackson.

'I suppose not,' I agreed, though the dripping seemed to beat a constant rebuttal. I finished my porridge. Amuda picked up my bowl and trundled back into the kitchen. Tilden had gone to check on Suarez and we were waiting for him to return.

'You haven't lost your appetite,' observed Stanislav.

'There's no reason to skip breakfast.'

'The expression "had your oats" springs to mind.'

'Victor,' said Mrs Jackson sharply.

'It's all right.'

'An observation,' said Stanislav, 'that's all.' He sipped his coffee. 'And these hallucinations?' he asked.

I shrugged my shoulders. 'I don't want to sound like a lunatic. But then it seems I'm not the only one.'

'Are they the same as Tilden's?'

'I don't know. I expect so.'

'Do you know why you haven't seen them?' Mrs Jackson asked Stanislav.

'Because I don't believe in such nonsense?'

'No,' she replied, 'it's because you're sleeping with Sasha. If Harry's right, then they're only preying on men who sleep alone.'

'The *they* being Lilith's daughters, the demons that have taken Bateman and O'Neil?'

'It's what I think,' I answered. 'And they were snatched when they were trying to leave. Trying to leave while it was dark.'

'The dark, the night, it's their element,' said Mrs Jackson. 'Perhaps they've always been with us, hiding in the shadows, waiting. Preying on the lost and forgotten, killing to sustain themselves, trying to avoid suspicion. Not everybody who walks out into the night returns. Now they're being drawn to their mother, congregating around her cell, her prison.'

'And you think we can find them lurking in the shadows,' said Stanislav, 'these demented daughters?'

'If we take enough lamps we'll be safe,' I said.

Stanislav was grinning. He said something to Sasha, but she didn't smile.

An anxious-looking Tilden entered the mess.

'Is he coming?' asked Mrs Jackson.

278

'He's not in his room.'

'In the washroom?' suggested Stanislav.

'No, I've checked.'

'Well, he can't have left the house. Fowler's men are on the gate.'

'I asked them. They haven't seen him.' Tilden stared at me. 'Did you hear anything?'

'Nothing.'

'Someone should tell Fowler,' suggested Mrs Jackson.

For what it was worth I offered to check the photographic studio. Stanislav went to the *antika* room.

It took no more than a couple of minutes to search the house. The cook hadn't seen him, and neither had Amuda, though the boy had noticed that his door was ajar when he'd gone to wake Tilden.

'He's been taken,' declared Mrs Jackson. 'He was alone . . .'

'Nonsense,' replied Stanislav as convincingly as he could. 'He's run away. That's all. Fowler will find him in Mosul.'

37

We sheltered under two umbrellas on our way up the hill. Mrs Jackson had slipped her arm through mine, while Stanislav did his best to hold his umbrella over Tilden. Trailing behind us was the Indian private. He was carrying his rifle. His turban was soaked and his face was dripping. 'Poor sod, he must be wondering what he's doing here.'

'At least the cook has company,' said Mrs Jackson. Beneath the drumming rain conversation was difficult and it was hard to see ahead. Everything was either grey or brown: a grey sky, a brown land. Rivulets of mud and sand ran between our boots.

The first pile of stones appeared halfway between the house and the ziggurat. I felt my arm being squeezed. 'Her daughters have returned,' said Mrs Jackson. I peered out from beneath the umbrella. There they were; scattered like dung across the landscape, clumsy-looking pyramids that had spent half the night being washed clean by the rain. I started to count those that stood beside the track: six, seven . . . every three or four yards there was another one.

'We're in the middle of it,' she cried.

They were on either side, multiplying in number as we trudged towards the half-buried ziggurat.

'Succubi,' she exclaimed.

'And her sons,' I asked, 'what about her sons?'

'Incubi,' she answered.

'But where are they?'

She shook her head. 'I don't know. Perhaps they're on their way. Boys are always slower on the uptake than girls. Even if they were to appear I'm sure they wouldn't bother someone like me. Only Susan . . .'

I glanced up and saw the entrance lay twenty yards ahead; a gaping mouth leading into a subterranean darkness. A face suddenly emerged from the ragged blackness and I fell back, almost tripping over my feet as I fought the impulse to run. Mrs Jackson held my elbow and steered me forward. 'It's Bilal, that's all. He's no demon.'

I looked up and saw that she was right. He stood there with his son, beckoning us towards the entrance. The ziggurat seemed to shine in the rain. Rippling tides of water ran down the building and collected at its base. The soft mud made our way to the entrance difficult. Planks had been laid across the final few yards, but they were sinking into the waterlogged sand.

Bilal and his son were waving us on from the shelter

of the upper chamber. Stanislav was the first to climb through the gap in the brickwork, the foreman enthusiastically slapping his back before he was even halfway through. 'Too familiar, much too familiar,' muttered Tilden as I followed him inside.

Paraffin lamps flickered round the hole in the stone floor. As we stood, shoulder to shoulder, Bilal explained to Stanislav that the others were too frightened to return. The Tigris was rising and the pontoon bridge had been washed away before. Nobody wanted to be on this side of the Tigris, not even the Yazidis. Not in the storm, not at night. There was also talk of a fever sweeping the city. Children were dying.

'It sounds like cholera,' said Stanislav. 'Their milk's contaminated.'

'You can't be certain of that,' said Mrs Jackson.

'It's happened before.'

'But not this time; this time it's far more serious.'

'That's enough,' said Tilden. He had one hand on the first rung and had switched on his electric torch. I inched towards the ladder. I was feeling apprehensive yet I was also aware of the mounting excitement that surrounded me. Tilden led the way, his torch cutting through the darkness below. We followed him down the ladder, each one of us clutching a lamp. The whole place had a decayed and abandoned air, yet there was also something else. In the blackness there was an overwhelming sense not of horror, but of grief and sadness, as if the cold, perspiring walls were weeping.

When we reached the floor above Lilith's tomb Tilden ordered Bilal and his son to pick up the two ladders that had been bound together in order to give us the required length. It was a precarious affair and Hassan, a slender boy of about thirteen, was chosen to test its strength. The boy was followed by his father, then Mrs Jackson. Photographs were needed and so I followed Tilden, while Stanislav, much to his chagrin, was told to remain above in the fourth chamber.

As I descended I heard Tilden again murmuring to himself. Bilal and his son were speaking to one another. Their voices were hushed, their tone communicating something akin to reverence. Their three lights were moving away from the ladder, spreading like fireflies between the columns. I stepped down from the final rung and forced myself to look around. The tomb was twice the height of the others and appeared to be square, about the size of a drill hall. There were two rows of brick columns, spaced at intervals of about four or five yards. The air was cold and damp. I raised my lamp and saw that the ceiling was vaulted. Particles of dust floated above my head, but through the dust and the gloom I could see three winged figures carved into the stone. The figures, bas-reliefs, appeared to be glowering down. One wielded a sword, the second clutched what looked like a snake in its hand, the third held an Assyrian bow, the string taut. They radiated out from the circular opening we'd made. Looking down was Stanislav's face, grotesquely lit by the lamp on the floor beside him. 'Photographs,' he called, a hand cupped around his mouth. 'Lots of pictures.'

284

In answer I held the camera case away from my chest and then turned to see Tilden holding his lamp in front of him. He was staring at a pictorial carving. Taking care not to tread on a clay urn or piece of bone, I walked over and stood beside him. It was a tranquil, pastoral scene: a banquet in a forest, musicians playing and a farmer carrying wood. With the help of his torch and Mrs Jackson's lamp I framed the scene and with a steady hand took two photographs. The fear I'd felt as we'd approached the ominous building had been replaced by wonder. I defy anyone, no matter how frayed their nerves, not to marvel at what we'd uncovered. In spite of what had happened it was thrilling to think that we were in a tomb untouched and unseen for nearly three thousand years. We were trespassing, poachers in a subterranean forest of brick and stone. I heard Bilal exclaim something in Arabic. I turned and saw that he and his son had wandered over to the sarcophagus.

'Don't touch anything,' cried Tilden. He pointed towards the ladder. 'Wait over there.'

They stared at him; a puzzled look, a moment's reluctance. Then Bilal took his son's arm and they picked their way back to the centre of the tomb.

'They mustn't touch anything,' Tilden was saying, as if repeating his order justified his decision. He gestured for me to lend him my arm. The discovery of the hidden tomb had lifted his spirits, yet he wasn't altogether well. In the dark airless cell he was finding it increasingly difficult to breathe. Together we slowly crossed the dusty floor to the sarcophagus. Shadows ran forward and then receded over the grey bones that Stanislav had mentioned. Tilden counted nine skulls and asked me to take a photograph of each one. Three skeletons were festooned with golden jewellery and lay close to the sarcophagus. The other six were wearing helmets of beaten metal and were lying apart from one another. There were copper spears and axe heads lying next to what I assumed were Assyrian soldiers. One axe head was propped against a brick pillar as if it had been placed there only moments ago, though all the handles had turned to dust. I wondered whether they'd been left to die in the tomb.

'They must have been alive when it was sealed,' said Tilden as though reading my mind. 'There's nothing uniform about the way in which they're lying. Within other tombs the corpses are laid out in a particular fashion, indicating that they'd been sacrificed on the steps of the ziggurat or taken poison in situ. Here they're strewn across the floor. See,' he said, moving his beam along the floor, 'their bones are scattered, lying as though casually discarded, no thought given to comfort or dignity.'

He gestured towards the sarcophagus. In the lamplight I could see that it was empty, except for beads of pale yellow that must have been plaited in her hair and several strips of cloth, which once could have been scarlet but were now the colour of clotted blood. With the help of Tilden's torch I took another photograph before he touched the fabric. It crumbled beneath his fingers. 'That's not unusual,' he remarked, 'though an empty sarcophagus . . .' He gazed around as if expecting to find the occupant hiding in the shadows. I watched him as he ran a hand over the smooth rim and then knelt down to touch the stone lid, half of which lay against the sarcophagus. 'Granite,' he said, 'split in two.' His breath was visible in the dank, cold air, and like a grey wraith it twisted above his head. There was the smell of incense, faint, but unmistakable. The fabric must have released the smell as it disintegrated. 'See here,' said Tilden, 'clay lamps beneath the lid. Those who were sealed in must have had a few hours of light.'

'Light to protect them?' I asked.

'Perhaps, albeit briefly. They were either here to serve or to keep whoever it was locked up; at least until they'd sealed the chamber above.'

'And we've let it escape?'

Tilden turned his head to look up at me, his furrowed brow visible in the sepia light. 'The sarcophagus's occupant must be amongst the corpses. She managed to escape, though didn't get far.'

'Breaking the lid?'

'It's happened before. A simple fault in the stone. It could have cracked when the sarcophagus was sealed, though for it to be dislodged . . .' He ran his torch along the length of the lid. 'That must have fallen from the woman's neck.'

I looked down at the golden necklace, its shining leaves tangled in the dust. Could it have belonged to a mortal

Lilith? Had she been a woman revered as a goddess, a goddess that had fallen out of favour?

'Look here,' said Mrs Jackson excitedly. She was standing on the other side of the sarcophagus and holding her lamp beneath her waist. 'Vessels of silver, stone bowls, clay jars; either for an offering or for sustenance, food for her jailers.'

Tilden, with my hand beneath his arm, managed to pull himself up. He was shaking his head. 'These aren't the usual artefacts; this isn't what you'd expect to find.'

'What do you mean?'

'It's almost bare. There are no golden cups, painted figures, wooden chests, statues. All we have are several pieces of jewellery, a handful of weapons, a few vessels strewn across the floor. Yet it can't have been robbed. There's no sign it's been entered.'

'Then it was a prison?'

Tilden stared pensively into the dark, one hand resting against a brick pillar. 'We need to take what we can back to the expedition house.' He clicked his fingers at Bilal and his son. Having silently watched our progress around the tomb, they now crossed the floor towards him. 'Strip it of jewellery first. You understand?'

Bilal nodded.

'Give each piece to Mrs Jackson. After it's been cleared of gold, all other artefacts are to be taken to the floor above.' He softly clapped his hands.

'Shouldn't I photograph each piece before it's moved?'

'No time for that,' he said. 'We need to get these things out of here before Fowler returns.'

'Why?' asked Mrs Jackson. 'You can't simply ransack the place.'

'Mina, if you want to assist me you'll stand over by the ladder.'

'This isn't how it's done.'

'I'll be the judge of what needs to be done. Here,' snapped Tilden, thrusting a small cotton sack into her hand. 'Just go and stand where Stanislav can see you.'

'This isn't right,' said Mrs Jackson.

'Don't be such a blasted funk and get over there.'

She glanced at me as though she expected me to intervene, but Tilden could do what he liked. I was curious, but I didn't want to linger there in the semi-darkness. Around the tomb Bilal and his son had already started lifting necklaces from the dusty floor. Bones were crumbling as they hurriedly searched for rings and brooches. It was a grim scene; shadows flickering over what was left, two dark figures, tripping stealthily, looting the dead. Mrs Jackson, unable to rouse even a pinch of sympathy, walked over to the ladder.

Tilden turned towards me. 'While they're busy let's see if the masons have anything else to tell us.' He was trying to sound jovial, but his tone rang hollow. I know what bravado sounds like: a voice that sails blithely forward, the cracks appearing just below the waterline, almost invisible. It was the wall behind the sarcophagus that he wanted to see. There was a carving, set in the same forest as the first, but now it was a scene of carnage. Severed heads, the women either raped or taken as slaves by demoniacal soldiers. Tilden cleared his throat. 'An Assyrian ambush,' he observed. 'They rarely kept male prisoners alive.'

It seemed bizarre for a civilisation even as barbaric as theirs to want to glorify the destruction of a once tranquil scene. 'A bloodthirsty race,' I commented in front of their celebration of wanton cruelty.

'The Assyrians had no qualms about killing civilians. In their world it was kill or be killed. Their morality – if you can call it that – was very different from our own.'

'I've never seen anything like it. Never such a graphic . . .' My voice trailed off. There were scenes, memories which, if allowed, could quite easily compete.

'They were ruthless, willing to face up to the reality of war. This was an ancient civilisation in crisis, operating under a fearful irrationality.'

'And that's what made them so vicious?'

'They wouldn't want anyone seeing it to feel sympathy for the enemy. They hated weakness.'

'As much as they hated compassion?'

'Hearts of stone, Mr Ward. The Assyrians despised compassion. Why do you think the carving's here?'

'As a warning?'

'A reminder. A reminder to others not to feel any sympathy.' He let go of my arm. 'I think I'd like to be in the next photograph, if you don't mind.'

'Of course,' I replied, though I disliked the thought of capturing the gruesome scene. Tilden passed me his torch and I brought the camera up to my eye.

After taking the photograph we carried on to the third wall. This was the most decorative. Its surface had a blue glaze and set within the left-hand corner was a pale disc the size of a carving dish. 'The moon's made of alabaster,' said Tilden, his fingers tracing the smooth edge of the circle. 'It's rising above a stepped altar.' In the background was the palm-fringed Tigris. In the foreground three priests were simultaneously pouring libations into the mouth of a female figure. She was naked, though where her feet should have been there were claws. Like Tilden, I couldn't resist touching the relief. With one hand I traced the voluptuous curves of the cold limestone. 'It's Lilith,' exclaimed Tilden, though I needed no introduction. 'The three libations are wine, water and oil: wine for the gods, water for purification and oil for the dead.'

Behind us Bilal and his son continued to trot backwards and forwards. We moved on, like gentlemen in a gallery, to the final wall. The figure, for there was only the outline of an awkward-looking creature, had been defaced. 'It's her nemesis,' explained Tilden, 'Pazuzu. The god of storms and winds. He defeated Lilith, though his own reputation is almost as dark. You'll see him on amulets fashioned to protect against her.'

'It's a savage attack,' I observed, running my finger down a long score across the figure's chest that was an inch deep.

'Those trapped within the tomb could have been followers of Lilith. If they were it's not surprising they attacked the image of the god that defeated her.'

291

'Or perhaps she killed those that were here, and then took out her anger on the carving.'

'I'm getting cold. I think it's time I took my leave. Take a photograph of the vandalised figure and the three magi on the ceiling.'

'The three magi?' asked Mrs Jackson, as he came towards her.

'Balthasar, Melchior and—'

'On the ceiling,' she interrupted, 'you mean the four.'

'Three,' I said, following in Tilden's wake.

'Four,' she replied firmly, turning her eyes towards the ceiling.

'But . . .' I glanced upwards, the breath catching in my throat. Tilden was pointing his torch at each one in turn. There were three winged figures. 'Caspar's such a ridiculous name for a magus,' he was saying over his shoulder, asking me if I agreed.

I ignored him.

'There were four!' exclaimed Mrs Jackson, clutching the sack to her chest. 'Where's the fourth?' Suddenly she wheeled round. It was such an unexpected movement that Bilal and his son turned to look at her.

'Did you hear that?'

'What?' I asked.

'It's up there.'

Tilden, his torch playing across the ceiling, was asking her if she was all right, if she'd seen anything.

I was breathing rapidly, trying to keep calm, trying to get across to the ladder without gazing into the shadows.

Suddenly Bilal called out. 'What's he saying?' shouted Tilden to Stanislav.

'I didn't hear,' replied the Russian. His shaven head had reappeared above me. Hassan had stepped out of my way. I was climbing, following Mrs Jackson. The stone ceiling was lit up, the three carved figures grimacing at the shadows below. Stanislav shouted something in Arabic. I heard Bilal reply from a corner of the tomb. He was cursing, using words that I hadn't heard since the war.

I was trying to slow my breathing down, moving from rung to rung, knowing the foreman had found something that had rattled him. I felt Stanislav's arm beneath mine. He was helping me up, pulling me into the chamber. Emerging from the tomb I heard Tilden's voice coming from the foot of the ladder.

'She's in there,' I was saying. 'They need to get out.'

Mrs Jackson was crawling away on her hands and knees. 'Stay in the light,' she cried. 'Keep out of the shadows. It's hiding in the shadows.'

Stanislav was calling down again to Bilal. Tilden's head appeared from beneath the floor. 'Is Mina OK?' he rasped. The climb or Mrs Jackson had drained the colour from his face.

'She thought she saw something.'

'It's Lilith,' I stammered, inching away from the entrance to her tomb.

'On the wall?' asked Tilden, thinking it was one of the carvings that had triggered her flight.

293

'On the ceiling,' she uttered, 'clinging to the ceiling. I saw four figures.'

'There are the three magi, that's all. There isn't a fourth.' Tilden climbed awkwardly off the ladder, Stanislav pulling him to his feet. 'There's nothing else.'

'She's in there.'

'The only people in there are the foreman and his son.'

'Get them out,' she cried. She was trembling, her lamp held in front of her face.

'Nonsense,' replied Tilden, though his words by now had lost all conviction.

'But they mustn't stray from the light.'

'There's no need for them to be afraid,' said Tilden.

'She's down there, in the shadows. They've got to get out.' She was angry, and her voice was shaking. I was telling Tilden that we should reseal the cell, that it wasn't too late.

'Once we've emptied the tomb we'll reseal it. It won't take long. How much jewellery have we got?' he asked, gesturing towards the sack.

'Enough,' she said, tossing it towards him. 'Just get them out.'

Tilden picked up the sack and pulled out a glittering pendant. He nodded, a look of satisfaction spread across his face. I saw him for what he was: little more than a graverobber. He wasn't interested in what Mrs Jackson had seen or what I had to say.

He asked me to help Mrs Jackson to her feet. 'Go back to the *antika* room. And take Mina with you.'

'She must be down there,' I said, 'hiding in the shadows.'

Tilden shook his head at me. 'There's nothing in there.' He ordered Stanislav to go down and see what Bilal was making all the fuss about. I tried to stop the Russian from descending, but he wouldn't listen. 'Go and develop your pictures,' he said. 'Make sure you've a record of our discovery.'

'You have to get them out,' pleaded Mrs Jackson. She'd grabbed hold of Tilden's sleeve and was trying to pull him away from the ladder.

'No,' said Tilden, 'you have to go. I'll stay here.'

'But—'

'No,' he repeated angrily, having managed to shake himself free. 'Just get her out, take her back to the house.'

I placed a hand on her shoulder. She was sobbing quietly, her back turned away from the entrance to the tomb. Tilden was telling us to leave, telling me he'd make sure nothing happened. I tried to explain, but he just laughed in my face. It was a nervous laugh, all bluff and bluster. He was unwell, anxious, caught up in the discovery, the elusive find. Stanislav was climbing down, disappearing into the dark, and I could hear Bilal calling. Mrs Jackson was climbing out of the chamber. Tilden was steering me towards the ladder.

I began to follow Mrs Jackson. They'd refused to listen. It had to be sealed before nightfall. Strip the cell, develop the pictures. Seal her in. I kept my gaze within the lamp's circle of light. I could hear the constant hammering of the rain on the stone ledge; the pouring rain ricocheting off the bricks.

38

I took off my jacket and unbuttoned my flannel trousers. I dried my clothes on a wooden clotheshorse by the stove in the kitchen. The act of undressing and dressing was a mechanical undertaking. My mind was a blank. I was losing the ability to think. It was the same as last time, the same fear of a thought process which could so easily lead me into some sort of vacant state, my identity left shattered. I closed my eyes against the self-induced apocalypse. I wasn't a coward, but I was cautious, aware of how close I was to becoming unhinged. The thought that Mrs Jackson had seen her kept returning. Lilith was there, waiting for the night.

A small curtained-off corner in the studio served as the darkroom. To remove the Leica's cassette I would close the door, pull down the blind over the one window and then step behind the thick curtain. I had to focus on my work. It was a straightforward process. I was about to begin when Mrs Jackson appeared.

'Are you all right? I asked.

She didn't answer, but stood there staring at me.

'The colour's come back to your cheeks,' I remarked.

'It was cold in the tomb.'

'What you saw . . .'

'It was dark, I thought . . .'

'But you're not sure?' Perhaps it was better if we could dismiss what she'd seen. It was necessary to trammel my thinking, to keep my thoughts under control.

'Tilden's given me the jewellery to catalogue.' She idly stroked my arm. 'Here's what I've catalogued so far.' Her face was powdered and on the lapel of her blouse she wore what appeared to be a diamanté lizard.

She suddenly became aware of me staring at her.

'Would you like a milk tablet?' she asked.

'If you have one.'

She slid a finger and thumb into the pocket of her cardigan and pulled out a tin of Horlicks milk tablets. 'A taste of home,' she said. 'I find it helps to calm the nerves.'

She opened the tin and I took a tablet.

'I'm sorry if I startled you,' she said. 'Back there in the tomb.'

'It doesn't matter.'

'I thought I'd caught a glimpse of something moving.'

I didn't say anything. The tablet was dissolving on my tongue. It slid from one cheek to the other. I started to place the artefacts she'd brought me onto the wooden

298

bench. There was a silver pendant, an elaborate necklace and inscribed amulets of gold and lapis lazuli. In amongst the glittering pile were several bronze figures. I carefully picked out one and saw that it was similar to the defaced carving.

'She was a wretched woman, more wretched than evil. They all worshipped her, Mr Ward.'

'Really,' I answered, though my thoughts were elsewhere. There was an eyelet behind the head, a place where a cord would have been threaded through. It was worn round the neck.

'Salome, Nitocris, Messalina, Agrippina, they all worshipped the Assyrian goddess. Semiramis was the first.'

'Semiramis?'

'The Assyrian queen. She had an insatiable appetite for the most handsome of her soldiers. She would seduce them and then have them killed. More than a hundred we're told.'

I turned the amulet over and held it in the palm of my hand. The face was almost triangular. The eyes wide open.

'Such a wicked abuse of power. If what they say is true, though no one's ever simply skin and bones.' She paused.

Was it made to protect against Lilith? Had they worn these in the tomb? Had it worked? Had they repelled the demon, slept with it watching them; died through lack of air or water?

'Perhaps you shouldn't sleep alone tonight,' she said.

I looked up. 'Thank you, but I'll be all right.'

'Well just make sure you keep a light burning.'

I needed time to think. Mrs Jackson said she'd bring the rest of the jewellery over when she'd finished cataloguing. I watched her leave the studio. My hand hesitated. There was no need to come to a decision. I'd sort out the others first. I looked away from the bench. I pocketed the bronze figure. Just for now, just for the darkroom, for the darkness to come.

39

Stanislav appeared just before they rang the bell for lunch. After wiping the rain off his spectacles, he clapped a hand on my shoulder. I showed him the artefacts I'd photographed. They lay in two wooden trays stacked beside me. He must have thought me a coward, but he could see that I was now working as if nothing had happened. He watched me as he described what Bilal had found. Apparently, half-buried in one dark corner of the room, he'd found the skeleton of a baby: the ribcage protruding from the sand like the claws of some hidden creature. Tilden wanted me to return after lunch and take more photographs.

I refused. Why should I go back to the ziggurat?

He tried to reason with me. 'It's a strain,' he said, 'recording everything as fast as we can. Tilden just wants the job done as quickly as possible. It's for your sake. He doesn't want to prolong the ordeal.'

I looked at Stanislav. He was lying. We both knew why Tilden was in a hurry.

'This rain,' he declared, glancing towards the open door. 'I've never known it like this.'

'Have you seen it?' I asked.

'What?'

'Lilith.'

'What do you think?'

I carried on working. I couldn't look at him. 'He has to seal the tomb before nightfall.'

'He's working as fast as he can.'

'But he won't be finished before dark.'

'No,' Stanislav replied. 'Though Bilal seems to share his sense of urgency.'

'He's afraid of her.'

'Perhaps you're right. All I know is he doesn't want Fowler interfering.' Stanislav picked up one of the bronze figures from its wooden tray. 'Your deserting us like that put the wind up them. You've fled before, haven't you? Felt the same panic?' His questions weren't accusations.

'Not while I was fighting.'

'Afterwards?'

It was almost impossible to answer. I couldn't simply cut through the cold rind of my reserve. The safest response was to carry on, to focus on the golden ring in front of me with its stone of sapphire blue. My hands were trembling. I grasped the Leica tightly, trying to steady it, pressing it against my face. But it was no use. The ring continued to shake. Yet it wasn't the blurring

302

of the picture that unsettled me. When the penny spins it's indistinct. When it stops spinning, when it falls and becomes fixed, that's when the screaming begins. Those were the visions that had haunted my nights: still, silent pictures of the dead; soldiers, their limbs torn apart by Turkish shells, sitting calmly at the end of my bed, a cigarette between their fingers. Their ghostly faces as pale as ivory, and their eyes always shining; eyes of polished mahogany, eyes the colour of the darkest bluebells in the wood.

My silence was an admission. I was shaking like a man with palsy.

Stanislav rested his hand on my arm. 'What I like about archaeology is the monotony of it.' His voice was low, comforting. 'Day after day with your own thoughts, digging, brushing, cataloguing. Putting the puzzle together. Before I came here, before Sasha, there was a time when I too had no moral compass.'

'You think I've no morals?'

'It's not that, though I think you're still hurt by what happened. It's what the war did to you.' He spoke softly, persuasively. 'We carry wounds that no one else can see.'

I tried to satisfy his curiosity with something which was easily understood. 'There was a time when a motor car backfiring would make me flinch.'

He grunted. This was no acknowledgement of what had happened. We both knew it wasn't uncommon to suffer such an affliction.

'I'm less susceptible to noises.' I put the camera down.

Stanislav had taken the bronze figures out of their tray and had placed them in a row on the bench. With one finger he was pulling each one to the edge. Pazuzu, but in different poses. I saw them lining up in front of me. 'Go on,' he said. He was looking down, concentrating on positioning each figure in relation to its neighbour.

I had to surrender. I had no choice but to let him through. I didn't turn to catch his eye, but watched his hand arranging the figures. 'There was a time when I imagined all sorts of things, terrible things. I would mutter to myself, and stare intently at bare walls. Not uncommon, I know, but enough for me to be packed off to a sanatorium.' There were seven bronze figures. The eighth was in my pocket. 'My father was a tailor. He doesn't drink. He was once very proud of his Christian soldier. My sister died after the war, influenza. My mother's still working. She lives by her sewing needle and scissors.'

Stanislav had started to examine each figure in turn.

I waited for him to speak.

Eventually he turned towards me, his voice still low. 'There were days when I would drink in my room in Petrograd.'

I leaned against the wooden bench, wanting to hear what he had to say.

'Days turned into nights and I drank. I had girls: girls with round shiny faces, hot-blooded Bolsheviks, kulaks sweating beneath blankets, even the wife of a Red Army officer. You know what beasts we can become?'

I averted my gaze. I didn't trust myself to reply.

'Some have a narrow understanding of beauty, but when I returned I saw beauty everywhere: in the folds of a dress, the smell of a girl's neck. I wasn't your melancholy drunk. At first I drank to celebrate. But the Bolsheviks had no time for anarchists. I'd fought the White Army for nothing. In order to be alone, to stop wasting what I had, I began to sleep by day, to read and study throughout the night. Free from distractions, from visitors. I had always dreamed of digging in the ruins, uncovering long-forgotten cities.' Stanislav paused. 'I've seen too many burials. This urge to uncover perhaps has something to do with that.'

'To resurrect the dead?'

'In a way.'

'I was buried once.'

'Explain?' said Stanislav softly.

I pressed my hands down on the bench, spread out my fingers. 'I was sent spinning by a shell, thrown into the mud. It weighed down every limb. I couldn't breathe.' The memory squeezed the air from my lungs, but I wanted Stanislav to understand, to know that I wasn't a coward. 'By the time they pulled me out I'd lost my sanity. I'd collapsed mentally; unable to move or speak. They sent me downriver, finally shipped me back to England. Doses of chloroform and faradic shock treatment were prescribed. When I finally regained what the doctor termed a neuropathic equilibrium I was told that I was as fragile as an eggshell. The breakdown I'd suffered . . . for months I wandered the street in my greatcoat . . . behaved strangely in teashops.' He gestured for me to continue. 'You don't have anything else to say?' I asked.

'What do you want to hear, that the crippled and the dead still haunt my mind? No, it's your turn. That's why I'm here.'

I allowed my hands to relax, and marvelled at their stillness; splayed and indifferent. 'I craved solitude, more than anything else. I began to use a camera, a camera to capture a moment's peace. A picture is something I can protect.' I leaned towards Stanislav, my voice a conspiratorial whisper. 'It's hard for me to say, but I'm not fit for the mating games that others play. This,' I gestured around me, 'was a self-imposed exile.' I turned to look at Stanislav. 'Or at least that's what I wanted.'

'We're both haunted by the past,' he said. 'You bury yourself in pictures. I hide my face in clay tablets, in Sasha's lap.'

'But sometimes I despise other people; all their talk of butter and beer. It all seems so petty, so insignificant.'

'Nothing makes much sense when you've seen so many slaughtered. The wine I drink is the blood of a comrade, each bottle brings me closer to levelling the score. Yet women,' he announced, 'women can help a man to lose himself, or to find himself, whichever you prefer. You should find Clara. When Fowler lets you go, when we have finished our plundering, you should find her. Sasha thinks she was in love with you. That she waited for you.'

306

He paused as I tried to take in what he had just said. 'Women are sometimes hard to understand.'

'Like Lilith?'

The Russian smiled. 'But this time you have an amulet to protect you.'

40

'It's an eerie place,' admitted Tilden as he sat down to lunch, 'but it all needs to be recorded. The work has to be documented. We can't reseal it until there's nothing left to understand, until there's nothing left unturned.'

'You know she's in there,' I said. 'It has to be resealed before nightfall. God knows what will happen if she's able to escape.'

'Are you too afraid to return to the tomb?'

'You've forgotten what's happened,' I said. 'If we haven't already released her from her lair then surely we should stop. Mrs Jackson, you understand the danger we're in.'

Tilden laid his hand on her arm. 'What we've discovered changes everything.'

'No,' I replied, 'it doesn't. Can't you see that you've been seduced by the discovery of something that should never have been disturbed?'

'This is why we're here, Mr Ward, and we're not running away because of bad dreams.'

'But you've had the same dreams, haven't you?'

'So what? Dreams are just dreams. I'm not running away. Besides, if it continues to rain the whole place could become flooded. We need to have a comprehensive photographic record. There's no time to sketch anything. You know it's a matter of getting enough light, the length of exposure.'

Amuda, carrying plates of cold chicken, moved silently around the table. Water continued to drip into the hearth.

'There are inscriptions running along the base of one of the walls,' said Stanislav. 'They're half covered by sand. One appears to be a list of those entombed; either as guardians or as a sacrifice. Another seems to be some kind of lullaby.'

'That doesn't surprise me,' said Mrs Jackson. 'Lullabies began as prayers or incantations to protect a baby from Lilith. Some even think the word lullaby stems from Lilith or Lilim go by, Lilim being another word for her daughters.'

Tilden ignored her and turned towards Stanislav. 'That's something else we need to explore. Where Bilal found the baby's skeleton the sand seems to go on.' He took a sip of water. 'Elsewhere there's a stone floor. I've told Bilal and his son to dig there. Perhaps something's buried in the corner.'

'What,' I asked, 'more buried treasure?'

'Wasn't Fowler supposed to be returning this morning?' asked Mrs Jackson.

'He was,' confirmed Tilden, albeit somewhat warily. 'Though I imagine he's hot on the case of the missing couple.'

'But he doesn't know about Tom, does he? Has anyone been to—'

'I've told the sergeant about his disappearance. Besides, I don't want anyone crossing the bridge while the river's still rising. Mr Ward, I'm just as uneasy as you about what has happened, but you don't seem to appreciate that what we've uncovered is incredibly significant. I'm not going to waste my time, or anybody else's, pursuing a Yank and his floozy.'

'That's unfair,' said Mrs Jackson.

'Perhaps you should ask Mr Ward what he thinks of Clara?'

'I think she had the good sense to get out while she could.'

'And there's nothing else you'd like to tell us about her, is there?' asked Tilden.

'Stop it, Henry,' said Mrs Jackson. 'You're really not helping. Now what if I said to you that I didn't see Lilith?'

'I'd say hallelujah.'

'The ziggurat's Lilith's, it's her tomb or prison, but what if it wasn't Lilith I saw? What if there's something else beneath the tomb?'

'Like what?' asked Tilden.

'Tablets and Hebrew scrolls mention a cave: Lilith's cave. Perhaps the whole edifice has been built above it, perhaps she's still trapped beneath the tomb and what I saw was one of her daughters.'

'I thought we'd agreed we weren't going to talk about what you did or didn't see in front of Mr Ward.'

'It's a little late for that,' said Stanislav.

'Then the sarcophagus isn't Lilith's?' I asked.

'It could have belonged to a high priestess,' said Mrs Jackson, 'or even to a daughter of hers, trapped for thousands of years. Just like the priestess at the temple of Bel.'

'This is all rather far-fetched,' said Tilden.

'I don't think so. No matter what you say, I did see something.'

He shrugged his shoulders. 'And you think there's a cave underneath,' he said, pushing his plate away. 'Then I guess we'll have to see if you're right. Bilal and his son will continue to dig until dusk. Tomorrow, if the rain stops, we should have others shovelling.'

'But this has gone far enough,' I exclaimed. 'We have to seal the tomb tonight. You've dynamite . . .'

'Don't be ridiculous,' Tilden snapped.

'We'll have to close the site when we've finished,' said Mrs Jackson, 'if only while we wait for the necessary permit, and if we're to ship any of the jewellery out of Iraq we'll need to give an account of what we've taken.'

'All right,' conceded Tilden, 'we'll seal it after you've taken your photographs. And you can sleep safe in the knowledge that Lilith isn't going to visit you, but I'm not abandoning the dig. As soon as the rain stops, as soon as Fowler thinks it's safe for us to leave the site, then you can be on your way.'

'And the generator's left running?'

'You mean throughout the night?'

'Of course.'

'All right, we can dock your wages for the extra diesel.'

'You think I'm worried about my wages?'

'Nothing is going to happen to you,' said Stanislav.

'How do you know? At least three men have disappeared.'

Tilden shook his head. 'Bateman was dragged out of the Tigris, and I'm sure Clara and Suarez have their reasons for wanting to get as far away from here as possible. Surely you must know better than anyone else why they're not here?'

'And Bateman? Did he drown himself?'

While we were quarrelling, Sasha had walked into the mess. Susan was running out of medication. In Sasha's opinion, according to Stanislav, she was getting worse. If Susan was no better tomorrow then she would have to be taken to the consulate.

'All right,' said Tilden, 'but if she has to leave then I'll see to it. In the meantime we all have work to do.'

41

Coraggio, bully monster. That's what was needed as we slugged our way up the hill in the pouring rain. The sky remained slate-grey and the wind whistled eerily across the dark piles of sodden earth. Stanislav had been urging me to face it squarely. There was whisky in the belly. Coraggio, bully monster. Nothing had happened to those who had entered the underground tomb. Nothing would happen to me. He did his best to hold the black umbrella over both of us. The air tasted of grit and our glistening cheeks were stinging from the elements whipping mercilessly against our faces. 'In Circassia,' cried Stanislav, 'you can buy a young girl for less than the price of a mule: a pretty, dark-haired slave to serve you for the rest of your life.'

'You're suggesting I buy a girl?'

'It's the marketplace. Everything has its price in

Circassia. A capitalist's playground, though it attracts unwholesome minds: beggars, thieves, mountebanks with their bears and their monkeys, all crying out for baksheesh.'

'And this is where you met Sasha?'

He laughed at the question. 'Not Sasha. She comes from a very strict family. They have honour, family pride in Slovakia.' With his left hand he slapped his chest. 'More than Suarez had.'

'What do you mean?'

'He was a hypocrite. He didn't want Clara, but he would never have agreed to a divorce. He valued the appearance of respectability, he was a slave to the worst sort of decorum. That was his trouble, and it's yours. You think you have to deny the truth, that denial is necessary. Denial of what you want, denial of who you are, and then denial when what is bound to happen happens.'

'How perceptive of you.'

'It happens and you deny it. You squash yourself. Do you want to know why?'

'I'm sure you'll enlighten me.'

'Because you're living a lie.'

'Is this about my mental state or something else?'

Stanislav tutted, as if I'd insulted him. He was about to reply when something in the sky caught his attention. 'It seems we have visitors.' He gestured with a jerk of his head towards the ziggurat. Flapping lazily through the torrential rain were three dark birds. They flew in a ring, one bird following at equidistance from the other two. We stood and watched as they wheeled slowly above the building.

316

'Birds of prey,' uttered Stanislav. 'If I was a superstitious man, I'd say it's an ill omen.'

'It doesn't require superstition to be wary,' I replied, trying not to let my trepidation show. We started towards them, our eyes glancing ever upwards. It was an ominous sight, made even more sinister when the birds began to make a choking, cawing cry that floated out into the rain-soaked sky. Beneath the shrieking birds was the black triangle. It was a crumbling shape, a sullen symbol of malignant sadness.

With mud clinging to the soles of our boots we climbed the sodden ramp leading to the entrance. I looked down into the moat which ran round three-quarters of the ziggurat. The brown water had continued to rise since the morning and now looked to be about four foot deep. By nightfall, if it continued to rain, the water would be covering the outside ledge, or what was the outer roof of the ground-floor chamber.

There was no one to greet us at the entrance and it was not until we descended into the dripping heart of the ziggurat that we could hear the sound of digging. We moved silently down from chamber to chamber. In the one that had been filled with water there was still the stench of a stagnant pond. In our pool of light I kept my eyes fixed on each rung. It was only in the corner of my eye, or on the back of my neck, that I could sense those hidden things, shadows impatiently waiting for their realm to envelop us.

Bilal didn't at first acknowledge our arrival, but continued to dig; the rags round his head dark with sweat.

317

Hassan briefly paused, shovel in hand. He smiled as we crossed the tomb to where they were digging. His teeth were perfectly white and his dark eyes shimmered in the light. As I walked behind Stanislav I felt the need to look up, to see again the three angels carved into the stone ceiling. The thought of seeing the fourth suspended above me flashed across my mind. Yet why go looking for its ancient face? Was it calling to me, watching me? I felt for the amulet in my pocket. My sight was blinkered by the light, fixed to the corner, to the bent back of Hassan. I saw the pile of sand, and the partly submerged Bilal, a hand half raised in greeting. We stopped at the edge. They were digging into a rocky mouth, a mouth that was stopped, or rather choked with sand. Stanislav knelt down and felt the shining, polished stone.

'It's cold,' he said, looking up at me, 'and smooth. Primordial waves . . . forgotten hands.' Then he looked beyond me. I saw his forehead crease, a hand shaded his eyes against my lamp. He stood up. He was gazing at the ceiling. On his face was a puzzled expression.

'You've seen it?' I said, flushed with a strange mixture of terror and relief. I was clutching the bronze amulet in my fist. He was baffled. I only needed to look at him to know it was there, somewhere above us.

He brushed past me, holding his lamp above his head, trying to see whatever it was he'd glimpsed. Bilal whispered something to his son.

Stanislav must have heard him. The Russian called to the foreman in Arabic. Bilal answered. 'Hassan thought

318

he heard something earlier,' said Stanislav, his back to me. 'Bring your lamp over here.'

I took a step or two towards him.

'Over there,' said Stanislav, 'there was something in the corner.' He pointed at my lamp. 'Hold it above your head.'

I did as he asked, my eyes drawn to the ceiling.

'Shadows overlapping. They looked like wings.' There was a moment's silence. I wondered if the foreman and his son were looking. 'No,' he said, 'no. It's gone. Did you see it?'

'No.' I turned and saw that Bilal was staring at me. He called to Stanislav. The lamp was by my side again, trembling in my hand. I began whispering the Lord's Prayer. The subterranean tomb was its lair. It was hiding, submerged in darkness, warily circling above our heads.

'Larger than a bat,' said Stanislav. 'If the generator was here we could string bulbs along the ceiling, flood it with light.'

'But you saw it,' I said, 'hiding in the shadows.'

'I thought I saw something. If there was anything it's gone.' Stanislav placed his hand on my arm. 'You've got your amulet?'

I held out the bronze figure.

Did it crane its neck to see, and recoil at the sight? Did I hear dust falling from the ceiling or was it simply the sound of earth spilling from a spade? The hardest thing to do was to stand still.

'Good,' said Stanislav, 'a little superstition isn't a bad thing.' He glanced above my head. 'Let's take the photographs.'

319

'All right.' I was desperate to escape from the tomb, but I needed to keep my thoughts under control. I gave Stanislav my lamp to hold and urged him to stay close as I took out my Leica. 'I need the light.'

'Follow me,' he said as he carefully circled the pit where Bilal and his son were digging. The entrance to the cave was narrow, though it was impossible to say how far down it went. What they had unearthed so far could have been just the roof of the entrance: a yard wide and roughly two yards high. I thought we'd already released Lilith from her cell, but as I stared at the choked mouth I started to wonder. 'This is one of the inscriptions,' said Stanislav, pointing to the lip of the cave that stood a foot below the wall.

I knelt down and, with my lamp held above my head, took a photograph of the cuneiform marks that appeared to have been hurriedly scratched into the rock.

'A dozen more,' said Stanislav, 'and we can go back to the house.'

42

There was nothing I could say that would make Tilden stop digging. The mouth of the cave was yet to be cleared and he refused to abandon the site, but he wouldn't prevent me from leaving the expedition house. In the morning, if Fowler failed to appear, Mrs Jackson was to drive me to Mosul.

Tilden wasn't happy about me wanting to leave, but, at the supper table, he was more annoyed with Stanislav for allowing the foreman and his son to leave the site an hour before dusk.

'I thought you would have had the sense to keep them there,' he announced irritably. 'Someone needs to guard the tomb. You had no right to send them home, no right at all.'

'There are boards across the entrance to the cell and Bilal and his son have covered them in sand,' said Stanislav.

'That's hardly going to prevent anyone getting in,' Tilden complained.

'It's better than nothing,' said Stanislav. 'Everything's been taken, and no one will cross the bridge tonight, not unless they're prepared to be stuck here.'

'That's not the point,' responded Tilden. 'I want someone there. Who knows what we'll find beneath the sand.'

'Why not have a soldier standing guard?' suggested Mrs Jackson. 'I'm sure we can persuade one of them for a few rupees.'

Tilden sat back. 'That's not a bad idea. I suppose Fowler wouldn't mind. After all, they're here to protect us and our interests.'

'You can't send a man up there,' I objected. 'Not at night.'

'Why not?' he asked irritably. 'You think they're scared of the dark?'

'But there's something in the tomb.'

'In the tomb, or in your head?'

'In the tomb, God damn it. Mrs Jackson's seen it and so has Stanislav.'

'Is that true?' asked Tilden. 'Did you see this mythical bird?'

Stanislav hesitated. 'There is something about this dig which is starting to worry me.'

'What, Ward's feeble-mindedness?'

'That's not helping, Henry,' said Mrs Jackson. She turned to Stanislav. 'Did you see it?'

'There's something about the tomb,' he continued,

'something wrong. You've had these dreams, Ward's had them too. It seems there's . . .' It was difficult for the empiricist to admit that there could be anything other than the physical world and yet this was what he was trying to say.

'They're just dreams,' Tilden replied scornfully. 'Too much cheese, or me worrying about Susan. Ward's hallucinating, that's all. He can't take the heat. I feel a lot happier now that we've found something. I just wish Suarez was still here.' He grinned. 'I'd love to see his face. Can you imagine what Chicago's going to say?'

'Let's not get carried away,' said Mrs Jackson.

'We've only just skimmed the surface. This could give us Genesis on a plate.'

'But what if that story's not an allegory?' asked Mrs Jackson. 'What if it's all true?'

'Genesis is *only* a story, written after the fall of Nineveh,' replied Tilden, 'one of thirty-nine taken from Hebrew scripture. We're just digging down to its source.'

'If you're right, we could discover something which sheds light on a whole host of contradictions,' said Stanislav. 'The Old Testament is full of contradictions: man created both on the sixth and seventh day; stories taken from different myths: Hebrew, Babylonian, Assyrian.'

'And that's what you're looking for,' I asked, 'something which underlines those contradictions?'

'Exactly,' answered Stanislav. 'The Bible means books, books that either complement or contradict one another.'

'And with Lilith,' said Mrs Jackson, 'we have an incomplete record of what happened. Sin and death entered the world through the gates of Paradise. Lilith wasn't there. If people believe that Satan exists, that angels exist, then why not Lilith? What if there was a war a long time ago? What if Lilith was defeated?'

'By Pazuzu, another fictitious phantom, and one that's not mentioned in the Bible, as far as I'm aware.'

'But where does monotheism come from?' she asked. 'It started in Babylonia. The Babylonian Marduk conquered all – he defeated the demigods, including Pazuzu. Throughout the Old Testament there are subtle references to other gods: the kin of God saw the daughters of men were fair and took them for wives; the *kin* of God, the daughters of *men*. Monotheism didn't just happen. They killed the other gods, the other demons – only one survived, the most powerful, Marduk.'

'And Lilith wasn't killed,' I said. 'Lilith was entombed, sealed beneath the ziggurat. This isn't a temple or a palace, but a prison. A prison for one of their gods.'

'Marduk, our god,' continued Mrs Jackson, 'destroyed the others, but one survived, one originally blessed with immortality. And we're digging down to her cave, about to unleash a demon that has been trapped for centuries.'

'Mina, just listen to yourself,' said Tilden. 'This is teacup theology of the worst kind. We're here to excavate, to delve into the past, not to entertain poppycock theories emanating from the delusional mind of a man who seems to be making a habit of running away.'

'Well I won't be going anywhere, not until the ziggurat's sealed.' There, I had said it.

'But I thought you wanted to plead your case at the consulate tomorrow?'

'I do, I want to get as far away from here as possible, but Mrs Jackson's right. Lilith is still trapped and I want to make sure that she never escapes.'

Tilden was shaking his head. 'And how do you propose to do that, by boycotting the dig?' He pushed himself away from the table. 'I'm not staying to listen to any more. I need to find someone to guard the ziggurat, unless any of you theologians want to volunteer? No, I didn't think so.'

43

It was the middle of the night and I could hear the rain beating down. I'd drunk far too much whisky and needed the latrine. In my pyjamas, and with my untied boots spilling over my ankles, I staggered round the courtyard. The door to the washroom was ajar and several moths were dancing in the light that spilled out into the yard. There was a tin bath, an enamelled jug and a pitted mirror that had once stood upon a chest of drawers. It was strange for someone to be washing after midnight and I glanced in as I went by. Crouching in the shadows was a woman, her back turned towards me. She was examining herself in a hand mirror. Her pale shoulders and wet hair were visible from behind, her body covered in a thin slip. I thought it was Susan, though her skin appeared to be almost luminescent beneath the bulb.

In the latrine I thought I heard a whisper, a voice calling

to me. I buttoned my flies and shook my head, yet as I left to return to my room I heard her voice again, Susan's voice imploring me to come to her. I paused outside the washroom. Her face was turned from the mirror. Her beauty seemed to shimmer, her velvet eyes were shining in an unearthly manner. She stepped nimbly through the shadows and out into the rain. Standing beside the lorry, she beckoned me towards her. She exalted in her sexuality and I watched her closely, desire of the filthiest kind coursing through my veins. I'd never noticed before how long her fingernails were. I glanced down at the muddy yard, trying to make sense of what was happening, where my thoughts were taking me. I saw her calves, her feet. Her slip dropped to the ground. Something inside made me want to look up, to dismiss what I'd seen, to tear my gaze away. Yet the sight of the brindled nails which covered her toes, now half hidden by the slip, startled me. Where were her feet? Why the pronounced claws of an owl? The lust I had felt transformed itself into fear, yet I was unable to tear my gaze away from her. The light from the washroom slowly collapsed in on itself. She walked with slow inevitability towards me. I tried to breathe. I lifted my head and felt a rush of air. Suddenly her face was merely inches away from mine. Her scarlet lips were parted, ready to press themselves against my flesh. I recall the scent of lavender, the warmth of her smooth cheek against mine. Yet there was the smell of her breath, the fetid, stale smell of a barn at the end of a summer's day. Something hot and moist was snaking between my

328

lips, into my mouth. I tried to pull my face away, but a hand firmly held the back of my head.

When I opened my eyes I was back in bed. The porter had found me in the middle of the yard. He'd summoned Stanislav, to whom he explained what had happened. The Russian sat at my bedside, lit by the paraffin lamp I had left burning. I tried to tell him that I'd seen Susan, that my overwrought imagination had twisted her into some sort of harpy. But as I was saying it, I knew I'd been tricked. One of her daughters had beckoned me towards her, caught me in her arms before I'd collapsed. My pyjama cord was loose round my waist. I let my hand slide beneath the brushed cotton. I was slippery and sore and I groaned at the thought of what must have happened out there in the cold yard. I looked at my hand and saw that the fingertips were rouged with blood. A grazing of skin, a back that ached from the pounding it had suffered. I turned my hand towards Stanislav. He winced at the sight of it, but offered no explanation.

'Do you need something to help you sleep?' he asked.

I shook my head.

'I'm going to check on the others. I'll be back later.' He picked up his lamp from the chest of drawers.

'The light,' I cried, reaching out towards him.

'You want me to leave my lamp?'

'Switch it on.'

'The generator's off. It's the middle of the night.' He flicked the electric up and down; a solid click, but nothing else.

'Tilden agreed. He said the light . . .'

'He promises a lot of things.'

I turned away to face the wall. My tormented mind was racing, trying to scale the corruption of my flesh, what was left of my soul. We forget what's under the appearance of life. We forget the blood and nerves working under the skin. The skin is all that most of us see. What had happened had soiled everything, every thought, every fibre in my body. A match flared behind my back, a match to light a candle. A hand briefly held my shoulder. I listened as he pulled the door shut, shifted my focus for a second onto his leaving; a second's respite from ignominy and self-loathing. I don't know how long I lay there trembling. There was no morality left, no right or wrong. Every time I tried to make sense of what had happened the shameless spectre leered at me, its greedy face trespassing through my mind. This time I had knowingly succumbed and I was fouled beyond redemption.

44

The gunshot didn't startle me. I was awake and knew at once what it was, what was out there under the cover of darkness. It echoed against the ancient bricks, and bounded across the desolate land. The soldier had fired his rifle. Silence, and then a second shot rang out. I heard voices in the courtyard. There was the voice of the sergeant. He was ordering someone to stay inside, pleading with them to get back from the gate. They ignored him. His skin was the wrong colour to be giving orders. The charade was over.

Tired of the wasteland where penitents wander, I climbed out of bed, curious to see how the tragedy would unfold. My back was bruised, but I stood up, one hand rubbing at my spine. A gust of wind hit the house, causing it to rock on its foundations, the doors to momentarily bow. My mind was spinning wild fantasies, but no one can remain terrified forever. I was beyond redemption and therefore there was nothing left to fear. I had nothing left to lose.

I opened my door. Mrs Jackson, wrapped in her dressing gown, was standing a couple of yards to the left of me. The rain had started again and she was sheltering beneath the overhanging roof.

'Are you all right, Mr Ward?' she asked, a look of genuine concern lit by her candle.

'Fine,' I lied. I had no grasp, no understanding of the value of life. I felt mine was spent and so there was nothing worth saving. The thought of Clara and what I had lost had made me mad. I pulled on my trousers and Bateman's mackintosh.

Tilden, holding his torch in one hand and waving his service revolver around in the other, was remonstrating with the sergeant. He was wearing little more than his own navy mackintosh, his pale calves visible above his boots. Stanislav was fully dressed and stood with a pummelled umbrella just behind Tilden. I could see the cook and porter watching from inside the kitchen. Sasha, in a pink slip and woollen cardigan, was leaning against the doorframe of her room. From each doorway there came a triangle of lamplight, softening and then merging in the centre of the yard. I steadily walked inside my illuminated path towards the gate. The mud squelched beneath my boots. I'd been foolish and unmanly. Shame and the fear of a breakdown had caused me to cower, to collapse. I'd reached my nadir. I was striding forward, wanting more than anything to be reckless and brave. If nothing else, Clara would hear that I fought against it.

Tilden had lost his temper. He was shouting at the sergeant, jabbing at him with his torch. 'I want you to go and find your friend and then I want the damn gate closed. You understand?'

The sergeant was saying that he should stay at the house. That he had to guard the house.

'That's my job,' said Tilden, his mackintosh falling open to reveal a grubby-looking undergarment. Unaware of the ridiculous figure he was cutting, he kept thrusting his torch aggressively towards the sergeant's chest. 'You go. I stay.'

'I'll go and see what's happened,' I said calmly.

'No,' said Stanislav. 'You're not well enough to go out there.'

'What did you say?' asked Tilden, channelling his frustration towards me.

'If you lend me the torch and the revolver I'll go and see what's happened.'

'Are you drunk?' he asked. 'Have you lost your mind?'

'It's out there, but I'm not afraid any more.' I pocketed the amulet and held out my hand. It wasn't exactly revenge I was after, such a thing I thought impossible, but what was driving me forward was some strange compulsion to face up to the fiend; damned, as it were, but not defeated.

Tilden hesitated. He didn't want to give over his revolver, especially to a madman.

'I'm not giving you the gun.'

'I'll go with him,' said Stanislav.

'I'm not giving it to you either. It stays here with me.'

The porter was standing by the gate.

'Then we'll go without it,' I said. 'Unlock the gate.'

The sergeant protested. He didn't want anyone to leave the expedition house.

'Unlock it,' said Tilden.

I stretched out my hand again. 'If you won't give me the revolver, then give me the torch.'

'Here,' he said, giving it to Stanislav. 'Make sure he doesn't bolt.' He turned to the porter. 'Let them out and then crank up the generator.'

'The soldier's name?' I asked the sergeant.

'Dhesi, Private Srujay Dhesi.'

The porter uncoiled the chain from between the bars and pulled the gate ajar. Stanislav followed me out of the yard and into the night. Neither moonlight nor stars were visible and in the pouring rain we paused to take stock of the walk ahead.

'I thought you said we shouldn't stray from the house at night,' said Stanislav, giving me the umbrella to hold.

'They've only taken those who've tried to cross the river.'

'Perhaps we should take the Ford,' said Stanislav. 'It'll be quicker. You can drive, can't you?'

In answer I turned back into the yard, and called to Tilden to give me the keys.

45

The engine shuddered then roared into life. I switched on the headlamps. The darkness leaped backwards. Those sheltering in front of the gate shaded their eyes and moved to the side. I put the lorry into gear and inched forward. We slowly rolled through the gates and followed the muddy track uphill. Outside the yard it was a quagmire and almost immediately the wheels began to spin.

'I thought we'd lost you,' said Stanislav in a voice that was barely audible above the noise of the engine.

I could sense his eyes upon me but, with the lorry sliding all over the place, I couldn't look away from the track ahead. 'You still don't think they're real?'

'I'd prefer to think of it as a memory or a dream.'

'That gives you comfort?'

'Memories can't kill, and neither can dreams.'

'But what I saw was real, what attacked me was real.'

'It seemed real to you.'

'I'll prove to you that they exist, that they prey upon men. This is some sort of physical manifestation, and it has nothing to do with what happened to me.'

'All right,' said Stanislav. 'I'm trying hard not to believe.'

There it was: the brick pinnacle of Lilith's prison. It was a dark, shining block climbing above the muddy ramparts. It wasn't the steepest part of the track but the lorry was starting to slide. The mud seemed to be thicker and the wheels had started to spin uncontrollably. It was rolling back and lacked the grip to take it any further forward. I judged we were close enough and, afraid of getting stuck if I tried to climb any more, stopped the lorry within fifty yards of the entrance. 'End of the line,' I announced as calmly as any conductor.

Stanislav switched on his torch and the beam lit up the cabin. Reflected on the inside of the windscreen were tired, impassive faces. 'Are you going to leave the head-lamps on?' he asked.

'Yes. If he's dead we'll be back within minutes, if he's alive . . .' I didn't know long the lorry's battery would last, but I was willing to take the chance.

As soon as we got out Stanislav unfurled his black umbrella in a vain attempt to protect himself from the rain. 'We shout. If we don't hear anything we head back to the lorry.'

In the headlamps our shadows reeled against the brick wall of the chamber as we squelched towards the entrance. The wind was gusting and the rain continued to beat

336

against the flapping umbrella. We were twenty yards away when Stanislav had to stop to wipe the film of water from his spectacles. Beneath our boots the track had turned to mud and rivulets of water were running down towards the lorry.

Stanislav said something, but the wind snatched his words away. He tried again, louder this time. 'What's the Indian's name?'

'Dhesi,' I shouted above the noise of the storm.

Stanislav swept the torch's beam through the slanting rain and across the muddy landscape. On either side of the track we saw stones piled in neat pyramids stretching out into the darkness. Beyond the ziggurat blackness enveloped everything. There was no sign of the soldier.

Stanislav called out.

For a split second, the hammering on the umbrella ceased; a silence made audible by its fleeting presence. We looked at one another, our faces lit from below in a ghastly manner. Had the wind carried the rain away? We would have felt it. No, something had flown above our heads. Tilting back the battered umbrella, Stanislav lifted the torch, illuminating silver drops falling from the invisible sky. Whatever had sailed across our path had gone, yet the beam from Stanislav's torch suddenly seemed to give little protection against whatever it was that had murdered the others.

'A cormorant,' said Stanislav, though we both knew the bird's wingspan was hardly large enough to stop the falling rain. And what bird would dare to fly through such a storm? The alternative was out there, gliding down towards the lorry, towards the house, an alternative too harrowing to contemplate. We continued to make our way up the track to the ziggurat. I didn't want to stop. What good would it have done us if we'd paused to consider our situation? We were out there to find the Indian soldier, to rescue him if we could.

Stanislav, his hand cupped round his mouth, called out again. Nothing; just the drumming rain and the howling wind. We started forward, the umbrella pointing ahead.

The track began to level out. In front, merely yards away, was the square peak of the ziggurat. It stood like a brick fist which had thumped its way out of the earth. We stopped at the wooden planks that crossed the muddy bridge to the upper chamber. The trenches on either side had become moats that were close to overflowing. 'We should look around,' I yelled. 'If he's here we won't have to go inside.' Was I more afraid of what was in the tomb or up in the night sky?

Stanislav wanted to get out of the rain, but he agreed to follow me. We started to circle the slippery banks of the moat; the piles of smooth stones glimmered in the torch's light. At first the way was unmarked, but then I noticed the watery outline of footprints in the thick mud. They were the soldier's, and beside them there were strange prints, claw marks, the padded paws of some predatory creature. 'You can't say they belong to a hyena,' I cried.

'What?'

'There.' I pointed at the patterns in the mud.

He acknowledged the footprints, but stubbornly refused to see anything else.

In the incessant rain we silently followed them around the ziggurat. The prints seemed to be everywhere. Either there was more than one, or whatever it was had been circling the place for hours. We stopped again at the wooden planks that led to the entrance and Stanislav called out again in every direction. There was still no answer.

Crossing the narrow bank of earth that connected the entrance to the ziggurat I glanced down at the swelling moat. With each gust of wind the surface of the water shimmered, rippling against the muddy banks and ancient bricks. I realised we could fill at least one of the chambers with water: the roof of the second chamber jutted out of the water, but the third and fourth were below the water-line. From the inside we could knock through. All that was needed was a hammer and chisel. If we hammered through the ceiling of the third chamber we could drain the moat. We just needed to seal the floor, to fix a cover back in place. It was a makeshift solution, but better than none.

'Do you want to go inside?' Stanislav asked.

'I'm not running away.'

He shone the torch into the chamber. Amongst the scattered paraffin lamps was the soldier's rifle. I let Stanislav clamber over the wet bricks and then followed him inside. He propped his umbrella against a wall while I picked up the rifle. There was a spent cartridge lying beside it. I shoved the bolt forward and the second cartridge fell to the floor.

'Pity we don't have any ammunition,' he remarked, his voice quieter out of the storm.

'It doesn't matter. I doubt bullets saved the soldier.' There was just something reassuring about the cold, heavy weight of it. I offered him the rifle.

'Keep it,' he said, 'and take the torch. I'll find a lamp.'

I stood up and slung the rifle over my shoulder. 'We should go down.'

'Should we?' he asked. We were speaking in hushed voices as if we'd suddenly become afraid of disturbing something in its lair. 'I don't think it'll do any good.'

'You want to go back?'

'How about we wait until daylight?'

I shook my head. His uncertainty was furnishing me with authority, giving me a courage I hadn't felt for a long time. I agreed to go first, so long as he kept the lamp above my head.

On the first few rungs my grip slid across the cold mud left by my boots, but I kept my eyes cast down to the brick floor. Looking back it's easy to say that I was reckless, that I was in too much of a hurry. It was only after he'd clambered down and joined me in the second chamber that I paused to consider what could be hidden beneath our feet. Through the entrance the headlamps from the lorry had illuminated a corner of the ceiling, and here the torch played powerfully against the walls. In the next chamber, which was twice the size, the beam would lose half of its intensity.

At the foot of the ladder I glanced nervously at Stanislav.

He cupped his hands round his mouth and, standing over the hole in the stone floor, he hollered down. 'Dhesi!'

There was no response. No sound other than our breathing and the rain above.

He called again. We were straining our ears.

Nothing.

'We're too late,' said Stanislav.

I wanted to agree, but couldn't betray myself again. My courage was starting to fail. Part of me wanted to leave the ziggurat and cower in the expedition house until it grew light. Yet I couldn't give up on the private. 'No. We have to press on.' I held the torch by my face, its beam streaming across my chest and legs.

In the third chamber we found what was left of the soldier. His body lay crumpled in a corner. From the ladder his greatcoat and khaki shorts appeared to be too large. His turban lay half unravelled across the floor. I waited until Stanislav was standing next to me before crossing over to the corpse. The first thing my eyes were drawn to was the ammunition pouch attached to his belt, though Stanislav's curse lifted my gaze to the private's shrivelled face. 'It's just like Bateman,' he said, his voice carrying the revulsion he felt at having made such a dreadful discovery.

I knelt down beside the desiccated corpse and looked into its dark eyes, which had settled back into the skull's pink sockets. Through the translucent skin the soldier's pale cheekbones were almost visible. It was a disturbing sight made even more gruesome by his thin lips, which

341

had fallen into a hideous grin. I reached for the young man's turban and folded a length of the damp cloth over his shrunken face.

'What could have done that?' whispered Stanislav, the colour having drained from his cheeks.

'One of Lilith's daughters.'

'It's blood they're after?'

'It has to be.'

'Did you hear something?' said Stanislav, turning.

'What?' I said, hurriedly unbuckling the soldier's belt.

'It sounded like a dog whimpering.'

Stanislav crept towards the opening to the chamber below while I quickly put the leather belt round my waist. He sat on his heels and listened above the ladder. I quietly loaded the rifle and then went and knelt down beside him.

'Listen,' he said.

I leaned over the gap in the floor, one hand supporting my weight. I was afraid to point the torch down into the black chasm beneath. At first I couldn't hear anything. Then, after straining my ears for what felt like several minutes, I heard a plaintive, snivelling cry. Whatever it was, it was afraid and in pain.

I shone the torch down into the chamber beneath. There was nothing to see. The whimpering had stopped. 'Look,' whispered Stanislav. I quietly shuffled round to see where he was pointing. The makeshift entrance to the tomb had been uncovered, and the boards had been split and tossed aside. The opening was a gaping hole: a hatchway to

Lilith's world through which we had to descend if we were to find the source of the miserable sound.

I stepped onto the ladder. Above me stood Stanislav, the lamp held above my head. As I descended the torch's beam cut swathes through the darkness. Trying not to think about what might have been hiding in the shadows I climbed off the last rung and lifted the rifle from my back. I gripped the wooden stock, and pointed the barrel towards the opening. Behind me I could hear Stanislav descending rung by rung. The lamplight was dancing on the walls above me. I couldn't say whether it was the noise of the ladder or the dancing light that stirred the wretch below, but suddenly the cries started again. There was an urgency about them. Soon I was grasping at words, at a voice that was at once familiar and yet, because of the ordeal he must have suffered, at a pitch that was almost inhuman. I called down and my cry was met with a yell of anguish, a yell that cemented my fear that this was someone I knew.

'Fowler,' I shouted, 'is that you?'

'Thank God,' he cried.

I shone the torch down into the cell and we saw him crawling on his hands and knees across the dirt. He was naked, his back, hips and thighs covered in deep, clotted gashes. With one hand he reached up towards the light, his face bruised and bloody. It looked as if his moustache was half hanging from his bleeding lips. 'Get me out of here,' he cried, 'for God's sake, hurry!'

'Where are the ladders?' I asked.

343

'There,' replied Stanislav. I looked down to where he was pointing and saw, behind Fowler's naked back, the scattered rungs and split wood. Each one had been torn apart. A sound floated across the chamber, the faint almost melodious sound of something softly chuckling to itself.

'Suarez,' Fowler was calling, 'is Suarez with you?'

'We need to get him out.'

'He was in the cave,' shouted Fowler.

'There's rope,' said Stanislav, 'back at the house.'

'You think we can pull him out?'

'Possibly, or we could use it to bind two ladders together. 'We'll have to get it.'

'We need to be quick. The light,' I said and lifted the torch. The beam trickled across the brick floor.

Fowler screamed and I immediately returned the fading light, bathing the wretched man below.

'They're in the shadows,' Fowler wailed, 'in the dark.' He stood up, though he was unable to straighten his back, and cupped his hands as if he could capture the torch's beam. 'Please,' he pleaded, 'get me out of here, get me out before they return.'

'We'll light the other lamps,' said Stanislav. 'We'll rescue him.'

What happened next made my heart lurch. From above we heard the snapping of wood and the tumbling of skittles. The sound was repeated, louder than the first, then again, closer, louder, the rungs falling on the floor above.

We'd both turned our faces at the sound of splintering wood and by the time the third ladder had been wrenched apart we were standing up. Fowler was screaming again, unable to appreciate why the light had suddenly deserted him. But we had no time to offer him an explanation. When we saw the last ladder, our only means of escape, being lifted from the floor and into the darkness above we threw ourselves across the chamber and grabbed hold of the last few rungs. Whatever held the other end had not anticipated the sudden change in weight and so the heels of the ladder fell back to the floor. Yet the struggle wasn't over. There were screams above now, unearthly, high-pitched screams, childlike in their annoyance and undisguised spite. They wailed in competition with those of the broken man below. The ladder started to lift again. How many there were on the other end was impossible to say. I could feel the struts being forced apart, the wood creaking as it was hauled and twisted. Though my arm was through the ladder, the elbow bent round a rung, I managed to guide the torch's beam towards the hatch. The effect was instantaneous. The ladder fell back with a thud and the screams from above fell silent.

'Keep it in the light,' cried Stanislav, though I had no intention of doing otherwise. 'We need to get out,' he said, 'before it's too late.'

'But they're down there with him.'

'And they're above. There's nothing we can do. We have to leave.'

Fowler was crying out in anguish, crying out to be rescued. 'We'll get rope,' I shouted, 'ladders . . .'

'Don't leave me!' he screamed from his subterranean cell.

But Stanislav, with his lamp held above his head, had already started to climb the ladder and there was nothing I could do but follow him. Fowler railed and cursed as the last glimmer of light disappeared. 'They're coming back,' he half sobbed, half yelled; we were leaving him to die. As the light receded his screams grew louder.

I climbed rung after rung, desperate to get away, yet wary of what must have been floating in the darkness. Stanislav helped me into the chamber. As he started to lift the ladder Fowler's screaming suddenly stopped. Silence. I glanced at Stanislav. With one hand I held the torch, with the other I steadied the rifle slung over my shoulder. A bullet would have had little effect, but the solid feel of the Enfield at least provided me with some sort of comfort. I shouted Fowler's name. I pointed the beam down into the chamber below and called again. There was no answer. His last cry had been so unnaturally high it could only have meant one thing. There was no point in returning.

Outside the rain continued to hammer down on the sweating landscape. The unlit lamps that had been left in the chamber had all been smashed, the glass and metal scattered across the floor. The torch was shining half as brightly. We had to get back to the house.

Without a word we clambered out and quickly shuffled our way across the slippery planks. There was something splashing in the moat. Neither of us dared to turn around to see what it was. We began to run heedlessly down the muddy track towards the lorry. The rain stung our faces, and the wind did its best to knock us off course. More than once a foot slid from under me and only by spreading my arms wide did I stop myself from falling. I was sprinting towards the lorry, into its headlamps.

We threw ourselves into the cab, the doors slamming in unison. Within seconds something hammered into the lorry, thumping down onto the cab's roof. Stanislav threw himself away from the door, cursing in Russian. 'Start the engine,' he cried, his hand clutching at the steering wheel.

I turned the key; the headlamps dimmed, the engine spluttered. It groaned, shuddered, turned over, and collapsed back into silence. The sound of claws scratching at the bowing metal could be heard just above our heads.

I tried the key again, twisting it as hard as I could, forcing it as far as it'd turn. Again the groaning protest, the revolving drum. My fingers were sliding across the key, yet I managed to hold it firmly in place and finally forced the vital spark. It coughed again and then, like a beast disturbed from its slumber, it began to roar. Stanislav cried out in triumph and let go of the wheel. I crunched the gear stick into reverse. There was blackness in the mirror. We were rolling backwards, turning, lumbering over mud. The brakes whined, I changed gear and sharply turned the steering wheel away from the house and then towards it. The headlamps arced through the darkness, sliced through shadows that went bounding for cover.

Silver rivulets were running on the slippery track. We

were sliding down the hill, one foot pressing lightly on a pedal, the other hovering above the brake. The thing must have taken flight. Stanislav was leaning forward, his nose almost pressed against the clouded windscreen. He'd seen enough to convince him that there was something out there, something beyond our comprehension. What had happened in the ziggurat was enough to persuade the most hard-bitten sceptic. It didn't need to be said. We'd heard them laughing and screaming from the shadows, felt their strength, and had witnessed their capability to destroy. Fowler was their plaything, their toy.

'Stop,' yelled Stanislav.

'Why?' I managed to utter before he yelled again and grabbed my arm. I hit the brakes and the lorry slalomed for some twenty or thirty yards. On Stanislav's side of the cab I glimpsed a crouched figure running towards us. A glance, even through the smeared windscreen, was enough to tell me it was white and naked. The lorry uncontrollably swerved towards it, causing the figure to backpedal. The softest of thuds and we slid to a halt.

46

Stanislav, holding the torch, shoved open the cab door and leaned out, his body twisted round in order to see what we'd left in our wake. 'He's there,' he said, before jumping down and heading towards the back of the lorry.

The motor was still running, the headlamps spilling their light over the cratered mud. Stanislav's door had been left ajar and I could hear the rain above the drumming of the engine. I wanted to pull his door shut, but I knew I had to get out. To see what it was.

I saw him kneeling down, cradling a head in his hands. He called out, beckoning me to hurry. The mud was thick and clung to my boots. I had no light and suddenly felt vulnerable. I ran as quickly as I could towards them. The torch's dismal beam lit the figure's hair, and a dim patina of light crawled across the man's bare shoulder, and his naked thigh.

'It's Suarez,' I exclaimed in disbelief.

'He's bruised, but I think nothing's broken,' cried Stanislav. It was Suarez, naked, yet half coated in mud, trembling and quietly sobbing.

He groaned as we lifted him to his feet. The wind continued to rage; the rain lashing at our hands, stinging our faces. With what strength we had left in our tired limbs we dragged him through the mud and back to the cab. I tried to hold him upright as Stanislav wrestled the door open. Together we pulled him up from his knees and managed to bundle him inside. He was whimpering, pleading for salvation. The Lord's Prayer was stuck in his throat. 'Deliver us,' he kept saying, the two words rushing in and out. His limbs were like jelly. Black shapes swirled around us, flapping above, crawling through the mud, but shy of the light.

I climbed into the cab. Suarez sat slumped between us, his head bowed, water dripping into his lap.

'What happened?' asked Stanislav.

No answer, other than an exhausted repetition of 'Deliver us from evil.'

'You escaped?'

The same response, though even with my head bent towards his it was hard to hear what he saying. I put the lorry into gear and it started sliding towards the house. There was no need to accelerate. We were crashing through the night, plummeting through rain and mud. As we shot through the gates I braked hard. The lorry

350

careered into the courtyard, narrowly avoided the palm tree, and skidded to a halt.

I turned the engine off. We sat and listened to the rain drumming on the roof, almost too afraid to open the doors. Condensation ran down the inside of the windscreen. Suarez's head remained bowed. We could hear his teeth chattering.

'Where are they?' demanded Stanislav.

I sounded the horn, but the courtyard remained in darkness. The deathly stillness of the house made us fear that something terrible had happened.

'Didn't Tilden have the generator running?'

Stanislav gripped the torch. 'Why don't you turn the headlamps back on?'

I did as he suggested. We weren't going anywhere.

Stanislav, the torch's light flickering across his thigh, opened his door an inch or two and started to yell. Silence, other than the beating rain. Then, from across the courtyard, a woman's voice called out. I turned to see a dim light coming from the common room.

'Over there,' I said, 'in the common room. We'll drag him out; make a dash for it. Are you ready?'

Stanislav nodded.

I flung open the cab door and, clutching the rifle with one hand, skated over the mud. Having wheeled round the front of the lorry I almost slid into Stanislav's door as he threw it open. I grabbed the handle as he jumped down and together we pulled Suarez from the cab and dragged him towards the common room. Sasha, a paraffin lamp in one hand, beckoned us to hurry.

Once we were inside, Mrs Jackson quickly closed and bolted the door. Susan, almost lost in the candlelight, was sitting perfectly still on the divan and appeared to be oblivious to the naked man who lay sprawled across the rug. 'My God,' cried Mrs Jackson at the sight of Suarez, 'what happened to him?'

'We found him outside,' answered Stanislav. 'He hasn't said much, other than asking for matches.'

'But you've found him,' she gasped as she bent down to rest a hand on the crumpled figure. Suarez, with his knees now tucked towards his chest and his arms wrapped tightly round his shins, said nothing in reply. Taking the blanket from the armchair, Sasha covered his shivering body.

'Here's whisky for him,' said Stanislav, passing Mrs Jackson a tumbler.

'He's seen her,' whispered Susan from the divan. 'Hasn't he? He's been with her.' She leaned forward as if drawn to his suffering. Her face was suddenly aglow with an awful interest in the shattered man.

Suarez, his damp head held by Mrs Jackson's hand, coughed as he swallowed the whisky. His dark, sunken eyes were looking up into hers. It was the first time I'd seen him open them since we'd rescued him. Mrs Jackson was murmuring soothing words, reassuring him while the nightmare rattled around in his head.

'You've been with her,' said Susan. She struggled to her

stockinged feet and stood swaying on her tiptoes at the edge of the Persian rug. 'He's played the filthy goat, and Clara will hear of this, she'll hear of the dreadful things he's done.'

Sasha moved across to Susan, ready to restrain her if she came any closer.

'But he doesn't belong to Clara any more. Does he?' Susan was staring at me. She repeated her question, and repeated it again and again until it became a demented chant.

'Who does he belong to?' I asked calmly, taking hold of her arm.

An incredulous smile flickered across her face. 'Why, he belongs to her, of course. But you know that. Her daughters have visited you. And Clara, Clara was just like them, wasn't she?'

'Clara wasn't the first,' Mrs Jackson exclaimed.

Susan bridled and clenched her hands; hard fists that wanted to rain down on the widow who sat stroking Suarez's head.

'And what do you know of her?' asked Stanislav.

'I know she visits my husband in the middle of the night,' she replied in a defiant manner. 'I can hear them, their filthy groans. I can smell her on his skin, his face. It makes me retch. These men,' she cried, 'they're rotten to the core, these shady monkeys that dress as men. And she knows them for what they are. This shambling horror is theirs, their fault, their guilt.'

'And where is she now?' Stanislav asked.

353

'Outside,' answered Susan. 'Outside with her daughters, waiting for the light to fail. Would you like to see her?'

'And where's Tilden?' I asked.

'He's with her, of course.'

'It was dreadful,' cried Mrs Jackson, 'just dreadful. While you were gone . . .' I waited for her to elaborate while Sasha told her husband what had happened. 'Dreadful,' Mrs Jackson repeated. 'It was there on the roof.'

'They heard footsteps,' explained Stanislav, 'just after the generator failed. The wind was howling, but the wailing that they heard was something else. They saw nothing, but running shadows. Then the banging of Tilden's door, screeching, the flapping of wings.'

Sasha spoke again. Even Suarez appeared to be listening.

'When the noise, the tempest stopped, they ran to one another. They ran here.' Stanislav asked her a question. 'She thinks the cook and houseboy are with the porter. She hasn't seen the sergeant.'

'The soldier?' asked Mrs Jackson, recalling why we'd left the house.

'Dead,' I said. 'Just like Bateman and . . .'

'And Tilden?' suggested Mrs Jackson.

'I don't know. Where is he?'

'He's in his room,' she answered. 'You must get him out.'

Susan, holding a handkerchief to her mouth, was whispering into the clenched ball of cotton, rocking backwards and forwards on the divan. Sasha had her arm round her

354

trying to comfort the woman. At first Susan's words were muffled, but then she lifted her head and looked directly at me. Her eyes were pink, her cheeks flushed by the memory. 'It was shining in the dark,' she said hoarsely. 'I saw it.' She began to cry. Sasha gently put a hand to Susan's face. She allowed her head to fall against Sasha's shoulder. 'I saw it,' she sobbed, her tears falling onto Sasha's blouse. 'Its black eyes were staring into mine. I saw them together and it was riding him, moaning, and he was smiling up at it.'

47

Tilden's door was ajar. Tentatively, with the barrel of the rifle, I pushed it open. Stanislav held the lamp aloft and we gazed inside. The mattress was half off the bed, the blanket and sheets strewn across the floor. There was no sign of Tilden, or the creature that Susan had seen. We entered the room.

A corner of the striped mattress lay against the cabinet. I propped the rifle against the wall and while doing so glimpsed through the bars of the iron bedstead a crumpled pair of pyjamas lying in the shadows cast by our lamps. But they weren't simply discarded pyjamas and I recoiled as they fashioned themselves into a corpse. It was the same shrunken figure we'd seen at the ziggurat. It was what was left of Tilden.

Stanislav, stepping onto the mattress, lowered his lamp towards the bed. There he was, stuffed in a corner, like unwanted jumble. The brick floor around where the skin and bones lay was smeared with blood.

'Poor bugger,' I said.

Stanislav retreated and I picked up my rifle. Together we threw the mattress back over the bedstead. 'Check the bedside drawer,' said Stanislav. 'Batteries,' he answered to my unspoken question.

Inside the drawer were two batteries, along with his penknife. I pocketed the items, my fingertips brushing the bronze figure of Pazuzu. On the floor was his revolver. I bent down and picked it up. 'It hasn't been fired.'

'I'll take it,' said Stanislav. 'You keep hold of the rifle.'

Outside there was a dreadful drumming in the sky. The lorry's headlamps were glowing, but casting little light. Better to switch them off and save what was left. Too afraid to look up, we hurried first to the cab and then back to the common room.

48

'How long had she been visiting Henry?' asked Stanislav.

'Before he arrived,' said Susan, her chin jutting towards me.

'You mean Ward?'

'Who else? It was while Stephen was here.'

'Bateman.'

'That's when she first appeared to him.'

'But this isn't Lilith,' said Mrs Jackson.

'Then what was it?' asked Susan.

'One of her daughters. Our digging has brought them here. Succubi have been sleeping with your husband, with Mr Ward. If Lilith hasn't escaped, then we still have a chance. Her forces have only just started to gather.'

'And Suarez,' I said, 'one of her daughters must have taken him.'

Mrs Jackson looked down at the man who lay upon

the rug. 'They probably wanted him as an offering, a sacrifice. Has he told you anything about his ordeal?'

'Nothing.'

His eyes were closed, yet he was whimpering like a dog in its sleep.

'They seem to be breeding and feeding,' continued Mrs Jackson, 'but once satisfied they could be preparing the way for Lilith.'

'Fowler was down there,' I said. 'He was caught, but we were too late to save him.'

'Poor man,' said Mrs Jackson. 'He was married with a family.'

A gust of wind pushed against the bolted door and the paraffin lamps flickered in the cold air. The fire was dying and there was the constant dripping of water into the hearth. Susan nestled into Sasha's shoulder, her red hair falling over her face.

'So we wait until it grows light,' said Stanislav.

'Unless you want to see what's wrong with the generator?' suggested Mrs Jackson.

I shook my head. 'I think we should stay together.'

'I agree,' said Stanislav. 'There's no point in risking our necks. The lamps should last till morning, and we have a torch. We just have to be careful. When it's light we'll—'

A short high-pitched scream interrupted the Russian. It came from somewhere in the house. Suarez shuddered violently on the floor, clasping his legs tightly against his stomach. We listened, hardly able to breathe. The wind continued to howl, water continued to drip while Suarez rapidly mouthed incoherent lines.

'It must have broken in,' whispered Mrs Jackson.

Stanislav and I went over to the door. Sasha said something, but her husband waved her warning away. We stood a foot from the door. I was leaning forward, trying to listen, when something punched at the wooden boards with such a force that they appeared to buckle. We reared back from the blow. Stanislav pointed his revolver at the door. Susan was shrieking. I could hear Sasha trying to calm her down, trying to restrain her.

Another scream from the other side of the door split the night.

Stanislav held the revolver in his trembling hands. I was shining the torch at the door, trying my best to hold it steady.

'Don't open the door,' Susan was crying, 'don't let her in. Not again. Not again.'

A wind began to blow from beneath the door and flecks of rainwater were scattered across the floor. The candles along the fireplace flickered. The flames in the lamps, although encased in glass, started to twist, to spiral downwards. What light there was, save for the torch, ebbed and flowed across the walls. There was something thumping above our heads, some blasphemous abomination stamping on the roof of the common room. The wind continued to circle round the room. Suarez, who was trying to crawl away from it, headed towards the divan. I gave the torch to Mrs Jackson and quickly retrieved the rifle from beside the chair. I put the Enfield against my shoulder and, with my finger on the trigger, pointed it at the door.

The candles had all been blown out, but the paraffin lamps still burned. The stomping and scraping above our heads stopped abruptly. The wind suddenly died and as the noise around us ceased so too did the cries of anguish within the room. We waited, the torch, revolver and rifle pointing at the door; those behind me were huddled together on the divan. For several interminable minutes we stood motionless.

I remember the weight of the rifle, the growing stiffness in my arms. Someone was whispering. I glanced round and in the dim light I saw we were all listening. It was coming from outside the room. A voice was quietly calling to us from the other side of the door. At first it was hard to catch what was being said, as if it was coming from far away. There was no hint of panic. It was just a rhythmic repetition of words. Then, suddenly cutting through the storm outside, it became clear. 'Susan,' it whispered, 'Susan, are you in there?' There was no mistaking the voice: it was Tilden's, her husband was calling to her. The door handle rattled. Something was trying to turn it. 'Unlock the door,' he cried. He must have been standing on the other side. The order was repeated, each time louder than the last, his lips only inches away.

'But he's dead,' whispered Stanislav.

'Are you sure?' asked Mrs Jackson.

'Yes,' I exclaimed. 'We saw his body.'

Tilden's voice continued to tell Susan to open the door. It was trying a different tenor. The calm, authoritative command had given way to angry words. And after the bitter reprimand came the plaintive cry, the thumping on the door. He was calling our names, a laconic, emotionless litany, reeling them off like a schoolmaster, including Clara's. Once he'd finished, the pleading began, pleading with us to let him in.

'What if he was only wounded?' asked Mrs Jackson.

'That's not Tilden,' I yelled. I was riled, maddened almost beyond endurance. 'He's not coming back.'

I could hear a struggle taking place behind me. Susan was trying to get up from the divan. Sasha was holding her back. 'He's dead,' Sasha was saying. 'It's not your husband.'

'Let him in,' Susan was crying. 'You bastards, he needs help.'

Mrs Jackson handed the torch to Stanislav.

I warned her to keep away from the door, but she had no intention of letting whatever it was inside and went back to help Sasha.

The thumping had ceased. The voice was fading, winding down. The words were becoming slurred, the sentences unfinished. 'If you won't let me in . . . join me . . . let me in. I want you . . . you . . . in . . . me.' It was still a voice, but hardly recognisable as Tilden's. There was the sound of something sliding down the door, then a final rattle of the handle. We stood watching the door for several more minutes. Susan had given up trying to wrestle herself free from Sasha and Mrs Jackson. She sat between them, quietly cursing everyone in the room. At the height of her struggle she'd tried to bite Sasha, but the young Slovak had slapped her hard across the face.

Outside it was quiet. I looked at my watch: two hours until sunrise. Suarez lay at the women's feet, his head turned away from the door. If we were to make it through the night then at least one of us needed to stay awake. I told Stanislav that he should try and get some rest. He understood the logic, and eventually agreed to sit in the high-backed chair, dragging it over to where he'd been standing. He fetched me the wooden stool. 'You sit, take the revolver. If I start to snore, then you wake me up.' He looked around. Susan had closed her eyes. 'And if anyone tries to open the door you have to shoot them, OK?'

'All right,' I agreed. I put the rifle down and took up the revolver. It was a threat that had already been made. No one was to touch the bolted door before sunrise.

'There are matches above the fireplace. We relight the candles if anything happens. We keep the lamps burning. The torch . . .' he said, switching it off, 'we keep in reserve.'

'You'll stay awake?' asked Mrs Jackson.

I picked up the stool and placed it where I could see the door and those on the divan. 'You get some rest,' I said quietly.

My legs were aching. I felt so tired, but I couldn't sleep. Voices came and went throughout the night. O'Neil's,

Fowler's, others that I didn't recognise. They would creep into my consciousness. Strange noises that would make me turn and look around. They were whispering, pleading, begging me to turn out the light and open the door.

49

At first I thought it was Tilden knocking at the door and that it was time to get up. I stumbled forward, the revolver sliding from my lap. With what sense I had I put out a foot to cushion its fall. I bent down and picked it up. Light was seeping in beneath the door. I saw Stanislav sitting in the chair, rubbing his face. My arms and legs were aching. The knocking came again. The three women were stirring on the divan, with Suarez, like a dog beneath its blanket, curled up at their feet. It couldn't be Tilden outside. I could hear a boy shouting in Arabic. Stanislav was unbolting the door. I was groggy, but working through what had happened.

'It's Amuda,' said Stanislav. The knocking was urgent, the boy's voice was pleading with the Russian to hurry.

I winced as the door opened and sunlight flooded in. Amuda embraced Stanislav, his shining face pressed against the man's chest. He was speaking quickly, relating what had happened. Stanislav was stroking his hair. Mrs Jackson was standing beside me. Sasha was speaking to Susan.

I turned to see Suarez climbing to his feet. His face was haggard, eyes restlessly scanning the common room. He fell against me as he staggered towards the light. I briefly held his arm, steadying his progress. He turned, like a drunk, and looked at me as he rolled forward, a glance which showed how much he resented my attempt to keep him on his feet. Clutching the blanket with one hand, he pushed past Amuda and stumbled into the courtyard. I watched him as he collapsed against the cab of the lorry. In a graceless movement he turned to face the sun, his back slumping against the door. He bared his teeth in a taut smile and shut his eyes against the glare. The dried mud was flaking from his pale body and livid gashes had begun to appear.

Stanislav was questioning Amuda in Arabic. He had a finger beneath his chin and the boy, his dark eyes glistening, was looking up at the Russian.

Mrs Jackson emerged from the darkness. 'Dear God,' she exclaimed at the sight of Suarez's wounds. 'We need to get you washed.' Suarez didn't say anything, but allowed himself to be gently lifted from the bonnet of the lorry and steered towards the washroom. Susan, shielding her eyes against the sun, walked towards me. Her hair was matted and her vacant eyes, half disguised by the shadow of her hand, stared into mine.

'Is he here?' she asked. 'Is my husband here?'

'Do you want to see him?'

'Won't he be hiding?'

'No, he's not hiding.'

'But he's done something terrible, hasn't he?'

I put my arm through hers and we crossed the yard to Tilden's room. The door was wide open and before we entered we could hear the buzzing of flies. I laid a hand on her freckled arm to hold her back. There was some sort of residual loyalty that had brought her this far, but did she really want to see what had happened to her husband?

The horror inside was all that I could think of as she brushed past me. I expected her to scream or to faint, but she did neither. As she stood staring down at the emaciated corpse she giggled and then quickly placed a hand over her mouth to stifle the sound.

In a grotesque twist, the body was now naked, except for his homburg. The head was almost hanging off the mattress, but the hat was pinned beneath an ear, the felt rim stretched diagonally from fallen cheek to sallow forehead. The flies, disturbed by our presence, were spinning around our faces. Susan waved her hand in front of her and then, gaining no relief, retreated towards the door. I took a final look at the mantis-like corpse before lifting the sheet and throwing it over the body. A cloud of flies scattered and I stepped out into daylight.

Susan had retreated to the palm tree and was looking at the ground. I went to see if she was all right. She asked

369

me if I had a cigarette. When I told her I hadn't, she wrapped her arms round the trunk of the tree. 'It doesn't matter that he's dead,' she murmured. 'I didn't love him. I couldn't after what they did.'

Mrs Jackson was leaving Suarez's room with a pile of clothes. She disappeared briefly into the washroom, then re-emerged and started towards us.

'You've found Henry?' she asked.

'We have,' I confirmed.

'He was a remarkable man; stubborn, but quite remarkable.' Her eyes glimmered.

'He's in his room, but I wouldn't go in, if I were you.'

Mrs Jackson sighed and drew the back of her hand across her cheek. If Susan hadn't been there I think she would have ignored my advice. Instead she put an arm across Susan's shoulder. 'I'm sorry,' she said, 'I know what it's like to lose a husband.'

I watched Mrs Jackson lead Susan towards the kitchen and then I wandered over to the washroom. Suarez was sitting on the muddy floor, his naked back resting against the tub. His eyes were closed. As he sat there in the morning sun I could clearly see the scratches on his arms, and round his neck. I squatted down on my haunches. As my shadow crossed his face, he flinched and a hand shot up.

'It's OK, I said, clutching his damp shoulder.

He took in a long wavering breath and blinked several times. 'It's you,' he said as though surprised to see me still alive.

370

'You're safe here.'

He was frowning in the sunlight. 'You think you've rescued me?' he said.

'Haven't we?'

He shook his head, though his dark eyes remained fixed upon my face. 'Nobody's safe, Mr Ward, nobody, but especially not you.'

50

We sat on a sheet of tarpaulin in the shade of the inner wall, a hundred yards or so from where we'd buried Tilden. The rain had softened the ground and, though the soil was as heavy as clay, it had taken less than an hour to dig his grave. There was no coffin. We'd used his bed sheet as a shroud and Mrs Jackson had uttered a short eulogy. A stoical-looking Susan had stood beside the grave, supported by Sasha. With her foot she'd gently nudged the first clod of earth onto her dead husband.

Amuda had spent the early morning telling Stanislav about what had happened to the porter and the cook. He knew nothing about the sergeant, but the porter's and the cook's fate was all too familiar. Amuda, when their candles had been blown out, had crawled into a cupboard and from his hiding place he'd heard the flapping of wings and the men shrieking in fear as they had been dragged out of the gatehouse.

Amuda was desperate to return to Mosul, but Stanislav had persuaded him to stay. Though the sun was shining, the ground around the site had become a fetid marshland. Each mound of sand was a dark muddy knoll and pools of brown water shimmered in every direction. Stanislav had taken the boy on a tour of the surrounding land. The pontoon part of the bridge had been washed away and a series of wide canals, built to bring water and to protect the ancient city from an attack from the east, had become flooded with rainwater. Suarez, wearing Tilden's trousers and one of his shirts, had suggested an attempt to wade through one of the canals. Stanislav had agreed that it was worth trying, but even if we had managed to cross one of the canals we would still have been on the wrong side of the Tigris. In the east there was nothing but wet scrubland and hyenas. In the north there were the Yazidis in the mountains, but it would have taken at least a couple of days to cross the plain. Could we have swum across the river? No, the current was far too strong. We had to wait for the bridge to be repaired or for the river to fall. How long would this take? No one could say. There were clouds gathering in the west, leaden clouds slowly rolling towards the site. It was almost midday and our respite from the rain wasn't going to last much longer.

'We can't just stay here. I won't let them take me back,' said Suarez. For some reason he was pinching his cheek, pulling it out an inch, then letting it fall back. 'This isn't how it's meant to be.' Each time he did it I could hear the quiet rasping of bristle, thumb and finger. 'We can't stay.' His dark eyes kept switching from those around him to the clouds in the west.

'What else can we do?' asked Mrs Jackson. 'Not all of us can swim and there's not a boatman in Mosul foolish enough to try and cross the Tigris as it is for the sake of a few white faces.'

'We're not stopping you, Tom,' said Stanislav. 'If you want to try and leave again, then go ahead.' He made a backward sweep with his arm as if inviting Suarez to strike out.

'You should stay,' I said, though he'd made no sign of leaving. 'You won't get far before dark. Out there you'll be vulnerable, exposed. They'll pick you off. Here, we can barricade ourselves in, keep the lights burning. Together we have a chance.'

'The generator's wrecked,' said Stanislav.

'But we have lamps, and candles.'

'You think we can survive another night?' asked Suarez, his voice full of contempt. 'They won't stay away, they'll be swarming back. They won't leave until they've taken what they want.'

'And they want?' asked Sasha.

Suarez narrowed his eyes. 'You mean you don't know?'

'She wants you to explain what happened,' said Stanislav. 'Why you're still alive when others have been fed upon.'

'They're gathering around her cell, feeding, mating.'

'And Lilith?' I asked.

'She hasn't appeared. They're calling for her, calling inside the ziggurat. Lilith, it seems, is buried beneath the tomb. I managed to escape. I had matches. When they brought . . .' Suarez paused.

'Brought who?' I asked.

'Someone else into the chamber. There was a commotion. I made it up the ladders, escaped from the tomb.'

'Who was it?' asked Mrs Jackson. 'Who did you leave behind?'

Suarez stared down at the tarpaulin. 'I don't know who it was. It was dark, he was unconscious. A soldier, an Arab; does it matter? I had to get out.' He suddenly looked up at me. 'You've been there. You must have seen who it was?'

'It was Fowler,' I said.

Suarez feigned surprise and dismay.

'It's as suspected,' said Mrs Jackson. 'The Assyrians must have returned her to her cave, built the chambers above it. The ziggurat's the prison gate, and the sarcophagus must have belonged to one of her daughters, but Lilith is beneath.'

'Then it's not too late. If we can stop her then we can contain what's been happening: the cholera in Mosul, the tormented nights, the killings.' I turned towards her. 'How many daughters can she have?'

'Their number's legion, countless scattered over the earth, and now they're returning to their queen. Whether or not they've all survived is something I can't guess.

Some may be stronger, others weaker, but they've all been waiting in the shadows, feeding when they needed to, watching and waiting.'

'We need to return to the ziggurat,' I stated calmly. 'If they're able to free Lilith, who knows what she could unleash.'

'A holy war,' said Suarez coldly, 'a slaughter that would easily eclipse the Kaiser's fury.'

'A war destroyed the Assyrians, and left only one victor, one god,' declared Mrs Jackson. 'There will be no bounds, no limits to what we suffer. This is a demon that cannot be killed, a demon that has been trapped for three thousand years, alone in her cave plotting and scheming, vowing revenge against man and the god that defeated her.'

'And what do you propose we do to stop her?' asked Suarez.

'We take light back to the chamber,' I said, 'stop her daughters, reseal the tomb.'

'Do you know how long it'd take to refill a chamber?' asked Stanislav.

'We can flood it with the water outside. We have to try.'

'And mix salt with the sand,' said Mrs Jackson. 'The devil loveth no salt on his meat. It's in every culture. Even the Japanese keep ghosts in jars of salt. Every level had a significance. The hidden tomb was to guard the cave, the one above was filled with sand and salt. The water must have been another element to hide or guard Lilith.

We can assume there must have been a fire in one of the other two chambers.'

'Of course,' exclaimed Stanislav. 'There was soot on the ceiling of the second chamber, a slight trace, but soot nevertheless.'

'Salt, water, fire are all very well,' said Suarez, 'but we need a sacrifice, someone sealed in the tomb.'

'I don't follow,' I said.

'If we're to trap any of her daughters then we need a tethered goat, a young man left alive in the tomb.'

'We're not going to leave anyone behind.'

'Then we'll all be haunted for the rest of our lives.'

'What if they've already got fresh meat?' asked Mrs Jackson.

'You mean the cook, the porter?' asked Suarez.

She nodded.

'I doubt they'd last very long. They'll be searching for others. A virgin, a soldier. Bloodied or unbloodied.'

'And if we manage to trap the daughters who are here, won't they just dig their way down to her?' I asked.

'They didn't three thousand years ago,' said Mrs Jackson. 'Her daughters are weak when they've nothing to feed on. Besides, we'll have salt on the ground and, if Suarez is right, something to distract them.'

'You mean someone,' I corrected, not wanting her to shy away from what Suarez was proposing. 'And are you volunteering to be buried alive?' I asked Suarez.

'What do you think?' he replied. 'Do you think I want to play the hero? No, I've had my turn.' He cast a glance at Amuda. The boy was lying on his back at the edge of the tarpaulin.

'You can't be serious,' said Stanislav.

'Why not? He's young, and isn't going to amount to much anyway.'

As if aware of the conversation Amuda said something.

'What did he say?' I asked.

'We should brace ourselves for wind and rain,' replied Stanislav. 'And murder, if we listen to Suarez.'

'So are you volunteering?' asked Suarez angrily.

'I'm not convinced we need a sacrifice,' I said.

'Then you haven't got a hope in hell of escaping this nightmare.'

51

The rain forced us to retreat to the common room. Inside we picked half-heartedly at figs and stale bread that Amuda had managed to find. Susan refused to eat anything. She sat listlessly on the divan, staring at the cold fireplace. It had been agreed that we needed to go back to the ziggurat. Sasha was to stay behind and look after Susan. Nobody wanted to return, but if we were to have any chance of defeating those already gathered then we needed to take the battle to Lilith. Suarez, however, was adamant that he wasn't going anywhere. He even accused me of plotting against him. There was very little he could do at the dig, but we couldn't leave him behind. Sasha would have her hands full looking after Susan, and couldn't be expected to keep an eye on Suarez as well. In the end we threatened to banish him from the house and the idea of spending the night elsewhere proved sufficient to change his mind.

Stanislav and I had agreed earlier that we needed to keep Suarez's hands away from the rifle and revolver. I had the rifle slung across my back and, like everyone else, I carried a lamp. Stanislav had a length of rope coiled round his shoulder like an Alpine climber. Amuda had put a tin of Morton's salt in Tilden's knapsack. It was Mrs Jackson's idea. We weren't sure what we were going to do, other than scattering the kitchen salt over the tomb's floor. There'd been talk of all kinds, but nothing had been resolved.

We drove the Ford up the hill in the rain, each one of us speculating on what lay ahead. In the back of the lorry were two ladders which we intended to bind together in order to make our final descent into the cell.

The ziggurat stood silently watching our progress, its dark bricks dripping in the rain. Around it was a sea of mud, a moat surrounding the pile of stone and suffering. Without pausing I crawled through the entrance. There was the ladder we'd used last night, ordinary and unbroken. I calmly descended into the second chamber, holding my lamp above my head, spying into the darkness. If her daughters were here they'd be in the tomb, hiding in the darkest recesses of the building. I could hear the others gathering above. Stanislav sent Amuda down, then Mrs Jackson, then Suarez. As each one appeared the light intensified. There was sand on the floor, spilled by the workmen as they'd emptied the fourth chamber. I bent down and sifted it through my fingers. Amongst the sand were gritty white crystals: sea salt. Mrs Jackson was right. I could hear the rungs of the ladder creaking. The light was fading. I turned and followed the party.

In the third chamber the air was markedly colder and the dank, fetid smell still lingered. In one corner lay the grim remains of the Indian soldier. At the sight of the mottled sack of skin and bones Mrs Jackson stifled a cry of anguish, otherwise we continued on our journey in silence. I followed Amuda down the ladder. His dark hair was a tangled mop and his nails were bitten. The thin brown arm which carried his lamp was shivering.

Silently we gathered round the entrance to the hidden cell. There was the faint sound of something scuttling away from the light, like the sound of a crab scurrying over rocks. All was quiet again, except for our breathing; shallow, rapid breaths. Stanislav shone his torch down into the black chasm below. The remains of the makeshift ladder were scattered across the floor, but there was no sign of Fowler. The deadness was starting to trouble me.

'If we're to carry on we'll need to bring the ladders down,' I said. 'Keep them where we can see them.'

'Do we need to go any further?' asked Suarez, his voice a whisper, his face pale, contorted with terror.

'We need to see inside,' I said.

'Why?' demanded Suarez. 'You think he might still be alive?'

'We have to know if there's a cave,' I answered. 'To see if they're there.'

'There's salt to scatter on the floor,' Mrs Jackson added, 'salt to rein in the succubi.'

'Don't listen to her,' said Suarez. 'This isn't going to be fixed by some spell.' He moved away from the entrance. 'We all know how we can solve this.'

Stanislav's hand was under the flap of the holster.

'Shove him down,' Suarez said quietly. 'It needs a sacrifice. They won't be satisfied unless they have a mate. Shove him down,' he repeated, staring at me.

I took hold of Amuda's arm, could feel the pimples beneath my palm. I held him for fear that Suarez would try and push the boy over the edge. 'We're not leaving him behind,' I said. 'He stays up here, guards the entrance.'

'Why should he get to stay up here?'

'Because we can trust him,' answered Stanislav.

'And what, you can't trust me, is that it?' Suarez was speaking loudly, his manner agitated. 'I swear I won't say anything.'

'Say anything about what?' asked Mrs Jackson.

Suarez ignored her. 'I'm not going down there. You can threaten to shoot me. I'm not going any further. If you're not leaving the boy, I'm getting out.' He went back to the ladder.

Amuda was anxiously watching the American, whispering to Stanislav.

'You're scaring the boy,' said the Russian.

'Do I fucking care!' screamed Suarez. He was peering up into the darkness; too afraid to ascend alone into the chamber above, petrified by the thought of returning to where he'd been kept. At first he seemed unable to do anything other than circle the ladder, but then he started

384

to advance on Stanislav. 'Shove him down the well,' he cried, 'leave the damn Arab behind.' Suarez paced backwards and forwards; each time he advanced he took a step closer to the Russian. 'It needs another sacrifice. This is no place for the righteous. Leave him. He's no help.' Suarez's face was only inches from Stanislav's. 'You've killed before. You know what it's like. Do it. Leave him!' The words were pummelling the Russian. 'He's worth nothing. Leave—'

With one hand I grabbed Suarez's lapel and twisted him round, with the other I landed a sharp uppercut to the jaw. Behind him I saw Mrs Jackson flinch as Suarez reeled backwards from the blow. He staggered a yard or two, with his hands half lifted towards his face. When he fell his head rebounded on the floor.

'He deserved it,' said Stanislav.

I looked down at Suarez. 'I just wanted him to stop.'

Mrs Jackson knelt beside him. 'He's out cold.'

I slid a hand beneath his head. It was sticky with blood.

52

We took Tilden's belt from Suarez's waist and strapped his ankles together. We used his shirt to tie his hands behind his back. It was Stanislav's handkerchief we used to gag him. We couldn't stand the idea of listening to him pleading for mercy. Mrs Jackson, who'd been wringing her hands throughout, thought gagging Suarez was excessive, but otherwise said very little in his defence. Once we were satisfied with the way in which he was trussed we left him with a trembling Amuda.

Stanislav led the way down into the tomb. I followed him, my lamp just above his head, bathing him in its golden light. I kept my eyes fixed on his shaven head. Above me I could hear Mrs Jackson, the rungs of the makeshift ladder creaking inches from my hand. Stanislav stepped down and, while waiting for me and Mrs Jackson to descend, he shone the torch over the walls. The stone pillars cast revolving rectangular shadows.

'We should stay together,' said Stanislav. 'The start of the tunnel's over there.' He waved his light towards a corner. Shades of darkness shuffled around, scurried this way and that. I heard something scuttle overhead.

Where was Fowler? There was no sign of the captain. No doubt what was left of him had either been discarded in some dark corner or lay in a crumpled heap just behind the sarcophagus.

I walked tentatively forward. Two shovels stood against the wall. The foreman and his son had made some progress. Where they had been digging the floor disappeared and we found ourselves teetering on the edge of a muddy crater. Stanislav shone his torch down into its mouth. To one side they'd uncovered two roughly hewn steps. Steps, like those in any ancient tower, leading to Lilith's cave. How many more steps yet to be uncovered: another ten, another hundred? The muddy floor that covered the hidden stairwell was dark and shiny. Something was rising up through the sand and mud. It was tar or oil; I couldn't say for certain. It seemed to be a seeping blackness, carrying the evil out, oozing its way to the surface.

'She's down there,' said Mrs Jackson, 'in her cave.' She slipped off Tilden's knapsack and I watched her as she unbuckled the canvas flap and lifted out her tin of Morton's salt. She poured it over the black morass, the stone steps. Beneath her swaying waterfall the blackness seemed to contract. Something hissed above our heads, but we didn't look up. Here was a housewife thawing the path to the coalshed. The contrast of the domestic and the supernatural made the scene almost comical. It was a pathetic, laughable, superstitious act. This commodity, packaged for the twentieth century and purchased across the counter, was a Roman's salary, Lot's wife, alchemy straight from the Bible.

'We should take the shovels,' I said. There was no answer, other than a soft growling that reverberated around the walls. Yet within our arc of light we were invincible. To see that the cave had not been uncovered made us almost giddy with success. We moved less cautiously, though the fear of being attacked had not quite disappeared. This world of light was our world, not theirs. They belonged to the nocturnal forest, the unlit yard. Waiting in the shadows, only travelling at night.

Why didn't we take pity on Suarez? His eyes were wide open. He was struggling to say something through the handkerchief. He shuffled, inching his way towards us across the grit and sand. Mrs Jackson studiously avoided him. Stanislav glanced in his direction, but didn't acknowledge his muffled cry for help. I like to think that I was able to convey a little sympathy. It was a desperate situation he was in. Would we have left him there if he'd shown a little more restraint, if he hadn't wanted to abandon Amuda? He was hysterical, kicking and squirming. Did we want to protect the vulnerable, to punish the

389

conceited? It wasn't murder. It was what he wanted. The sacrifice I was prepared to make. At least that's what I keep telling myself.

With Amuda's help we managed to shove the circular cover back over the entrance to the fourth chamber. The funnel-shaped stone slotted easily into the floor. There was the soft grating of sand, a muffled yell from below. It was a design which might have anticipated such an event. The only damage to the stone was chisel marks to the edges, ropes and a crowbar having been used to lift the ancient bung out of the floor. Stanislav pulled off his knapsack and unpacked the hammer and chisel he'd found in the porter's room. It had been agreed. Using the water that had gathered in the moat we would flood the chamber above Suarez.

53

During the night we heard the cries of a creature that hadn't been caught in the ziggurat. It was grieving for its loss. It bellowed into the night, scratched at the door, thumped on the ceiling. Susan was sobbing in her sleep. Stanislav and I took it in turns to listen, but long before dawn its wailing had stopped, as though the wind had torn its mournful howling from its throat.

In the morning the storm was dying and we walked down to the river. They had already started to repair the pontoon bridge and ferrymen were gathering on the opposite bank. Within a couple of days the workmen had returned. They were bemused by the new *khwaja*'s order to bury the ziggurat, but they didn't argue; the Kurdish women told their men that they shouldn't question the Russian's wisdom.

The cholera outbreak proved to be short-lived and soon

Mosul was back on its feet. The disappearance of Fowler and Suarez caused quite a stir, but the consulate found itself at a loss to explain what had happened. The most plausible explanation was that they must have drowned while trying to cross the Tigris. O'Neil's body was never found. The Indian soldiers were simply recorded as absent without leave. Eventually the whole tragedy was linked to some tribe or other and reprisals followed.

I remained at the site for nearly a month. Long enough, we'd agreed, to allay any suspicion. Stanislav, Sasha and Mrs Jackson stayed until the end of the season, while I accompanied Susan back to England. I had no idea that she was pregnant. I wondered if the child was Tilden's or Bateman's. There was the possibility that neither of them was the father, though this was something I refused to dwell upon, if not for the child's sake, then for what was left of my sanity.

Stanislav returned for another season, not out of curiosity, but to prevent anyone else from digging. At the end of the season he declared the site exhausted and buried what we'd uncovered. He returned to Iraq the following year to satisfy himself that it had been properly abandoned – and it had. Lost, I believe, from most maps and with little to recommend it.

54

And where was Clara? Since she'd fled from the site I hadn't stopped thinking about her. In London she seemed to be everywhere. The underground was thronged with slender women with jet-black hair and in public houses I was constantly catching snatches of her soft drawl. I was forever turning round, trying to determine a woman's height, the narrowness of her shoulders, the way in which she walked along the platform. At the bar I would study the crowd of flushed and leery faces, faces bent on ignoring the pale man with the hollow eyes and the unfortunate scar across his lips.

After three years of receiving merely the most circumspect of letters from Stanislav I couldn't stand it any longer. I had sufficient funds and had exhausted every line of inquiry this side of the Atlantic, all that is except for one.

Susan was living in a flat in Bedford Square. I spent the morning in the British Museum, walking through the Assyrian gallery, working up the courage to pay her a visit. In many ways it was a mistake, and merely served to accelerate her final collapse. She was barely present when I saw her, curled up in a thick dressing gown on a velvet-covered couch. We sat beneath a crystal chandelier and I remember the unfamiliar air of luxury and idleness, the tawny oil paintings and the bronze statuettes. I looked into Susan's vacant eyes, I sensed her guilty fear and noticed that her red hair had started to thin. Her maid, a buxom woman in her forties, was made to perch awkwardly on the arm of the couch. The two women regarded me curiously.

I began by talking of mundane matters. I inquired after her health, and made some remark about the unseasonably cold weather. It had been agreed on the ship that had brought us back to England that we would never see each other again and my intrusion baffled her. I soon gave up my attempt to put her at her ease, and told her it was Clara I was after.

'Clara,' she said, as though amused by my predicament. She repeated the name, looking at her maid as though she wanted her to share in her amusement.

'Have you heard from her?'

'After three years you've come to ask me this?'

'Yes.'

'Well, I can't remember.' Susan glanced again at her maid, but if she was looking for support she didn't receive it. She turned back towards me. We sat in silence, except for the ticking of a clock. The rays of the setting sun filled the room with a soft radiance. 'Yes,' she finally admitted, 'now that I think about it there was a letter . . .'

I repeated her last few words as though by repetition I was guaranteeing its existence. The strangest sensation, a feeling that the room was beginning to slide away, took hold of me. I put a hand on the arm of the chair for fear of toppling over.

'Yes,' Susan confirmed. 'There was a letter.'

'When?' I managed to ask.

'Oh, not long after we returned. I didn't think it wise to reply.'

I looked at the maid, but her face remained expressionless.

'Where is she?'

'She was asking the most impertinent of questions. As if I would stoop so low . . .' She paused, recalling what I had just said. 'You can't see her.'

'Why not?'

'She's far away.'

'Where?'

She flinched at my impatience.

'Where?' I repeated softly. 'Chicago?'

'I don't know.'

'Do you have the letter?'

She shook her head. I glanced at the mantelpiece, the writing bureau. I had the urge to empty every drawer, to ransack the flat in an effort to find it. 'You don't have her letter?'

'I don't want anything to do with . . .' She failed to finish her sentence. Her voice was becoming increasingly distant. 'It's getting dark. She'll be back soon.'

'Who'll be back?'

'My daughter.' She looked at me and her face suddenly blanched. 'You'd better go.'

The maid stood up and took a step towards me.

'Do you still see them?' I uttered.

She pretended not to understand. I asked again, the note of urgency in my voice increasing her alarm. The maid was standing over me, asking me to follow her downstairs. I tried to look past her apron, but couldn't. I stood up. Susan was cowering in her corner, as though afraid that I would strike her. I tried once more, but by now she was pleading with me to get out.

The maid had taken hold of my arm. 'Mr Ward,' she was saying, 'you have to leave.'

I felt myself being pulled firmly towards the door. 'I see them,' I cried defiantly. 'They come at night. I try to hide, but there's nowhere . . .' All the while the maid was guiding me to the door. 'Her daughter—' I began, but the maid was hauling me downstairs, telling me to hush, her hand up to my mouth, an inch from my lips.

At the door I refused to leave until I'd written down my address. I thrust the scrap of paper and a shilling into the woman's palm. 'Where's the letter?' I asked.

'How should I know?' She saw that I wasn't satisfied. 'That's not to say there never was a letter, that it's not somewhere.' A smile pulled at her face, there to ease me back outside.

I took the crumb of comfort, but I wasn't ready to leave. 'And her daughter?'

The maid shook her head. I shouldn't be asking. 'Her daughter,' I said again, louder this time.

She motioned for me to be quiet. She didn't want a commotion. I agreed never to return and urged her once more to respond. She turned slightly away as though too ashamed to look me in the eye. 'You honestly don't know?' she whispered.

'Know what?'

'That it was a healthy-looking babe,' she glanced up. 'But there was no way of knowing. The doctor said she'd be fine.'

'What happened?'

'She doesn't sleep well.' Again the furtive look.

'Were you there?' I asked.

'Of course I was there. It was one of the hottest nights I've ever known.'

'And what happened?'

'She died, just after dawn. Screamed her heart out, poor mite. It just kept growing louder and louder. The nurses, the doctor, they were all at a loss. Nothing they could do to stop her. Mrs Tilden held her at the end. She kept singing this one lullaby. Even after it was all over. Three hours of life and then . . .' The maid quietly clicked her fingers.

Epilogue

To the ignorant I am nothing more than a malingerer. I try not to think of what I was, or what once lay ahead. Life as a clerk or a schoolmaster is not for me. There are ghosts in the air, in my thoughts. They echo in my words. At night, the shifting fingers tap lightly at the window and muffled footsteps run behind.

Recently I've been hearing a voice – a young woman's voice. There is a girlish, whispering quality to her speech, a quality which draws the listener near.

'Listen,' she says, and I picture her head slightly tilted to one side. 'Listen. Can you hear it?'

'Hear what?' I ask.

'Why, it's the sound of solace; your lover as she speaks,

the laughter of your children, the sigh of one who longs to be set free.'

'No,' I reply, 'you can't be her. You've got the wrong m-m-man.'

She ignores what I have to say and begins to recount our sins. Her chanting is as unstoppable as death. Yet her lust is without malice or spite. She haunts me, but doesn't terrify me. She is possessive, but not jealous; revengeful but no longer murderous. Motherless, she taunts me with her whispering, her laughter, her soft weeping.

This is the sound of the boarding house as it settles down: the rattling of pipes, the soft footfall in the corridor . . . whether it's light or dark, it doesn't matter now, she's always there. I don't know if praying does any good, but I kneel and pray and during the day I try and sleep.

In the evening I wake with a sense of disquiet and remorse. I wake to coughs and noses being blown, filthy mattresses pressed against one another. I am surrounded by Lithuanians and Poles, the smell of sweat and boiled cabbage. A sickly wind rattles the window. Outside it is dull and deathly cold, yet I venture out into the frozen stockyards to look for her. I walk amongst the canning factories, cross the railroads, ride the trolley cars, stare at the jumble of fire escapes and pipes. I pound the snow-covered pavements and sing Hosanna. Others think of me as utterly alone, yet my yesterdays slide alongside and keep step beside me. Suarez's face peers over my shoulder. In shop windows I glimpse his lifeless reflection. He asks me why, but I think he understands. For him there was

400

the chance of redemption. He studies my face and sees there is no guilt – guilt is a dead thing in the damned. For me there is no salvation. Only the thought of finding Clara spurs me on. I avoid dark alleys and call at saloons and boarding houses. Hostility and mistrust dog me. The streets are congested with every type of vehicle and the air is thick with acrid smoke. Through frosted lashes I watch the snow begin to fall. It drifts beneath the street lamps and covers every sign. The icy wind blows and I let it carry me through the half illuminated neighbour-hood. With the bronze figure of Pazuzu safe inside my woollen reefer I have learnt to let it be. Twice it has steered me along Ashland Avenue and there must be a reason why. Even the most rational of men will look for meaning in the fall of a sparrow.

And in my pocket is a photograph. A photograph I've studied for countless hours. It found its way to me after I'd visited Susan. The box camera is pointing at the mirror, her hands are cradling it an inch or two from her waist. Slender hands that with their straying tenderness awoke a passion that consumes my soul. She sits in front of a dressing table, staring into the mirror. Her smile is uncer-tain, lips slightly parted. The same searching eyes and jet-black hair. It's an innocent photograph: a seated woman in a school-monitor style of dress.

Innocent, until you look beyond her shoulder to the narrow bed behind. The shadow of the fire escape falls in diagonal lines across the counterpane while the curtain lies in a swelling horizontal. The sun makes the thin curtain almost translucent in comparison to the cast-iron bars of the fire escape. I try to fix my eyes on her pale face, her hands, the swell of her bosom beneath the grey fabric of her dress. Yet there's something else, framed inside the squalid room, visible neither on one side of the curtain nor the other. It's a darker shadow, innocuous unless you're looking for it, unless you believe it's the silhouette of something crouching on the floor.

Author's Note

The Devil's Ark interweaves fact and fiction and it may interest the reader to know where the narrative endeavours to establish links with the past. Nineveh is an ancient city which lies just across the Tigris from Mosul. Its history is well documented and archaeological excavations by the British were carried out during the 1920s. Lilith is mentioned in Isaiah, though modern translations obliquely refer to her as the 'night monster' or 'night hag'. In Wycliffe's translation it uses the Latin, Lamia, and speaks of her 'flying serpents' and their 'temples of lust'. She is identified as the original woman in texts which pre-date Genesis, and is mentioned in the Dead Sea Scrolls. For readers interested in Lilith I recommend Barbara Black Koltuv's *The Book of Lilith* (Nicholas-Hays Inc. 1983). For anyone wanting to know more about attitudes towards women in the ancient Near East there is

Gwendolyn Leick's *Sex and Eroticism in Mesopotamian Literature* (Routledge, 1994). Leonard Woolley's *Ur of the Chaldees* (Penguin, 1929) and Agatha Christie Mallowan's *Come, Tell Me How You Live* (Collins, 1946) contain authoritative accounts of British and American archaeologists working in Iraq in the late 1920s and early 1930s and references to Woolley and Carter are, as far as I am aware, entirely accurate.

The character of Harry Ward was shaped, in part, by Peter Barham's sympathetic account of those driven mad by war in his *Forgotten Lunatics of the Great War* (Yale, 2004) and Robert Palmer's *Letters from Mesopotamia*, letters which were initially published for private circulation but are now freely available from the Gutenberg Press. For a wider understanding of the fighting in Mesopotamia two books are worth mentioning, A. J. Barker's *The Neglected War, Mesopotamia 1914–1918* (Faber, 1967) and Wilfred Nunn's *Tigris Gunboats, The Forgotten War in Iraq 1914–1917* (Melrose, 1932), the latter explaining why, without any obfuscation, the British landed in Basra.

Finally, many people have supported the writing of this novel and I would like to take this opportunity to thank the following: John Wordsworth, the commissioning editor at Headline; Frances Doyle; Mrunal Sisodia; Dr Tracey Bywater; Niki Waugh; colleagues at BMS; Andrew Grimshaw; the British Museum; the Wellcome Trust; my agent, Charlotte Robertson; Dr Jane Kocen; and, last but not least, my family for their patience, help and encouragement.